Stepping back, Candace pulled down the covers on the bed, then sat on the edge. Alice moved naturally between Candace's knees, leaning down to resume the wonderful kisses. She wanted to say she couldn't believe this was happening to her, that for the first time in her life her desires made sense, but kissing was too good to stop for mere words.

She wiggled her hips as Candace hooked her thumbs into her pantyhose, helping the process along. She wanted to be naked too. Candace's hands were warm and firm as they massaged and squeezed her hips. Alice already felt as if Candace had touched her body more than anyone else ever had before, and this was, she thought with a shiver, only the beginning.

—*From "Next-Door Neighbors" by Karin Kallmaker*

ॐ

Aidan scanned the table as five different hands pushed chips into the betting circles. Some dropped them carelessly. Others aligned them precisely in the center. The new arrival let them fall from the funnel of her fingers one at a time with a *snick snick snick* that reminded Aidan of the sound of sex. She had watched those hands every night of the cruise—fingers flicking the edge of a card, caressing the faintly corrugated edge of a chip, tapping the felt delicately with a firm, round fingertip. Beautiful hands, strong and deliberate. She imagined them skimming her body with casual possessiveness, a fingernail grazing her nipple.

Aidan dealt the cards and her clit grew hard.

—*From "Count Me In" by Radclyffe*

Visit

Bella Books

at

BellaBooks.com

or call our toll-free number

1-800-729-4992

In DEEP WATERS

Volume One · Cruising The Seas

Withdrawn

KARIN KALLMAKER
and RADCLY*f*FE

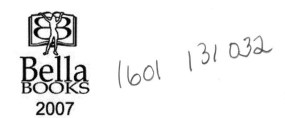

Bella
BOOKS
2007

1601 131 032

Bella Books, Inc.
P.O. Box 10543
Tallahassee, FL 32302

Printed in the United States of America on acid-free paper
First Edition

Editor: Cindy Cresap
Cover designer: LA Callaghan

ISBN-10: 1-59493-111-9
ISBN-13: 978-1-59493-111-6

For all the nice girls and the naughty ones too.
A project like this would not be possible without both.

~Karin Kallmaker

To Lee
Who Makes Every Trip Worth It

~Radclyffe

Contents

Welcome Aboard the Riviera Andante!

HIGHLIGHTS OF THE WEEK

Port	*Shipboard Events*	*LOVE Entertainment*
Saturday: Depart	Venice Captain's Reception	Comedy by Zelda with a Z!
Sunday: Bari	Toga Party	Marcy Chastain
Monday: Olympia	Pastry Chef Extravaganza	The Bottoms Up!
Tuesday: Santorini	Roma means Romance	Talent Show
Wednesday: at Sea	March of the Gladiators	Lip Sync
Thursday: Lesbos	Taste of America Pool Party	
Friday: Dubrovnik	Black & White Dinner Dance	Mashell Cordoba
Saturday: Venice	Disembarkation	

SPECIAL ANNOUNCEMENTS FROM YOUR LOVE STAFF

- The *Sea Side Video Lounge* will feature continuously running films of special interest to lesbians. Erotic films after ten p.m. sponsored by *Toyz Toyz Toyz*.
- Heavy metal sensation *Chain Maille* will perform nightly in *Medusa*.
- Check the daily schedule for pool parties and games, *Celebrity Bingo*, our unforgettable scavenger hunt and the *Newlywed Game*.
- Sheets and directions to create your own toga will be delivered to staterooms on Sunday afternoon.
- Tryouts for the Talent Show and Lip Sync contest Sunday at 4 p.m.
- Last minute addition: *Fashion Show Monday night!*
- Excursion desk will open Saturday at 5 p.m. Additional times will be posted.
- Guest artist recordings and books are on sale at the *Andante Boutique* located aft in the *Via Condotti*.
- The *Ladies on Vacation Enterprises* staff is here to make your holiday the best of your life! See any staff member or visit the *LOVE* desk in the *d'Argento Atrium* between 8 a.m. and 10 p.m. daily.

Panorama
Karin Kallmaker

"I can't believe that Italy is behind me and a ship full of lesbians is in front of me." Sissy scooted her carry-on suitcase a few inches ahead as the queue for the gangplank moved slowly forward.

"I can't believe half our vacation is already over." Gab sipped again from her water bottle and offered it to Sissy.

After a refreshing swig—the gangplank access was airless and muggy—Sissy handed the bottle back. "I'd rather think that we have half our vacation still to come. I loved Venice and Italy, but I am looking forward to the next week even more."

"I know what I'm looking forward to."

"Pool games? The Lip Sync contest?" Sissy looked up from the newsletter highlights they'd been handed after their passports and booking documents had been checked.

Gab gave her a level look.

"Oh." Sissy flushed. "Yes, well, the walls were very thin at that bed and breakfast, weren't they?"

"I'm hoping a ship is a lot more private, yes." Leaning close, Gab whispered, "I know you don't have as much fun when you have to be so quiet."

Sissy whispered back, "It wasn't having to be quiet, it was having to be still. The bed creaked *so* loudly. I thought it was going to fall apart under us."

Gab nodded, a smile broadening over her round face. The sun of the last week had put a lovely glow on her cheeks, Sissy mused, making her even more adorable. "Okay, that did stifle my creativity. I say we go directly to our cabin and do it like rabbits."

Sissy reveled in the shiver that started in her spine and danced across her shoulders like hot sunlight. "Okay, it's a deal."

After a thoughtful pause, Gab muttered, "The lube is in the luggage and who knows when the stevedores will get it to our room."

Since it wasn't often that she could zing the far more flirtatious Gab, Sissy just smiled until Gab said, "What?"

"Honey, we're not going to need lube." Sissy watched Gab swallow hard, and she smiled with satisfaction.

The queue was long, but finally they stepped past the welcoming line of ship's officers, consulted the map and found the nearest stairs that would lead below deck. Sissy gazed around in awe. Any other time she might have been looking at the lush carpet or the gleaming brass and marble of the ten-story atrium, or gazing raptly at the sensuous sculpture of dancers suspended in mid-air above their heads. What registered instead were the clusters of women and nothing but women, all kinds of women, every size and shape. Her gaydar started pinging and just wouldn't shut off.

There were at least a hundred women and they were *all* gay.

Gab said from behind her, "I don't think we're in Kansas anymore."

Sissy grabbed Gab's hand and dragged her toward the stairwell. "Let's go prove it, babe."

They descended a flight, passing a dining room, casino and a series of lounge areas, only to be confronted by a chain across the next stairs down and the polite missive *To allow for prompt delivery of your luggage, we request that you remain above deck at the present time.*

"Oh, heck." Gab fiddled with the chain. "It's only a request. We could still go down." She rolled her eyes when Sissy giggled over her word choice.

"I don't want to get into trouble our first hour on board," Sissy said. "We'll just have to wait, won't we?"

For an answer, Gab leaned her gently against the steel of the door frame and kissed her. It wasn't a light kiss either and, after a moment, Sissy pushed her away with a furtive glance to both sides.

"We're not in Kansas," Gab repeated. "If anybody's looking it's because they approve."

"Oh. Sorry." Sissy ducked her head. "Force of habit. Topeka is a long, long way away."

"Yes, it is," Gab said, and she kissed Sissy again.

It took a conscious effort to conquer her fear of being seen, but when Gab's hands slid around her hips with a possessive grasp, Sissy gave herself over to the tingling magic that she tried so hard not to let show in public. It was okay here. It was safe here.

"Honey, this is going to be a long wait," Gab murmured against her lips.

"You got that right. You want to explore?"

"Sure. Let's celebrate with one of those blue drinks with an umbrella in it and check out the pool."

The Talia Lounge was filled with yet more women, and Sissy tried hard not to gawk. Lesbians, all of them, and most were holding hands or standing close . . . Shut off the gaydar, she told herself. You don't need it.

Drinks in hand, they wandered through the sumptuous Piazza Casanova then traversed the length of the Cleopatra deck, encountering polite but busy staff bearing the blue and gold logo of the Riviera Andante on their otherwise pristine white uniforms. A number of other women were doing exactly what they were. Every time they passed another couple, Sissy had to forcibly restrain herself from the usual elbow nudge she would give Gab at the sight of another pair of lesbians.

A skirl of raucous music drew Sissy's attention to the Medusa Lounge, whose dark entrance was flanked by placards proclaiming that Chain Maille would be performing later. The band photo featured three women in heavy metal leather, two with guitars strapped on suggestively low. A powerfully built brunette emerged from the club and brushed by them, her spiked hair and vivid tattoos making her easy to recognize as the lead guitarist in the band photo.

They were so very definitely not in Kansas anymore.

"Oh my word . . ." Gab had stopped at a picture window and was looking down to the deck below.

When Sissy joined her she almost couldn't breathe. She finally managed to say, "How did they all get their swimsuits?"

"Maybe they knew to have them in their carryon stuff. And not everybody has a suit."

"Oh. Wow." Twin pools separated by a raised whirlpool were surrounded by women. To the far aft was a water slide arriving from the deck above—two women wrapped around each other toboggan style arrived with a huge splash.

At first Sissy didn't know why she felt . . . shocked. It wasn't the cluster of topless women, even, that stunned her. It was something more basic. None of these women cared who looked at them as they held hands or kissed. Sissy saw more than one purring as a friend—lover, she told herself, use the right word—rubbed suntan lotion on a bare back. It wasn't that anyone was doing anything she hadn't seen done at any public swimming pool she'd ever spent time at. It's just she'd never seen two women showing that easy and simple familiarity that het couples showed all the time, whether they knew it or not. There was laughter and flirtatious tips of the head, gleaming bodies . . . She stepped back abruptly.

"What's wrong?" Gab looked away from the panorama. "You okay, honey?"

"Yes. I just . . . wish we could go to our room." In her head she had no trouble at all imagining every pairing on the pool deck tonight, all those lesbians, having lesbian sex in every stateroom on the ship. Her whole body throbbed at the idea—all that love, all that energy. She felt giddy and high.

"Me too." Gab's gaze flicked to the wall behind Sissy, and she took Sissy's hand. "Why wait until we get to our room?"

"Gab! Nobody's doing it in plain sight."

"There's a restroom right behind us." Gab pulled her close and whispered, "You're all flushed, honey. I can practically smell you. How about a little something to stave off the fever?"

"Gab . . . we'll get caught." Even to her own ears, her tone screamed *yes*.

Gab let go of her and headed for the restroom. Sissy looked after her and then couldn't help but follow.

They were a long way from home and the air seethed with freedom, but that didn't mean they had to get arrested. Did they actually arrest people on cruises?

The restroom was opulent by any standards, with chilled marble walls and floors. It was also quite unoccupied. She followed Gab into the stall at the very end, feeling shy and not at all certain that anything more than frustrating gropes could happen. "I don't think this is going to work. I'm sorry."

Gab shushed her as she locked the stall door. "Just a little something, honey." She pushed Sissy against the wall and kissed her hungrily this time, hands cupping her face.

Enhanced by the cold wall against her back, goose bumps

started in Sissy's toes like they always did, running like chilled fire up her legs to her thighs. She tried to fight it back, but Gab was whispering hot little words in her ears. It wasn't that she wasn't turned on, but she was used to not allowing feelings like these to blossom outside of their bedroom. She'd not realized until now that the habit was so deeply ingrained.

"Come on, honey," Gab whispered. "Let me touch you. I want to lick you everywhere. Let me inside you." Her hands swept around to firmly squeeze Sissy's bottom. "A little taste of what I'm going to do to you later."

"Heaven above, Gab. You're making it hard to say no."

"Good."

A quickie in a public restroom was in every lesbian erotic anthology she'd ever read, almost as if it were a rite of passage, but she'd never thought it was something she could do. It wasn't safe—and that was part of the thrill, she had to admit as Gab pushed her shorts down slightly—but it was as safe here as it was ever going to be.

The goose bumps swept up her tummy, over her chest, and Gab smiled into their long, wet kiss.

"What?" Sissy gasped against Gab's mouth as fingers slipped down the front of her shorts.

"I love it when your nipples get hard like this. I can feel them burning holes in me. Later, honey, later, I'm going to give them all the attention they want. But right now, this."

A surprised, loud moan escaped Sissy before she could stop herself, echoing off the marble walls. Gab's fingers were warm and direct, and the sound of pleasure Gab made as they kissed again added more fuel to the fire.

"You're so wet, honey."

"I want you." Sissy frantically unbuttoned her shorts and shoved her clothing down. She'd never had her panties all the way off in a public restroom before. She hoped it didn't shock Gab. There was something more than the heat of the moment happening.

Gab went to her knees with another sound of ravenous pleasure and Sissy flattened against the wall, trying not to fall down as the heat of Gab's tongue seared over her clit. Then Gab's fingers were pushing her open, slipping inside her, and Sissy realized that even if she heard someone enter the restroom, she couldn't stop now.

Gab gave a smothered laugh of delight and pushed in harder as her tongue continued its dancing circles. I'm making her happy, Sissy thought, with the little part of her brain that wasn't overwhelmed by the ripples that had begun to pulse between her clit and the deep place that Gab was massaging with her fingers. Gab knew her body so well, knew just what to pleasure and tease and stroke.

She was distantly aware that her cry of climax reverberated off the bathroom walls. She wound her fingers into Gab's hair as she jerked against her mouth, two, three, four times, then just as Gab began to let go of her, one last time accompanied by a surprised giggle.

Gab, being Gab, made a show of licking her lips, then wiping off her mouth. "Will that help you last until we can get to our stateroom?"

Sissy seized Gab in a comfortable, pleased embrace. "Yes, you wild woman." I do make her happy, Sissy thought again. It suddenly seemed abundantly unfair that the only place she felt safe to do so was behind a locked door.

Gab helped her step into her panties and shorts, and gave her clit one last parting kiss. "I love you, honey," she said somewhat shyly as she pulled Sissy into her arms. "Thank you for letting me do that."

"Thank you for wanting to. Thank you for . . ." She struggled to find just the right words. "For not being afraid. At home—"

"But we're not there." Gab's face smelled like really good sex as they kissed again.

Sissy pulled Gab out of the stall after her. "Let's go ogle some more dykes."

"You bet." A glance over her shoulder confirmed for Sissy that Gab was strutting. It felt for a moment like her heart would burst with happiness.

When they emerged into the corridor there was another couple at the glass looking down at the Solarium deck. One of the women turned to study them for just a little bit longer than a polite glance.

Oh hell, Sissy thought, how loud was I?

Then the woman grinned, ear-to-ear, and gave them a friendly nod.

Sissy couldn't help but blush a little in response to the other woman's knowing look. Nevertheless, she maintained the eye contact and grinned back as she took Gab's hand in her own. She thought, with the surprise that comes from realizing that the truth had been there all along, that this was the world the way it ought to be.

Uncharted Course
Radclyffe

"Here you are," the purser said, handing two passports and a folder across the counter. "Have a great cruise."

"Thank you, I'm sure we will." Cynthia Wilson stepped aside so those in line behind her could take care of their pre-departure paperwork. She recognized a starry-eyed couple who had been waiting to board with her earlier and recalled overhearing one enthuse to her girlfriend, "I don't think we're in Kansas anymore." Scanning the crowd of women in all sizes, shapes and colors that spilled out into the atrium, Cyn had to agree. Definitely not Kansas, and for a second she let herself drift on the over-the-rainbow excitement everyone seemed to be infected with.

Reality intruded as soon as she searched for her employer and discovered her, not surprisingly, in the midst of an animated conversation with Jessica Parry, their very attractive tour director. After serving as Rian James's administrative assistant for almost three years, Cyn didn't know why it still bothered her to see Rian with yet another new woman in her thrall. Rian was not only a successful corporate headhunter, but also a prominent lesbian activist, and drew attention almost anywhere she went. At thirty-five and single, not to mention drop-dead gorgeous, she was considered one of the country's most eligible lesbian bachelors. Cyn was used to seeing her with beautiful women, *many* beautiful women, but she just wasn't in the mood to witness a new conquest. Deciding to slip away with the excuse of viewing Venice from on deck as the *Riviera Andante* left port, she was almost at the door when she heard Rian's husky alto.

"Cyn! All done?"

Fixing a smile, Cyn turned. "Yes." She had little choice but to join Rian and Jessica. Rian's deep brown eyes, Cyn realized, were marred by smudges beneath each one, and her cream-colored linen pants looked loose on her lean frame. *She's lost weight. She needs this vacation, even if part of it is work.*

"I was just going to the cabin to make sure the luggage is taken care of," Cyn said while indicating the folder in her hand. "And I need to put this away."

"I'll come with you," Rian said.

Cyn slid a glance at the decidedly voluptuous redhead by Rian's side, but couldn't detect any sign of displeasure. If she had glimpsed the makings of a liaison, neither Rian nor Jessica gave any sign of it. Still, it was her job to see to the travel details, not Rian's. "That's not necessary. I'll take—"

"Cyn," Rian murmured, as she slid an arm around Cyn's waist and guided her subtly but firmly into the hall, "you're on vacation too. We agreed on that before we booked the cruise."

"You know neither one of us is going to be completely on vacation." Cyn tried not to shiver from the heat of Rian's hand searing through her blouse. The light pressure of Rian's palm wouldn't have been quite so hard to ignore if she didn't know exactly what Rian's hands could do to her body. For a few brief minutes one night almost six weeks before, she'd felt those hands inside her. Determined not to think about that one night, a night to which neither of them had ever subsequently referred, Cyn injected a note of mock reprimand into her voice. "You've got two ship-to-shore phone conferences and one onboard meeting scheduled, and we haven't even left port. I'm lucky I held you to that."

"As I recall," Rian said, her fingers drifting up and down Cyn's side, "you were quite forceful, and I had no choice but to submit."

Submit. Is that what Rian had done when Cyn had seduced her in a limousine on their way to a fundraiser? Rian had let herself be taken, had let Cyn kneel between her legs and tease her with her hands and her mouth until she'd come. But it hadn't felt like *Rian's* submission when Cyn had curled up in Rian's lap and Rian had slipped her hand beneath Cyn's black vintage Dior and caressed her to orgasm. Even now, the memory of the shattering pleasure was overpowering, and Cyn shuddered.

"Tired?" Rian asked gently. "It was a long flight and I know you were up half the night finalizing that last prospectus."

"No, I'm not tired," Cyn said brightly, trying unsuccessfully to slip out of Rian's grasp. "Just excited . . . about the cruise."

"Me too." Rian's voice was throaty and warm.

Cyn realized then that it had been a mistake to book a suite, even if their beds *were* in separate rooms. How she'd ever thought she could be in that kind of proximity to Rian for a week, she had no idea. Well. She would just have to get through it the way she got through every day—by doing her job. After all, Rian had made it clear by not mentioning their encounter that she wanted to keep their relationship strictly professional. "We've got four hours until the Captain's Reception. I want to make sure your suit gets unpacked. It's bound to be wrinkled—"

"It'll be fine." Rian unlocked the door to their suite and held it open for Cyn, then followed her inside. "I don't suppose you packed that Dior, did you?"

"I . . ." Cyn turned quickly away and pretended to look out the double glass doors to the veranda. God, she was in trouble when just the mention of the dress she'd worn the one and only time they'd made love could make her blush. Not just make her blush, but make her wet. She folded her arms around her middle. "No."

"That's too bad," Rian said from somewhere very close behind. "I'm very fond of that dress."

Stepping sideways, Cyn pivoted and managed to get around Rian without touching her. She crossed the room to where the porter had left their luggage standing in front of the closets, and turned the larger piece onto its side. She knelt to open it and then grew still as she realized Rian had come to stand beside her. Without looking up, she said, "I'm going to get these clothes put away. Why don't you relax for a while?"

In the other room, Cyn thought desperately. *Somewhere, anywhere, where you're not so close to me. Somewhere where I can't smell your cologne. Somewhere where I can't see you and want to . . .*

"I think we should make a deal." Rian clasped Cyn's hands and drew her to her feet.

Cyn made the mistake of looking into Rian's eyes then and found that she couldn't look away. She'd seen Rian under every circumstance imaginable in the last three years, and she knew every nuance of her expressions. She recognized the subtle tightening of the muscles along her jaw when she was angry, and the glint in her eyes when she was about to close a deal that was far more to her advantage than anyone realized, and the slow, lazy way she smiled when she saw a woman she wanted. And once, so painfully briefly, she'd witnessed Rian's look of utter abandon when she'd come. This afternoon, however, the look in Rian's eyes was one she couldn't decipher. A fierceness she'd never seen, even in the heat of corporate battle. Unnerved, Cyn brushed at the chestnut strands that fluttered over the collar of

Rian's shirt. "I should have scheduled a haircut for you before we left."

"The deal," Rian went on, apparently undeterred by Cyn's non sequitur, "is that you don't take care of any details this week. In fact, you don't take care of anything to do with me at all."

"I don't understand," Cyn whispered, aware that Rian's mouth was mere inches from hers. "If you didn't need me, why did you suggest I come with you?"

"Because we both needed a vacation and I enjoy your company." Rian shook her head and smiled as if Cyn had missed some very important point. "And because I wanted to be with you when I wasn't your boss."

Cyn felt her face flaming again and tried to extricate her fingers from Rian's grip. "Well, since I'm here, then it only makes sense that I should do my job."

"No," Rian said. "I think, since we're on vacation, we should do something completely different."

"Like what?" Cyn said, thoroughly confused. She couldn't think clearly with Rian's body nearly pressed against hers. Somehow, without her realizing it, Rian had let go of her hands and lightly clasped both arms around her waist. Cyn's legs trembled, and she felt another wash of arousal.

"This week, you're going to be in charge, and I'm going to take care of you."

Cyn pulled away and laughed uncomfortably. "I'm afraid you'd find that very boring, very quickly."

"Really?" Rian leaned against the dresser and put her hands in her pockets while giving Cyn an appraising glance. "So what were you planning to do between now and the reception?"

"After I unpacked, I was going to—" Cyn broke off, ambushed by an image of herself stretched out in the bathtub, head back, eyes closed, bringing herself to orgasm while she fantasized about Rian making love to her.

"What?" Rian teased. "You're blushing again."

"Just the usual things that a girl does before going out to a formal reception," Cyn said haughtily, hoping that Rian would let it drop. "You know."

"I have no idea. What sort of things?"

"I'm not going to tell you that!" Cyn pointed toward the adjoining bedroom. "Go in there and read or something, and let me get some work done."

Rian shook her head. "No, I don't think so." She pushed away from the dresser and caught Cyn's hand. She turned her toward the bathroom. "I told you, I want to take care of you this trip. Starting now."

When Cyn felt Rian's mouth against the side of her neck, she closed her eyes. Then Rian's arms circled her waist from behind, and she leaned back into the embrace. It was beyond her power to resist when Rian's mouth was on her skin and Rian's hands gently caressed her stomach, but her mind was still functional enough for her to understand the message. *You're going to be in charge. I want to take care of you.* "I have quite a lot to do to get ready."

"Tell me." Rian sucked Cyn's earlobe as she carefully loosed Cyn's blouse from her slacks. "Tell me what you need me to do."

"Why don't you draw a bath for me?" Cyn instructed. "And then, perhaps I will."

Rian dropped one last kiss onto Cyn's neck. "All right. I'll take care of that right now."

When Rian disappeared into the bathroom, Cyn quickly shed her clothes, sorted through her luggage until she found a short, aqua-blue silk robe, and pulled it on. She'd chosen it because it was a match to the color of her eyes. She glanced in the mirror and saw the flush of arousal on her neck and chest. Rian would surely see it too, but she couldn't help the fact that her entire body hummed with anticipation. She pulled out the band that held her shoulder length blond hair back and flicked her head to shake out the curls. When she turned toward the bathroom,

Rian was framed in the doorway, watching her with an expression Cyn *did* recognize. Hunger.

"Is it ready?" Cyn asked with a nonchalance she didn't feel. The sensation of silk gliding over her hard nipples as she walked toward Rian turned her liquid inside.

"Almost."

"If you're going to help me with my bath . . ." Cyn stopped in the doorway opposite Rian and traced her fingertip along Rian's jaw and down her neck, enjoying the way Rian tensed and caught her breath. "You should get out of these clothes. In fact, I think you should strip down to your underwear."

Wordlessly, Rian unbuttoned her shirt and pulled it from her pants. As much as Cyn wanted to watch her undress, ached to see her completely nude when previously she'd only caught glimpses of her, she turned away and walked into the bathroom. She couldn't look at her now without giving away how much she wanted Rian to just take her. Her stomach quivered and her clit throbbed insistently. She was so excited she was afraid if Rian touched her anywhere at all, she'd come.

"You will not," she whispered fervently to herself. Whatever this was, she was going to make it last as long as she possibly could.

"What was that?" Rian asked quietly.

Cyn glanced behind her and almost moaned. Rian wore nothing except a pair of black bikini briefs. Her breasts, high and firm and round, were tipped by small dusky nipples. Small very *erect* nipples.

Oh God, she's excited, too—and even more beautiful than I imagined.

"I said," Cyn said sharply, ignoring the sensation of her clitoris stiffening, "I'd like to get started while the water is still warm. I need to wash my hair."

"I'll take your robe." Rian slowly and deliberately untied the sash, allowing the robe to fall open and expose the inner surfaces of Cyn's breasts. She skimmed her palms beneath the silk and over Cyn's breasts on her way to easing the robe from Cyn's shoulders.

Cyn gasped at the fleeting brush of Rian's hot skin and swayed toward Rian. She was forced to brace her hands on Rian's bare shoulders to catch her balance. Aching to ease the painful pressure that centered just beneath her nipples, all she wanted was to rub her breasts over Rian's. She was so aroused her inner thighs were wet. Rian's face was very close, her eyes very intense as they looked into Cyn's. If she kissed Rian now, Cyn knew, she could have Rian inside her within seconds. She remembered the feel of those long, slender fingers filling her, the way Rian circled her clitoris with her thumb as she stroked her, fucking her deeper and harder with each thrust as she masturbated her clitoris, finally making her come with every part of her cunt exploding. How many times had she replayed those few moments, alone in the dark, or once, with a woman who looked very much like Rian? But no memory or stranger could give her what she really needed, the sound of Rian whispering, *You feel so wonderful, Cyn. I want to feel you come, come just for me.*

"Better get in," Rian murmured just as Cyn was about to give in to the wild need churning in the pit of her stomach.

"Yes," Cyn said hoarsely, keeping one hand on Rian's shoulder as she turned and stepped into the hot, soothing water. The steam held a fragrance of vanilla, and she realized that Rian had used some of the complimentary essential oils that she'd noticed on the bathroom counter. The special touch surprised her, although she wasn't certain why. Despite Rian's lethal aggression during business battles, she had always been attentive and kind to Cyn. In fact, she never treated Cyn like an employee. Perhaps if she had, Cyn wouldn't have fallen . . . No, that was one place she couldn't afford to go. Cyn tipped her head back and dipped her hair below the surface to wet it. "You can shampoo me now."

"I'd love to." Rian sat on the wide edge of the built-in tub and poured thick golden liquid into her hand. Then she spread her fingers through Cyn's hair, caressing her scalp.

Cyn tipped her head back and watched Rian through slitted lids as Rian bent forward, both hands buried in Cyn's hair, her breasts swaying inches from Cyn's face. If Cyn lifted her head just a little, she would be able to capture one of those teasingly tight nipples in her mouth. She wanted to so badly. She wanted to bite down and make Rian whimper, make her ache to come as badly as Cyn ached now. The play of Rian's fingers over her scalp and the back of her neck did nothing to quiet the urgency in her cunt. The warm water lapped around her clitoris, teasing it with every slight movement as if a tongue gently licked her. She imagined Rian's mouth closing around her swollen clitoris, sucking gently, and she moaned.

"Good?" Rian asked, her voice deeper than Cyn had ever heard it.

"Oh God, yes."

Rian bent lower, dipped an arm into the water, and circled Cyn's shoulders. "Tilt your head back and rinse."

Cyn arched and submerged her hair, turning her face as she did and brushing her mouth over Rian's nipple. She heard Rian's swift gasp and smiled with satisfaction. Then she pushed herself upward with her arms outstretched on either side of the tub, lifting her breasts from the water. "Now lather the rest of me."

Cyn had never been able to come just from breast play, but she feared she might now as Rian's soapy hands massaged her breasts, lingering on her taut nipples, pinching them so lightly she might have imagined it, but she knew she hadn't. Her clitoris twitched in time to the sharp points of pleasure spearing her breasts. *A little more, just a little more, just a little harder.* Her head fell back and she closed her eyes. She needed to come. It didn't matter that it was too soon, she needed relief. Rian's fingers etched slick circles on her stomach, moving lower. *Oh, yes. Just touch me and I'll . . .*

Rian's hands disappeared at the same instant as her lips skimmed Cyn's mouth. Cyn's eyes flew open, but by the time she focused, Rian was sitting up on the edge of the tub, smiling softly. Her expression was calm, almost casual, but her breasts rose and fell rapidly, and her nipples, if possible, stood out even more than they had before.

"I was afraid you might fall asleep," Rian said.

"No," Cyn said weakly. "No, not likely." She reached beside her and opened the drain on the tub. Her legs felt heavy, listless, and she wondered if she could stand. She held up one hand. "Rinse me with the shower massage?"

Rian's eyes widened for an instant, then she took Cyn's hand and guided her up. "I may have to stand in there with you . . . to reach everything."

"Then we're lucky the suites have roomy tubs." Cyn glanced down as Rian climbed into the tub. Rian's arms and chest were wet, and thin rivulets ran down her stomach and dampened the top of her black bikinis. Cyn traced a wandering trail of water with her fingertip and Rian's belly tensed and quivered. "Are you wet?"

"What?" Looking stunned, Rian bowed her head, her gaze riveted to Cyn's hand.

Cyn flicked a nail beneath the top edge of Rian's bikinis, and Rian grasped Cyn's wrist with trembling fingers. For one brief second, Cyn thought Rian was going to push her fingers between her legs. She wouldn't have resisted. She had tasted Rian, there on her knees in a limousine. She had felt her grow hard and urgent between her lips, had felt her pulse to the brink of release and then shatter with a rush of sweet come that had filled her mouth and left her hungry ever after.

"These," Cyn repeated, tugging lightly on the material between Rian's legs. "Did we get you wet?"

"Soaked," Rian said roughly.

"Then take them off."

In seconds they were both naked. When Rian reached around Cyn to turn the dials on the handheld shower massage, their breasts brushed, then melded, and Cyn allowed herself the fleeting indulgence of dragging her mouth down the column of Rian's throat, licking the sweat and scented water from her skin. Rian quivered, and Cyn wanted to beg.

Finish me now. Fuck me make me come. Fuck me fuck me fuck me.

Rian leaned back, her thighs brushing Cyn's, and played the spray over Cyn's chest and breasts. "Too hard?"

Cyn shook her head, her throat too tight for words. The pinpricks of water striking her swollen breasts sent electric echoes to her clit, and she rubbed her needy cunt over Rian's. She couldn't stand it. She was losing control but she didn't care. "Oh God I need to—"

"Spread your legs," Rian whispered as she knelt in front of Cyn.

"Rian," Cyn said as she opened her legs and steadied herself with her hand cupped against the side of Rian's face, "be careful."

"I'll stop whenever you say." Gently, Rian spread Cyn's lips with her thumb and finger and directed a warm, gentle spray over her lips. Cyn twitched and moaned softly.

"Mmm, wonderful." Cyn's thighs shook and her cunt contracted slowly, then pulsed steadily. "Rian."

Rian removed her fingers for an instant and Cyn heard her ratchet the dial on the showerhead. Then Rian fingered the hood away from her clit and directed a steady stream against it.

"Oh God." Cyn shuddered. "Oh, you can't do that. God, Rian. Stop. Stop before you make me come."

Rian twitched the water away and gazed up. "You're incredibly wet and your clit is so hard. Don't you want to come?"

"Yes, yes. So much."

"Then tell me. Tell me, Cyn, tell me what you want."

Cyn rubbed her thumb over Rian's mouth. "This. I've dreamed of your mouth on me."

Wordlessly, Rian leaned forward and delicately kissed Cyn's clit. Just a brush of her lips and then she was gone. Cyn whimpered. Standing, Rian whispered, "I want to take my time."

Quickly, Rian turned off the water and stepped out of the tub. She rotated the dial for the overhead heat light and spread out a large fluffy bath sheet on the edge of the tiled tub surround. She held out her hand to Cyn. "Sit here."

Cyn settled onto the warm, soft towel as Rian knelt between her legs. She couldn't think of anything except Rian's mouth and how much she ached. She curved one hand behind Rian's head and pressed the fingertips of her other hand against her mons, bearing down until her clit rose up. "There. I need you there."

Rian moaned and rubbed her check against Cyn's thigh. "What would you like?"

"Lick me," Cyn said, her voice breaking. "Lick me and . . ." The first sweep of Rian's slick, hot tongue sent shivers along her spine and her vision immediately blurred. She felt the pull of Rian sucking on her clit, and her cunt clenched painfully. "Yes, yes, your tongue feels so nice. Oh . . . slow down. Slow down or you'll make me finish right this second. I don't want to."

Cyn pulled Rian away from her clit with a hand in her hair. Rian looked dazed, her mouth swollen and wet.

"I need you," Rian groaned. "Please."

"Go slow. I'm almost ready to come."

Cyn guided Rian's mouth back to her clit, whimpering as soft lips closed around her. Her clit stiffened with the constant attention, and she fought not to let go. Rian's mouth was hot and her tongue worked Cyn's clit back and forth, faster and faster, just the way she needed it manipulated to come. She couldn't help herself. She had to come.

"I'm going to . . ." Cyn tried to warn her, but her hips lurched and her clit spasmed, and she couldn't do anything to stop it now. "Oh, it's so good."

Cyn closed her eyes as pleasure erupted deep in her belly and flooded through her. She cried out, writing against Rian's face with each wrenching beat of her cunt. When she sagged forward Rian stood quickly and cradled her against her body. Gasping, still trembling with aftershocks, Cyn rubbed her face over Rian's breasts and caught a nipple in her mouth. She sucked it as her clit continued to twitch.

"Cyn," Rian groaned. "Oh Cyn. I need . . ."

Cyn pressed her palm to Rian's stomach, felt her body jerk, and slipped her fingers lower. Rian groaned again when Cyn found her clitoris and began to fondle her. Within seconds, Rian's thighs turned to stone.

"That's it," Cyn crooned, "come."

Rian shuddered and came in a hot gush on Cyn's hand.

"I like this trip already," Rian sighed.

"The itinerary isn't quite what I expected," Cyn said, searching Rian's eyes.

"Just a slight change of course." Rian kissed her softly. "I've been wanting to do that for the last six weeks."

Cyn rested her cheek against Rian's belly. "What, give me a bath?"

"Make love with you again when we were just us." Rian laughed. "But now that I know how enjoyable a bath can be, that too."

"I'm glad you liked it." Cyn kissed Rian's stomach, then grinned up at her. "Wait until you see how much fun it will be to shave my legs."

Music on the Wind
Radclyffe

Anna woke in the dark to the sensation of a cool, damp wind blowing across her face. She reached for Graham and when she didn't find her, shot upright, her heart racing. The cabin glowed with the eerie blue-gray cast of moonlight in the midnight sky, and it took her only a second of glancing frantically around the strange space to realize that the doors to the balcony were open, and she was completely alone.

"Oh my God." She lurched from bed, grasped her robe in one hand and hastily pulled it on as she ran outside. "Graham!"

Graham Yardley turned her face away from the ocean and toward the sound of Anna's voice. "Anna? What's the matter?"

"I couldn't find you," Anna gasped, pressing her hands to Graham's chest. With the moon and ocean behind her and her face in shadow, Graham's chiseled profile and blade-thin form appeared like a rent in the fabric of a dark and dangerous painting. Searching for something to say that wouldn't betray her terror, Anna said, "Darling, your shirt is soaked."

"I'm surprised at how much spray there is all the way up here." Graham covered Anna's hands with hers and bent to kiss her. "We're quite high up, aren't we?"

Anna shivered, thinking just exactly how high above the water their suite was situated. From the balcony where Graham had stood alone, it was at least a hundred feet to the surface of the ocean. Had she fallen . . . Anna pressed her face to the curve of Graham's neck and wrapped her arms tightly around her waist. "How long have you been out here?"

"Not long. Ten minutes." Graham stroked Anna's hair and gathered her close. "You're upset. Why?"

"I wish you wouldn't take midnight tours without me, darling," Anna said lightly.

"After five years you don't trust me to walk around by myself?" Graham tilted Anna's face up with a finger beneath her chin and kissed her again, skimming her tongue lightly between Anna's lips before drawing back.

"There's no one in the world who knows as well as I how independent you are," Anna murmured, resting her cheek on Graham's shoulder. "But it's our first night and we've never been on a ship like this before. Graham, you can't realize what it's like out here—it feels as if we're a tiny city adrift in an endless, uninhabited universe. There's nothing around us except the stars overhead. The seas are quiet right now, but if there were turbulence and you lost your footing, you wouldn't be able to—"

"Anna, love," Graham whispered, "I've seen the ocean. I've even seen oceangoing ships." She reached beside her and curled one hand around the balcony railing. "And I can hold on quite adequately."

"I know, but you haven't seen *this* one, and I'd feel better if you got acquainted with it a little more before you started investigating on your own."

"Well then," Graham said, "let's take a walk and you can show me."

"Now? It's the middle of the night." Anna laughed, realizing she was the only one exhausted by four months of nonstop touring on three continents. Graham never seemed to tire of the hectic concert schedule, and performing only seemed to invigorate her. "You're not tired at all, are you?"

Graham smiled. "Excited. We haven't had a vacation together in a very long time."

"It seems to me that we've been in every major European city in the last few—"

"It's not a vacation for you when I'm touring, I know that. I'm distracted and self-absorbed, and you worry that I don't eat enough." Graham slid her hands inside Anna's silk robe and caressed her breasts. "And I'm not very attentive."

Anna caught her breath, ambushed by the sudden swelling of her breasts. Every part of her responded to Graham's touch, as if her body were as precisely strung as the strings on Graham's concert grand. "Graham, darling, you are very attentive when you're touring because all the passion that wells up in you when you play is still there after the performance." She kissed Graham lingeringly. "And I'm always waiting."

"I still don't feel like I take enough time with you." Graham clasped Anna's hand. "Let's explore."

"I need to change." Anna skimmed her fingers over Graham's shirt. "And so do you. I'll find you something."

"I'll wear my jeans," Graham said, following Anna's gentle lead back into the cabin. "Then I'll know I'm really on vacation."

Anna smiled to herself as she opened the suitcases they hadn't yet unpacked. She found a pair of black denim jeans and a soft cotton navy V-neck sweater. Graham had never worn casual clothes off the rack before they'd met. Her wardrobe had been custom-made all of her life, because she'd been performing all of her life. She'd only stopped playing after a car accident left her blind and she'd gone into seclusion for a dozen years. But now, she had returned to the concert stage and to life. Their life.

"Here," Anna said, turning with the clothes in her hands. She stopped, startled despite how many times in their years together the same thing had happened. Graham held out one of Anna's favorite lounging-around outfits, a pale green, scoop neck sweater and tan cotton slacks. "I don't how you do that."

Graham grinned, momentarily softening the austerely handsome planes of her face—a classically beautiful face marred by a diagonal scar across her forehead that extended into one eyebrow. That mark of past tragedy only made Anna desire her more.

"I know the way they feel from touching you in them," Graham said. "And I plan on spending a lot more time touching them this evening."

Anna's legs felt suddenly shaky and she laughed self-consciously, as if they weren't longtime lovers but newlyweds on their wedding night. "Stop," she said softly.

Graham cupped Anna's cheek and smiled. "You're blushing."

"I was just thinking that there's something about being here, away from our normal lives—if anything about our life can be called normal—that makes me feel as if it's our first time together. I can't . . ." She feathered her fingers across Graham's mouth. "I can't wait for you to make love to me."

Graham grew suddenly still, her clear dark eyes focused unerringly on Anna's. She parted Anna's robe and skimmed it off her shoulders, dropping it behind them on the bed. Then she curved an arm around Anna's waist and pulled her close, caressing her breasts as she kissed her. Anna moaned and leaned into Graham's embrace.

A moment later, Graham glided her lips along the rim of Anna's ear. "Perhaps the tour should wait until morning."

Anna's heart pounded and her stomach tingled in that "wanting to be touched" kind of way that always made her long for Graham's talented hands. Shaking her head, she gently disengaged. "I want to walk with you for a while and think about how wonderful you're going to make me feel later."

"It's a clear night, isn't it? A little bit cool."

"Yes," Anna said, slipping the sweater over her head, loving the freedom of having nothing against her skin except the soft, familiar fabric. "How can you tell?"

"The air is very sharp and crisp, despite the salt spray. It feels as if there's nothing between my skin and the stars except the night."

"There isn't. When we go up on deck, I'll point them out to you. The stars."

"I'd like that."

Anna brushed a lock of dark hair back from Graham's forehead and laughed softly as it promptly fell back. Graham's hair, though carefully styled for the concert stage, was still casually roguish. Traces of gray streaked her temples now, and although she was naturally pale and slender, she radiated vitality and passion with every breath.

"I love you," Anna whispered. Not that long ago Graham had nearly slipped away, and Anna would never forget the agony of almost losing her.

Graham looked up from buttoning her jeans, and as always, Anna felt her gaze. Graham couldn't see her, had never seen her, but she had never felt so known in all the ways that mattered.

"I love you." Graham held out her hand. "Are you prepared to be my tour guide?"

"Always." Anna threaded her fingers through Graham's. "We are in the center of the main room of the suite right now. The bed—a queen size, very nice—is behind us. To your left are—"

"Two sets of double doors to the veranda, which faces the bow and overlooks the port side of the ship. We're on deck nine—Pegasio, which is the highest level containing passenger cabins. To our right is the sitting room and the door to the bath."

"I told you all this earlier, didn't I?" Anna said, laughing.

"You did. If you hadn't, I wouldn't have gone out onto the veranda."

"Uh huh," Anna said with a hint of disbelief. She tugged Graham toward the door and opened it. "The hallway is ten feet wide with cabin doors opening every twenty feet or so along it. We're at the very front of this deck, so if we walk down the corridor to the central foyer, we'll reach the elevators."

Anna waited while Graham closed the door, her right hand on the handle, and pivoted to face the direction in which they would walk. Although Graham had not been born blind, she had developed an unerring sense of herself in relationship to her environment and adapted very quickly to new surroundings. Still, she could not see and that made her vulnerable, and Anna was intensely attuned to that fact every moment of the day. And every moment of the day, she worked hard so that Graham would not sense her worry.

"Ready?" Anna asked.

Graham took Anna's hand as any lover would upon embarking on a stroll. "Yes."

"The ship is almost nine hundred feet long, which is almost . . ." Anna hesitated, working on the math as they walked.

"A little bit over an eighth of a mile." Graham tucked Anna's hand in the bend of her arm.

"Something like that." Anna laughed. "Now, this deck actually overlooks one of the main restaurants two decks below." They reached the end of the passageway and Anna stopped. "Have you been counting?"

"Yes. To the right are the elevators?"

"That's right. And to the left is the open balcony that rings the restaurant below. Halfway around in that direction are the doors to one of the outside pools. There's also a cabana and bar out there, but they're closed tonight, of course." Anna wanted to tell Graham not to attempt navigating anywhere in this area by herself, but she refrained. In all likelihood Graham would not go anywhere without her. As independent as Graham might be, she wasn't foolhardy. "We can go down to the lounge now, or check out the decks where the health spas and casinos are located, or we can go outside and see the stars."

"We'll have plenty of time to explore the rest of the ship tomorrow," Graham said, draping her arm around Anna's shoulders. "I opt for stars tonight."

"Good." Anna encircled Graham's waist and tilted her head against Graham's shoulder. "Let's find a deck chair to cuddle up in."

Once outside, Anna chose a deck lounger out of the wind and away from the few couples who stood at the rail on the far side of the pool, apparently taking in the view. She tilted the back of the lounger so that it was nearly reclining and said, "You lie down first."

Graham stretched out and Anna settled between her legs, her back to Graham's chest. When Graham's arms came around her, she clasped them and nuzzled her face against Graham's neck. "Perfect."

"Are you cold?" Graham murmured with her lips against Anna's ear.

"No, not with you holding me this way."

"Can you count the stars?"

Anna laughed. "There are thousands."

Graham eased one hand free from Anna's grip and slid it underneath the bottom of Anna's sweater, spreading her fingers over Anna's stomach. "How many can you see directly above us?"

"Oh," Anna mused, realizing how many small stars there were between the bright points of the constellations. "Hundreds."

"Even the wind is different out here," Graham said, tilting her head to one side. "It ebbs and flows as if the sky itself were breathing. Or playing for us."

Anna closed her eyes, hoping to capture the refrain that Graham heard in the night sky. The stars still sparkled beneath her closed lids and her skin tingled, stirred by Graham's fingers moving rhythmically on her bare stomach, recreating the wind-song on her skin. Graham did that unconsciously when a melody formed in her mind, her pianist's fingers playing chords as the music came to her. Anna had fallen hopelessly in love watching Graham play and had lost her heart to the woman whose music was life. Now, years later, she fell in love with her all over again every time Graham played. Tonight, she felt her play.

"Your hands are so warm." Anna shifted her hips between Graham's legs, feeling the heat spread from Graham's hands throughout her stomach and settle deep, deep inside.

"Your skin is so soft." Graham skimmed her other hand beneath Anna's sweater, this hand cooler than the first had been. When Anna tensed, Graham stilled. "Too cold?"

"Mmm, no. It feels wonderful." Anna kissed Graham's neck, then, eyes still closed, she arched one arm back and slid her hand behind Graham's neck, tugging Graham's head lower so she could find her mouth. She kissed her, exploring her lips and inside her mouth as if her tongue were all she could see or touch her with. When Graham lightly sucked on the tip of her tongue, Anna moaned. "I think we should go back to our cabin."

"I think you should let us play for you, the wind and I." Graham cupped Anna's breasts and rippled her fingers over the nipples, scoring the melody, note by flowing note. "Listen, Anna."

Anna strained to feel what Graham heard, her body electric with silent sound. A sliver of cool night air licked her belly where Graham's wrists tented her sweater, and she tightened inside. Or was it Graham's fingertips, as soft and clever as her mouth, gracefully tracing a phrase over her breast, striking a cantabile deep in her flesh that ignited the familiar ache? Anna couldn't tell. Like a countermelody, elusive and sweet, she felt Graham's hands in places beyond her body and her blood. Her passion brimmed and pulsed, as fluid and graceful as the chords that flowed beneath Graham's hands on the concert stage. Pleasure pierced her nipples and converged in a single point between her legs. She floated on the music flowing in and around her—the distant rush of water, Graham's heartbeat, her own breathless moans. So much beauty to hold, too much pleasure to contain. She ached to spill into the night, onto the wind, over Graham's hands.

"Graham," Anna gasped, trembling in the curve of Graham's body, "what you're doing to me. I can't keep it all inside. I need to . . . oh, God I need to let go. Will you make me come?"

"Yes," Graham breathed against Anna's ear. "Anything. Always."

Anna fumbled to open her slacks. "It won't take very long. I'm so ready for you."

"Don't hurry." Graham slid her hand down Anna's stomach, beneath her shorts, and cupped her tenderly. "Tell me what you see."

"Lights sparkling everywhere. Endlessly." Anna arched her back and pressed herself to Graham's palm. She was wet and open, aching to be filled. "Please put your fingers on me . . . oh, I love when you touch me . . ."

"Is the moon very bright?"

"Yes, very . . . oh, there, that's perfect . . . just keep touching me there and I'll—"

"What else?" Graham caressed her lingeringly, then fleetingly, now harder, then softly, coaxing every note from her flesh.

"Wisps of cloud . . . there, oh you're prefect . . . touch right there . . ." Anna whimpered when Graham's fingertip circled the spot on the underside of her straining clitoris that always made her come. She needed to come so badly she couldn't think, couldn't speak, but still she tried. She wanted Graham to see. "Clouds . . . like a veil obscuring the face of a beautiful woman . . . I'm going to come soon, darling."

Graham stroked faster, massaging the place that made Anna moan. "You're my night sky, Anna," Graham whispered, "and the light of all my days."

Anna's orgasm played in her depths, a teasing melody she couldn't quite grasp. "Inside . . . I need you inside me . . . darling, please."

"Do you hear it, love?" Graham entered her, one finger after the other until Anna tightened around her and tossed her head in wordless pleasure. Groaning, Graham pressed harder. "You will always be the music, Anna."

"You'll make me . . . oh, God, I can't . . ." Anna pushed down against Graham's hand, forcing her deeper. "More . . . bring me, darling . . . oh, I'm so close now . . ."

"Listen, Anna," Graham urged, thrusting smoothly, her movements a glissando that carried her lover toward climax. "Listen to the . . ."

"I'm coming," Anna cried softly, burying her face against Graham's chest. She sobbed her joy into the night and the wind carried her song to the stars. "I love you. I love you with all I am."

Graham held Anna tightly, her mouth skimming Anna's. "I love you. When I touch you, I . . ." Her voice drifted off as Anna kissed her throat and worked a hand inside her jeans.

"You what, darling?" Anna cupped and squeezed with a slow, steady rhythm, the last notes of her own orgasm still drifting through her body. Graham was hot beneath her hand, her slim form vibrating with tension. Graham always needed release right after she made Anna come, needed Anna to finish her quickly and hard. "Can you still hear the windsong?"

"Yes," Graham groaned, covering Anna's hand and guiding Anna's fingers to the hard ache between her thighs. "Anna . . . Anna . . ."

"What, my love?"

Graham cupped Anna's cheek as the first surge of release broke through her. "The sky," she gasped, shuddering helplessly in Anna's embrace, "the sky is beautiful out here, isn't it?"

"So beautiful." Anna took care that her tears did not fall on Graham's face. As much as her heart ached for the hurt that even her boundless love could not heal, she rejoiced in knowing that their love song was eternal.

Cruise Crews
Karin Kallmaker

"I don't speak Italian," Wendy said in the other woman's ear, hoping at least that much of her English would be understood.

Apparently it was, because the strong arms around her tightened with a little shrug, and the smoky-eyed officer went back to kissing Wendy as they swayed on the discotheque floor.

It was after two a.m., and some members of the crew—female members—had evidently just gotten off duty. At first Wendy wondered if they'd showed up just to check out the queers, but when two began dancing with each other and several more flirted with potential playmates, she'd revised her opinion of their interest.

By now, her ex-best friend Brittany was probably underneath the Chain Maille drummer. It was the first night out, and hanging in the disco on the chance one of the musicians might show up to dance had been Wendy's idea. When the band's dead sexy drummer, Lila, had strolled through the door, she and Brittany had done a little femme dance for her amusement—also Wendy's idea. When Lila got bored and left, Brittany had gone chasing after her like a lapdog while Wendy was in the bathroom.

They might be groupies, but even groupies had some pride. Abandoned, Wendy had blown their first night's drink budget in less than an hour, but then the white-uniformed women had started showing up. The one holding her right now had bought Wendy her last drink. So maybe she couldn't kick it with Lila or JoJo or Reo. A hot woman in uniform was most certainly the next best thing.

The woman said something, and for all Wendy knew she'd just described some kind of gastrointestinal difficulty. It didn't matter—everything she said sounded seductive and romantic. The kisses were deep and wet.

In between the next round of kisses, Wendy put her hand on her chest and repeated her name.

"Sophia," was what she got in reply, and they merged again. Sophia's hands were starting to wander and Wendy didn't mind in the least. Normally she would be a bouncing ball to a Paul Oakenfold remix, but their rhythm had nothing to do with the music that pounded out of the speakers, or the lights that pulsed in the floor beneath their feet.

What, Wendy wondered, did an officer wear under her uniform? If she unbuttoned the form-fitting jacket, would she discover a non-regulation lacy bra? A sexy tattoo? Adventurous piercings? Did it matter as long as there were nipples and skin and nerves underneath all that pristine white? If there was a driving beat and a scream of pure living before the night was done, Wendy would be a happy woman. She leaned into the kisses, hoping her tongue was speaking a universal language.

Though the music made it hard to hear anything else, Wendy heard someone shouting in what sounded like Italian. It took her a muddled moment to realize that the tirade was directed at Sophia—and her, it seemed. Sophia immediately launched into a counter-tirade, and Wendy watched helplessly as a bleached blonde with seriously bad black roots slapped Sophia hard enough to leave a handprint across her cheek.

Wendy might have received the same, but Sophia got between them and pushed the still shouting woman toward the exit. Wendy didn't know what *ficona* meant, but she was certain it could not possibly flatter her.

And Wendy thought she'd seen some dyke drama in her day. Dyke drama in a foreign language was a whole new level.

Left standing in the middle of the dance floor with all eyes on her, Wendy wanted to say, "I didn't know she had a girlfriend," but what was the point? She gathered up her tattered dignity and went to the bathroom in the hope that Sophia and the madwoman had gone somewhere far enough away that Wendy could return to her cabin without encountering either of them.

The splash of cool water on her face helped calm her frayed nerves. Brittany was going to pay for abandoning her, and pay double if she actually managed to get laid. Wendy's chances of first night nooky were nil at this point. What a total waste of a bikini wax and Wonder bra it had turned out to be.

The flash of a white uniform behind her made her gasp and turn in alarm.

The newcomer was one of the other officers who'd been eyeing the dance floor since arriving. Taking Wendy's hand, she said something that might have been about the threat of global warming, but whatever it was she said, it was with a kind smile and an air of apology, followed by a roll of the eyes that clearly indicated that other people were nuts. All Wendy understood for sure was the hand on the chest and, "Carmella."

She repeated her name, and Carmella nodded and gave her a little bow.

"Scuse," she said, or something that sounded like that, then she disappeared into one of the stalls.

Wendy finished dabbing at her face. She was trying to repair some of the damage to her makeup when Carmella joined her at the sink. After washing her hands, she leaned against the counter, watching Wendy in the mirror.

She met Carmella's gaze in their reflection and smiled politely. Carmella nodded back but didn't leave. Wendy filled in her smudged eyeliner, then glanced again at Carmella, who smiled even more broadly and went on watching.

"What?"

Her annoyed question was lost on Carmella, who shrugged without comprehension.

Wendy gathered her makeup back into her purse and headed for the door. A long arm opened it for her before she got there. She muttered her thanks.

"Bibita?"

"I don't speak Italian."

"Bibita," Carmella said again, and Wendy stopped to give her an even more annoyed look. Carmella mimed drinking and gestured toward the bar.

"No," Wendy said. "I've had too much." Carmella raised her hands helplessly, so Wendy put a hand to her head. "I'm going to bed."

"Scorta." Carmella gestured at the exit and offered her arm. "Escort?"

"I don't need—" What if the crazy woman was lurking outside, she thought. She could at least get safe passage out of the line of fire. She tucked her hand under Carmella's arm and accepted the gentle guidance to the exit.

Just the other side of the door was Sophia and her no longer angry girlfriend. At least Wendy presumed she was no longer angry because her skirt was up and Sophia's hand was down. They didn't even notice Wendy going by. She wondered if they did that little scene all the time because the make up sex was hot.

Which would be pretty twisted, Wendy thought. She was glad of Carmella's arm.

"You know," she said for no reason at all, except that walking in silence seemed bizarre. "It's the first night of my vacation, and it didn't have to end quite so crappily. I know I won this trip for me and Brittany, but just because it was free doesn't mean I shouldn't have fun. Brittany couldn't believe it when one of our choices for the cruise was this one. Chain Maille, and we'd be within feet of them. Maybe even seated near them at dinner. Run into them at the pool or something."

They descended a flight of stairs. Carmella made the gesture of putting a key in a lock, and Wendy dug in her purse for the cabin key. Carmella examined it, gave it back and turned them toward aft.

"I know that being a groupie isn't a long-term life choice. I've only got one more year of college and then I won't be able to do this anymore. I'll have an internship to finish and all that shit. We could have dug on Melissa, you know. We were just looking for something fun to do on our vacations. Then we get here and my best friend dumps me in the bar."

With Carmella leading the way Wendy didn't have to worry about finding the correct stairs. She was still completely turned around. The ship was beautiful and all that, but every time she went up or down a deck she lost her sense of which way was which.

"I mean this is a drag. I came on this trip to be wild and crazy, and I was well on my way to a one-night stand with a perfect stranger. But no. No, I have to pick a perfect stranger with a jealous girlfriend."

They encountered no one as they strolled the Via Condotti. It really was a lovely ship, and while Wendy had no real sense of what an Italian villa might look like, she was willing to accept this was a good facsimile, if Italian villas had casinos and shopping concourses. The sculptures of Medusa that circled the atrium on every floor were awesome.

She paused to look more closely at one of them. "Personally,

I think Medusa was just having a bad hair life. She didn't want to be conventional and ends up getting her head cut off by some jerk on his own hero quest. It's really kind of sick that a lot of the hero stories in great literature include at least one instance where the dude earns his dudeness by killing a woman."

Carmella was listening politely when Wendy glanced at her. She couldn't have been even five years older than Wendy was, and Wendy had no idea what the two thin blue stripes on her sleeves meant.

"You don't understand a thing I'm saying." Not quite against her will she smiled at the woman. "But you're cute."

Her smile was returned, and Wendy felt a lot better. Carmella's gaze did a slow, suggestive glide down Wendy's front, and Wendy thought maybe the bikini wax and Wonder bra weren't a total write-off. Jesus, could it be that women in uniform were just about as attractive as heavy metal guitarists? It was a heretical thought, but at the moment the reality more likely to result in fun before sunrise.

She turned toward the shops. "I can't really afford any of the clothes down here, but that little pink number there is a wow. I mean I can picture myself putting it on and then some wonderful woman peeling it back off me. But with my luck, I'd be getting myself out of my clothes one more time."

She paused for a moment to give the pink halter dress a long look. No doubt about it, her nipple rings would show and that would look pretty damned hot. It probably cost a semester's tuition. "Don't you think a girl ought to get some action if she wants some? On a ship full of women who like just what she does? I guess I don't really have much to complain about, though. I'm here for free. I'll get to see my favorite band in concert all week. So what if I can't find someone to hold me down and do me until we both scream? Even if I haven't been with anyone in almost six months." She sighed. "Bad breakup. Never date the ex of an ex. That's just asking to get double-fucked, and not in the good way."

Carmella patted her hand, and Wendy wondered if "fuck" was one of those words that sounded the same in several languages. If so, there was a chance of being partially understood.

"Sure, there's something good that comes out of any relationship, but it's usually not enough to balance out the bitterness and lies. So she showed me just how crazy it made me to get fisted, and that was some of the best sex I've ever had and maybe ever will have. She was still a nut job. I just want to find someone who can do the sex part and leave me alone so I don't have to endure the crazy shit."

Carmella pulled her a little closer to her side when the ship did one of its odd lurches in mid-rise. After the floor under them steadied, Wendy didn't move away. Carmella didn't seem to mind at all.

"I really miss her mouth and her hands. You would think I could find some woman on this ship, this week, who can eat me and fuck me silly." Her little laugh was unamused. "Not to mention one who likes a lot of the same in return. Good, hard sex. What's so bad about that?"

Carmella said, "A girl like you should get whatever she wants."

After she scraped her jaw off the floor, Wendy accused, "You speak English!"

"Sophia doesn't. She was getting somewhere without English." Carmella's shrug was elegant. "I might as well try."

"That wasn't very nice." In spite of herself, Wendy found it hard to stay mad when Carmella was smiling so charmingly. "I was telling you all my secrets."

"You are very articulate." The more Carmella said, the more Wendy loved the edges of the Italian accent that softened her words. "I was taking notes."

"I'd have never said that if I thought you could understand me."

One eyebrow lifted. "Isn't that typical of modern communication? We're only clear about what we want when we think there's no chance anyone will understand."

Wendy opened her mouth to deliver a clever retort, but nothing came to mind. She closed her mouth again, tried to find a good glare, failed, so she admitted defeat. "You're right."

"How about we be very clear about what we want?"

"I already have been," Wendy reminded her. "It's your turn."

Carmella's hands slid around her waist. "When I heard we would be hosting a LOVE trip, I was hoping to find someone who wanted, as you say, good, hard sex. Someone who would let me get a year's worth in a night."

So far, so good, Wendy wanted to say, but Carmella's hands had moved from her waist to her ass. "Uh huh."

"Someone who, if I said I knew of a little room, over there, would find that exciting. Would enjoy me fucking her there."

"Uh huh."

"As usual, Sophia got to the hottest woman in the room first. What a shame someone called Leta to tell her to go look in the disco." Carmella's eyes were shining with laughter.

"Oh, what a shame." Wendy tugged lightly on the lapel of Carmella's jacket. "Then there was the bereft damsel needing an escort."

"Yes. Needing an escort. Needing much more."

Carmella pulled her in tight for a kiss that started soft but quickly escalated to a question that Wendy eagerly answered. All she had wanted was a playmate and Carmella fit the bill.

"About that little room," Wendy said when she was able. "How far is it?"

For an answer Carmella lifted Wendy off her feet, wrapping her legs around her waist. The concourse was empty as she carried her past the first shop and bumped open an almost invisible door with her shoulder.

"It's right here." She set Wendy down on a counter and

flipped on a light just before the door shut behind them.

Wendy had an impression of a janitor's closet before Carmella kissed her so hard that only the important facts remained in her head. For the rest of the cruise she would walk past this door and remember Carmella frantically unbuttoning the sheer blouse and unhooking the Wonder bra. She would get turned on all over again recalling Carmella's grin at the sight of the nipple rings and the way she flicked both before hiking Wendy's skirt up to her waist.

"This is what you want." Carmella looked down at the thigh-high stockings and lack of panties.

"Yes." Wendy spread her legs and put Carmella's hand on the aching heat between them. "Just so we're communicating clearly, I want you to fuck me good and hard."

Carmella's eyes had gone almost completely black with lust, and her response wasn't in English.

"I didn't understand that," Wendy said.

Carmella swallowed noisily. "I said that I want to fuck you with my hand until you scream."

Wendy leaned up for a kiss that ended with a nip of Carmella's lower lip. "We are communicating perfectly."

"Your pussy is hot."

"You're going to need to take that jacket off and roll up your sleeve, baby."

Carmella gave her a smoldering look as Wendy undid the buttons. She draped her jacket over the same chair where Wendy's blouse and bra now rested. Wendy unbuttoned the white dress shirt too, hoping for more skin.

She got skin. Carmella's small breasts were tipped with hard, deeply red nipples that responded to being pinched. A tattoo of a voluptuous angel spread over her shoulder in purples, greens and blacks. Wendy would have taken the time to appreciate the artist's work, but Carmella stepped back long enough to pull off her shirt, then her hand went directly to Wendy's cunt and she pushed inside, at least two fingers, and hard enough to make Wendy groan in anticipation of more.

"Good and hard was the request, yes?"

"That's right." Wendy rested back on her hands and spread her legs. "Fuck me good and hard."

Carmella's grin was lust-soaked while her eyes danced with delight. She pushed in more fingers. "You feel me, don't you?"

"God, yes."

She rolled her hand so the back brushed over Wendy's clit. "Soaking wet. You are dripping."

"So fuck me."

"Beg for it."

"Fuck me! Come on, you know you want to shove your hand in me." Struggling to keep her balance on one hand, Wendy pinched one of Carmella's nipples again. God, they were perfect for that.

"Beg for it!"

Wendy could already feel the first ripples of climax from the thrusting of Carmella's fingers. "Come on, please. Shove it in. Fist me!"

Something in Italian. Then, "That's right. You want it, here it is."

Wendy cried out, loudly—it felt that good. There was nothing that meant sex to her more than the layers of sensations as Carmella's hand pushed all the way inside her. Full. Stretched. Filled. Fucked. When Carmella curled her hand into a fist, Wendy's muscles adjusted again, clamping down and flexing at the same time. She trapped Carmella's hand inside her and arched her hips to make it clear she could take a good, hard fuck like this.

Carmella pulled Wendy upright enough for a bruising kiss. "Now we're going to fuck, *amica*."

Wendy met Carmella, thrust for thrust, groan for groan. Her cunt was completely filled and every nerve inside her was massaged by Carmella's knuckles and wrist. It felt so damned good and she didn't even want to come. She wanted to fuck for a very long time.

Carmella didn't seem to mind that idea at all. She twisted and turned her hand inside Wendy, grinning lustily at what she felt. "I have never been inside a woman who responded like you. Who could take it hard the way I want to give it."

Panting, Wendy pushed back. "This is what I wanted. God! Don't stop, fuck me good, fuck me good."

She tried to stay upright, but Carmella was winning the contest of strength. Another dozen strokes and Wendy was on her back on the counter. Carmella pulled Wendy's legs onto her shoulders and leaned in, fucking even deeper while Wendy lost the control she'd had. Her muscles were pushed open now. Her cunt felt like a river of wet. She was going to come, she realized, she was going to come and come, she didn't have a choice about that now. Carmella was pounding her with a driving beat and the only response she had left to give was a scream of pleasure as she climaxed. She screamed with pure life, with all of her senses focused on what her body could experience.

"*Dio santo*," Carmella said as she pulled out her hand. "*Dio santo.*"

Brittany stumbled across the Via Condotti toward Wendy, avoiding the women milling around the shops. She also seemed to be avoiding anything bright and noisy. Wendy didn't really have any pity for her.

"You look like you had a rough night. I'm on the way to the pool. The tour doesn't leave for two hours."

"Yeah," Brittany said with a smug grin. "I had a rough night. Will you wake me up in time to get dressed for the tour? I wouldn't want to miss wherever the fuck we are today."

"Bari. We're going to see some beautiful old buildings."

Brittany obviously would not remember much of this conversation, Wendy thought. "Go ahead. I'll be your alarm clock."

"You're pissed."

"I'm not."

"You look like you got a good night's sleep." Brittany's smug expression deepened.

"I got the night I wanted." She grinned when Brittany looked skeptical, and her gaze flicked to the door that likely only she knew was there in the paneling between two shops. "I feel like a million bucks and I'm ready for a great time."

Brittany continued her hung-over journey toward their cabin, and Wendy turned her steps toward the Apollo Lido. Along the way she passed a white-uniformed crewwoman answering a passenger's questions. It wasn't Sophia or Carmella, but that didn't matter judging by the reaction of Wendy's pulse.

Brittany could have the musicians. They were expensive to chase and hard to attract. Women in uniform, on the other hand . . . yes, Wendy thought. She was ready for a great time.

Return Passage
Radclyffe

"Hi, you've reached Darla Ames, cruise director. How may I help you this morning?" Darla tucked the phone between her ear and shoulder as she shuffled papers. "Today's excursion is to the Basilica of St. Nicholas. You'll find information about where to get the shuttle in the itinerary package you received when you boarded yesterday." At the sound of light tapping on the glass door to her office, Darla smiled at the voluptuous redhead standing out in the hall and motioned her visitor inside. "Yes, local guides will meet your group once you reach the island, but you should check with your tour director for the exact times." Darla pushed an errant strand of shoulder length blond hair away from her face and pointed to the chair in front of her desk. "Oh, you'll be back in plenty of time for the toga party tonight."

"One of mine?" Jessica Parry whispered as she sat down across from Darla and crossed her legs. She didn't bother to pull her skirt down when it rode high up on her thighs.

Darla shook her head and mouthed *Rainbow Adventures*. "That's all right, it's no trouble at all. Have a wonderful trip." She hung up the phone and pushed her paperwork aside. "You're up early this morning."

"You know how first days go," Jessica replied. "I wanted to make the rounds and make sure my group was all set for the day trip to Bari."

"It's so good to see you again." Darla came around the front of her desk and leaned against it. When she braced a hand on either side of her hips, the motion pulled her silk blouse tightly across her full breasts. "Sorry I didn't get much of a chance to talk with you at the Captain's Reception last night. We booked quite a few new tour groups for this go-round, in addition to the regulars like yours, and I had to chat up all the virgin tour directors. This cruise is getting popular."

"Not *too* popular, I hope," Jessica said softly, watching the small round prominences in the center of Darla's breasts tighten and protrude. She ran the tip of her tongue lightly over her lower lip, thinking of the way Darla's breasts flushed when she was excited and how, when she sucked on Darla's nipples, the pale pink areola deepened to rose. "How was the Caribbean run?"

"Mercifully uneventful," Darla replied, her gaze on Jessica's mouth. "You had the Alaska trip last, didn't you?"

"Mmm," Jessica said, absently trailing her fingers over her own nipples and smiling as she saw Darla's eyes widen. "I always enjoy that cruise, but this one is my favorite."

"Really?" Darla's voice grew husky, and her breasts rose and fell rapidly. "Why is that?"

"Because I've never found anyone who can suck me the way you do," Jessica whispered, pinching her nipples through her cotton top. "It's been a very long four months."

"A popular tour director like you, working with one of the biggest lesbian agencies in the States?" Darla licked her lips.

"Don't tell me you don't have *friends* on the other ships who can help you out."

"Oh," Jessica laughed. "There are a few with talent, but you've got a magic mouth."

"The minute I saw you leading your group on board yesterday afternoon, I was wet," Darla confided. "I hardly slept last night thinking about the way you taste."

Jessica spread her legs and tilted her hips just enough to pull her skirt up another inch. Darla gasped, and Jessica knew that she had caught a glimpse of her smooth, bare pussy. From the way her clit throbbed, Jessica imagined her lips were red and wet right now. "I've been thinking about this all night. When I woke up this morning, the first thing I thought about was how much I needed to come."

"Did you masturbate?" Darla whispered. "Did you rub your clit and make yourself come?"

"No. I'm saving it for you." Jessica drew her index finger up the inside of her leg and skimmed the channel between her thighs. She held up her glistening finger. "I haven't come for a week."

"Your excursion isn't scheduled to leave for three hours."

"I know." Jessica slid a little lower in the chair and squeezed her pussy. "I could make myself come for you now. It won't take much." Breathing hard, she spread herself open. Her clit tingled as the air hit it. "Can you see my clit?"

"Yes," Darla gasped. "Oh God, you're so swollen already." She lifted her gaze to Jessica's, her expression plaintive. "You do need to come, don't you?"

Jessica nodded eagerly, two fingers poised over her clit. "Should I?"

"Not that way. Not yet. You want to come in my mouth, don't you?"

Jessica nodded, her breath coming fast. "You know I do."

"Then let me suck you."

"You will." Jessica dared to tap her clit lightly and moaned. "Oh, I really do need to come."

Darla looked at the clock. "I'm due for a break."

"Are you sure?" Jessica caressed her slit, skimming just along the sides of her clit. "I could just do it for you here."

"No," Darla said hoarsely. "I want to lick you. I want to make you come all over my face."

Jessica laughed softly. "Maybe *I* don't want you to suck me just yet. Maybe I just want to make you watch me do myself."

"Then I'll lick you while you masturbate."

Jessica's hips twitched and she closed her eyes. "You'll have to do me soon. I'm so so horny right now." She gazed up beneath hooded lids. "I really need to finish before I scream."

Darla leaned over her desk, retrieved her phone and pushed two buttons. "Chrissy? I'm going to be out of the office for a while. I'll have my pager if you need me." She hung up and pushed away from the desk. "Let's go to my cabin."

"And then what?" Jessica asked, rising unsteadily. Her vision was the slightest bit blurry, and she felt as if she might come just from the pressure of her thighs closing around her throbbing pussy.

Darla laughed. "Then I'll give you five minutes before you're screaming my name."

"I've waited months for this," Jessica said. She glanced quickly behind her, saw no one through the doors, and ran her tongue along the edge of Darla's ear. "I'm not giving it up until I'm damn good and ready."

"We'll see," Darla murmured. "I'm going to take you on a trip around the world."

"I've been around the world," Jessica said, catching Darla's hand and pushing it under her skirt for an instant. "Now I just want you to fuck me."

When Darla withdrew her hand, her palm was shiny with come. "If you don't want me to fuck you silly right here, you'll behave."

Jessica smiled sweetly and touched her tongue to Darla's palm. "Did I say I didn't?"

"Cabin. Now." Darla hissed and dragged her away.

Most of the passengers were on deck or at breakfast, and the halls were mercifully clear. Five minutes later, their clothes lay in an untidy path from Darla's stateroom door to the bed where Darla was stretched out naked. She spread her legs and slowly circled her clit with one finger. Her engorged pussy gleamed as red as the polish on her smoothly sculpted nail. "Bring your beautiful clit over here so I can suck it."

"In a minute." Jessica leaned over, pushed Darla's finger away and delicately kissed the hard clit that stood straight up from the folds. "Mmm. So nice."

Darla's belly rolled and she groaned. "Do me a little," she pleaded. "Watching you play with yourself got me so hot."

Jessica kissed her clit again and toyed with her opening without entering her. "Should I lick you a little?"

"God, yes."

Jessica licked very, very slowly, stopping at the undersurface of Darla's rapidly stiffening clit to tease it with light, fluttering strokes. When Darla started to writhe, she pressed one fingertip down on the top of Darla's clit and massaged it while she licked all around the end.

"Oh, I'm going to have to come." Darla twisted a handful of Jessica's thick red curls around her fingers and pushed Jessica's head down. "Lick me faster. There. That's good. Yes. Yes, oh God."

"Oh, no you don't. You've got work to do first." Jessica pinched Darla's clit roughly and pulled away. Then she climbed onto the bed and straddled Darla's face.

Her expression dazed, Darla stared up the length of Jessica's body poised above her. "You bitch."

"We'll see who's the bitch," Jessica murmured, opening herself wide with both hands. Her thumbs framed her clit. "Suck that."

Darla lifted her head slightly and kissed Jessica's exposed clit quickly, then drew back with a sly grin. "Payback time."

Smiling tremulously, Jessica watched through half-closed lids as the very tip of a moist, pink tongue toyed with the end of her clit. Each tiny flick made the plump shaft pulse. It was already too stiff to twitch. In between licks, she squeezed it lightly. "Come on. Suck me," she whispered.

"In a hurry all of a sudden?" Darla teased, pushing the tip of her tongue firmly against the shaft of Jessica's clitoris.

"Put your lips around it." Jessica slid a finger on either side and pulled the hood back harder. Her belly quivered from just that little bit of pressure and, moaning, she fondled her clit faster. "Suck the head. Oh yeah, that feels so good."

While Darla toyed with her clit, Jessica cupped her breast and pulled on her nipple. Her fingers flew on her clit and her hips pumped faster. "Suck harder."

Darla let Jessica's hard clit pop out of her mouth. "You're going to make yourself come," Darla warned.

"No I'm not," Jessica panted. "I'm not ready."

"You need to come in my mouth. You know you want to." Darla pursed her full, ripe lips. "Let it go right in here."

It was all Jessica could do not to jam her tense clit between those wet, perfect lips and come all over Darla's face. "Not. Yet. Lick. Me."

"I can make you give it up, you know," Darla said with a laugh and stretched out her tongue.

Flick, flick, flick—the beat of Darla's tongue on her blood-filled clit made Jessica's hips jerk wildly. Her come flowed like a river, coating the inside of her thighs and dripping onto Darla's neck. Through clenched teeth, she groaned, "Put your lips around my clit and suck me, God damn it."

Darla's green eyes darkened. "I can tell you're dying to

come." She raised her head and licked the top of Jessica's clit as Jessica squeezed it between her fingers. "You know as soon as I suck you, you're going to, so why are you waiting?"

"I'll come," Jessica gasped, rubbing the undersurface of her clit back and forth over Darla's outstretched tongue, "when I want to come. Now suck my fucking clit."

Darla made a circle of her lips and closed them around the head of Jessica's clit. At the same time, she reached down and rolled her own clit between her fingers. She whimpered and the vibration worked through Jessica's stiff clit, making her toss her head back and moan. Darla slid her own clit back and forth between her fingers, forcing the blood from the base toward the tip. The more excited she got, the faster she sucked on Jessica.

"That's good that's good," Jessica chanted. When Darla started whimpering and writhing beneath her, Jessica focused on the mirror above the built-in dressers across from the bed. Darla's legs were splayed and trembling, her fingers tugging spastically on her clit. The sight of Darla getting herself off made Jessica's cunt spasm and she looked back down, grinning tightly. Darla's eyes were open and glazed, her cheeks hollowed from sucking so hard on Jessica's clit. Jessica forked her fingers around the base of her clit and pulled it out of Darla's mouth just a little.

"Suck the head. Just the head. In and out. In and out, that's it. Oh Jesus, like that." Jessica plucked the base of her clit while she watched Darla suck her. Her clit suddenly swelled and got very hard and she felt the tingle of an orgasm starting. Holding her breath, she got ready to drag her clit free so she wouldn't climax yet, but Darla saved her by letting go of her.

"Oh God." Darla's head fell back and she twisted wildly between Jessica's legs. "My cunt's exploding! Oh my God, it feels so good."

Jessica smiled, feeling Darla's breasts heaving against her buttocks as she bucked into her come.

"Oh! Oh fuck," Darla cried, her mouth twisting with stunned pleasure, "I'm coming all over everything."

Jessica masturbated furiously, her clit barely an inch from Darla's mouth, as Darla shuddered and moaned. When Darla's face slackened as the last of her orgasm dwindled away, Jessica leaned forward and rubbed her clit over Darla's wet mouth. She grunted softly, holding the hood back so she could slide the head between Darla's lips. "I'm going to come in your mouth now, you little bitch." Her thighs trembled so badly she could barely support herself. She vibrated the base of her clit rapidly between two fingers and shoved as much of it between Darla's lips as she could. "Suck me now. God damn it, suck me suck me hard." She caught her breath as Darla regained enough strength to work her clit with purpose.

"You're sucking me off," Jessica moaned, unable to hold back as Darla dragged her clit deeper into her mouth and tongued it. Eyes closed, Jessica cried out helplessly, her belly undulating. She held one breast and twisted her nipple, the other hand holding her clit to Darla's mouth.

Darla laughed around the bulging clit and gripped it lightly with her teeth.

"Harder . . . bite it hard . . . oh fuck . . . feel that?" Jessica's eyes snapped open and she stared into Darla's dreamy green ones, grinding out each word as she struggled not to scream. "Look what you're making me do. I'm . . . coming . . . in . . . your . . . mouth." And then everything she'd been holding back for days broke free and she gushed over Darla's face, in her mouth, down her neck.

Darla kept swallowing until Jessica rolled off, collapsing on her side with one arm flung across Darla's middle. "Oh my God. That was so good."

"It was," Darla murmured contentedly. She turned her head and smiled a self-satisfied smile. "I have so got your number."

"You think?" Jessica arched an eyebrow and tweaked Darla's

nipple. "Like you didn't just come like crazy."

"It makes me really hot to get you off," Darla admitted.

"Then you should be on fire right about now." Jessica reached down and cupped Darla's pussy. "Oh yeah. You get so wet when you come."

Darla bumped her pelvis into Jessica's palm. "You're getting my clit all hard again."

"I noticed." Jessica propped her chin in her hand and toyed with Darla's clit. "I've been waiting four months for a return voyage. I'm not hardly done yet."

"We've still got a little bit of time." Darla licked Jessica's nipple, then grazed it with her teeth. "And you know how busy things can get."

"Uh huh," Jessica murmured, her hips rolling to the rhythm of Darla's mouth working her nipple. She stroked Darla's clit faster and Darla moaned. "Who else do you have your eye on this trip?"

Darla moaned and moved to the other breast. "You're a tough act to follow." She closed her eyes and arched her back. "Oh, that's going to make me come."

Jessica hooked her thumb around Darla's clit and slid her fingers inside her. She stroked her clit and fucked her in firm, steady thrusts. She wanted to be sure she had Darla's attention, so she kept her pace just slow enough that Darla couldn't quite come. "I saw you cruising that guitar player yesterday. I bet you'd like *her* to fuck you, wouldn't you?" When Darla didn't answer, Jessica stopped moving.

"Oh please," Darla moaned, sucking frantically on Jessica's breast. "I'm almost coming. Please. Please don't stop."

"Don't forget," Jessica whispered, pounding into Darla's cunt again, "*I* booked this return passage a long time ago."

Darla gasped as her cunt squeezed down around Jessica's fingers and her belly heaved in a series of hard spasms. "Oh God, oh God, I'm coming."

Jessica gathered her close and milked her clit until the last pulsations quieted. She kept her fingers buried deep inside, knowing Darla would be ready again soon. "You can play as much as you want, with whoever you want," she whispered as Darla twitched and sighed, "but I've already reserved this room for the rest of the cruise."

"Consider that itinerary confirmed," Darla murmured. She roused herself to kiss Jessica languidly. "Do me again?"

Jessica laughed and massaged the trigger spot that made Darla moan. "I believe we've got time for one more quick excursion."

Cruising Solo
Karin Kallmaker

"Brandy! Can you help me get these cases to the lounge?"

I turned back from my errand to check yesterday's sales with the gift shop manager to give Mel a hand. The rolling amps weren't that heavy, but they were awkward, as I'd learned yesterday.

"How's the busman's holiday so far?" Mel put one stocky shoulder to the back of the amp again, and I steadied it from the other side.

"I'm loving it. I just wish my girlfriend hadn't broken her ankle. She'd be loving it too."

"At least you got a room to yourself."

I wasn't happy with the empty bed at night. "Ship to shore costs a fortune, doesn't it?"

"Not all that bad," Mel said. "But on our wages it is."

I'd already blown most of my spending money on a beautiful necklace of Venetian glass for Tess's birthday. The brief stints with the Internet hookup available when we were in port would have to do.

Mel grappled to keep control of the amp, but I caught it before it ran into the wall. "I know why we don't have two sets of these, but moving them from venue to venue is a royal pain."

I averted my eyes from the sight of Mel's rippling biceps. She was about my height but probably carried twenty pounds more muscle—a fine figure of a woman in an A-shirt and shorts. When I'd met her my first thought had been "power butch" and that had proven quite accurate. She also liked to play, if the gossip during the staff lunch was anything to go by. There had been a time when I'd have issued her an invitation or accepted one in a heartbeat.

We finally muscled the amp into the lounge and went back for the second one. Once it was in place, the rock band's sound woman took over and Mel and I caught our breath. Just as we were leaving, two of the musicians passed us, one saying to the other, "Tuesday night—but invitation only."

The other answered, "Oh, I have my eye on someone to invite already, if I can wait that long to do her."

"I wonder how I could get an invitation to *that* party," Mel said to me as the lounge door closed behind us.

The image of Mel and the heavy metal girls all having a really hot time left me feeling a bit weak in the knees. Tess would laugh—the older I got the more I understood her cat scratch fever hormones. My kitty was in major need.

Mel was regarding me with that mixed expression of cool interest and playful impishness I knew so well from the many times I'd had the same expression. Before I'd left on this trip, Tess had said, her ankle wrapped in that damned heavy cast, "As long as you come back home to me, I don't care if you have some fun. I don't own your body or your brain, Brandy. Just your heart and your future. Don't do anything that'll cost me either one."

Thankfully, before Mel could actually start the conversation I could tell she was considering, I recalled my original errand.

"Jessica wants to know how the CD sales went yesterday. If you see her, would you tell her I got slightly delayed?"

Mel nodded and headed aft while I went up a flight to the shopping concourse. There were times I forgot I was on a ship, but then there would be a slight hesitation in the rise or fall to remind me. Tess would love the stores, even if we couldn't afford anything in them. There was a turquoise bikini in one window that reminded me vividly of the one she wore for sunbathing, the one that I had removed many, many times so I could worship the unbronzed parts of her.

The gift shop manager had the previous day's sales records all ready. I glanced down the list and could see that all of the artists had sold a few CDs, but I had no idea if the numbers were strong or lackluster. I hoped Jessica would explain and I'd get a chance to show I had a brain for this sort of thing. Tess and I had hopes of joining the Ladies on Vacation Enterprises staff. We could settle into an apartment of our own instead of the two studios Club Sandzibel allotted us. The work was hard but very fun so far.

By the end of the day I was exhausted in a good way. I'd also overheard a fairly noisy couple having a tryst in the fitness room restroom, which brought back a lot of fond memories. Then there was the couple losing their clothes on the way to their stateroom. They caught me looking and did not seem to mind. After the late-night comedy act finished, I swear the ship levitated on the lust endorphins alone as the corridors slowly emptied and the guests found warm beds for the night. In some cases, I was certain, the beds they found were not their own.

Feeling sorry for myself, I sat in my stateroom and tried not to miss Tess. I was perfectly capable of arranging some fun—that is if everyone on the prowl hadn't already been claimed—but I was pretty tired. No energy for conversation and flirting at that level.

I decided that a quick tryst with my vibrator might be just the thing and claimed it from the dresser drawer. A search for the nearest outlet to the bed only increased my frustration level. The bargain cabins where staffers stayed were so small there was just one outlet, in the bathroom, which was so tiny there wasn't even room enough to lie on the floor. Mel had joked the shower stalls were converted coffins.

And, dang it, I had never mastered the art of having a full-blown, knee-shaking, muscle-clenching orgasm standing up. Twenty minutes later I had ascertained that there was no miraculously appearing extension cord in my suitcase. The corridor outside was empty of any other human beings, let alone one with an extension cord slung over one shoulder. I was tired and cranky and no longer in the mood to let my vibrator have its way with me.

I went to bed, and it took nearly fifteen minutes to fall asleep.

Monday. The home of the Olympic Games. Herding women onto tenders because the ship was too large to dock. Answering the same question two hundred times. Herding women into the shade, herding them onto shuttles and greeting every minute with a big smile and endless energy. By the time I got off the very last tender back to the ship, Jessica had already thanked me twice for my help, and praised my quick thinking when a guest had abruptly succumbed to heat stroke. I hoped she remembered I was the one whose girlfriend—as ideal an employee as I was—had broken her ankle two days before our planned flights. I was playing it low-key for now, but I wasn't planning to leave for home without pigeonholing her and giving her the full Brandy and Tess credentials.

Sweaty and tired, and off-duty for the rest of the night, I bumped into Mel on the way to my cabin. She, too, had been herding women all day and looked as tired as I felt.

"Want to get dinner to go and eat somewhere far away from the guests?"

"Sure," I said easily. We did just that, too. Then, feeling like recalcitrant children, we snuck into the kitchen and helped ourselves to some of the savories and sweets prepared for the pastry extravaganza. I left with an admiring backward glance at beautiful, 3-D swans made from phyllo dough and glistening with sugar. A dozen multi-tiered cakes frosted in rainbow colors hadn't yet been cut. But the cinnamon and chocolate puff I'd swiped was light as a feather and filled with a rum-flavored custard—tasty enough to have me licking my fingers.

Mel had that look again as we leaned against the railing and watched the ship splitting the sea dozens of feet below us. "You can tell me to take a hike," she began.

I shrugged. "My girlfriend and I have an understanding."

"Which is?"

"I can be borrowed." If she was here, I didn't add, there wasn't a chance in hell I'd want anyone else. But Tess wasn't here. So maybe for one night I could be the old Brandy.

Mel laughed. "I like that way of looking at it. I'm not the stealing sort. But I don't mind borrowing."

I pulled the bandeau off my hair and let the wind finish ruining it. The damp air only made it more curly, and tomorrow morning I'd have some serious work on it ahead of me.

"You're the first white girl I've ever seen with hair that kinky." Mel touched it briefly and then caressed my neck lightly.

My nipples tightened in response. The old Brandy was very close to the surface now, and I wondered what it would feel like to go down on Mel, what her cunt looked like and if she liked having every furl and ripple between her legs thoroughly explored. Or would she want it hard and fast? Was she a butch who liked to be fisted? Or was she stone and wanting to spend the night pleasuring me?

I shook suddenly with a feeling of being unleashed. I loved sex and had always enjoyed a new partner. Exploring women, learning them, had for years been one of the highlights of my life. Women are simply the *best*. And here was one ready to play with me, more butch than any I'd ever been with, and I was quite certain there would be more than one new experience with her.

In the three years I had been with Tess we'd had our understanding about borrowing. Mostly it was a recognition that while we wanted to be all the other ever needed, if in some circumstances that just wasn't the case, talking about unmet needs and how they might be fulfilled was better than doing anything behind the other's back. Tess had been the one who pointed out, too, that expecting our bodies to never change and our self-knowledge to be static was unrealistic. Certainly her self-knowledge had evolved, and that was why she was with me and not a guy. I didn't expect her to never change. I did expect her to want me to be part of those changes.

Given that we worked and lived side-by-side, it wasn't surprising that neither of us had taken advantage of the agreement. Any way that we might be changing, such as my unexpectedly strong hormonal drive that I still said I'd caught from her, we'd adapted to together. Here I was, however, eager to be with someone else. Thinking that the experience would be something to tell Tess about. Wondering if the telling would get us in the raunchy mood we both relished.

Mel pulled me into her embrace. The kiss was very nice and suggested that there could be real heat and real play. "I have a roommate," she said, "so if you'd like, we could go to your cabin."

"It would be a shame to waste it."

"I could pick up a few things from my cabin on the way."

I was about to suggest an extension cord, if she had one, when she cupped my face and kissed me again, harder this time. My skin was tingling as I leaned into her. All that muscle and strength was feeling very, very good to me.

One hand slipped under the waistband of my shorts, gripping my hip.

And I had the thought I could not ignore: *Tess didn't touch me quite like that.*

And then I realized the woman kissing me wasn't Tess. Of course she wasn't. I knew that. It was Mel. Who wasn't Tess.

She touched me, kissed me, and my body responded, no doubt about it. But my infernal brain kept thinking her fingers would move there, or her tongue would touch here, because that was how Tess touched me. Tess who knew my body now better than I did. Tess who possessed every key there was to me.

Fuck a duck, I hate having a brain.

Mel let go of me and gave me a puzzled look. "Are you sure about this?"

"Actually, I'm not." Mel was very nice and I didn't want to hurt her feelings, but only the truth was going to suffice. "You'd just be a stand-in for my girlfriend. I'm sorry."

"I don't care. I get the feeling you're a really fun time."

"I think you probably are too. But . . ." The truth was inescapable. "I love my girlfriend. And while parts of me want you, all of me is only going to be happy with her."

She took my refusal with good grace. I suggested there was plenty of time to cruise the folk singer's show or the late-night dance scene. She left me at the railing with a cheery smile, and I was fairly certain that the rest of the week wouldn't be awkward between us because of the last few minutes.

I was most of the way to my cabin when I realized I still needed an extension cord.

Fine, I thought, sitting on my bed, all alone. I was being a good girl. Kisses from Not Tess women were useless. I was an old married woman, settled down, constrained, giving up the happy life of soul-wrenching ecstasy through any and all means by which I could find it. And for what?

For a chick with long arms—I could hear Tess saying that to

me clear as day in my head. I fell back on the bed, ruefully laughing. I gave up the footloose and fancy-free life for a woman who some nights could not get fucked enough and all nights could not hold me enough. For a woman who was generous and kind, thoughtful and wise, hot as a firecracker and, frankly, smarter than I was.

I gave up nights with Not Tesses for breakfasts and brownies and tomorrows *and* hot sex with Tess.

Damn, I wanted an extension cord.

The slam of a nearby cabin door brought me to my feet. Peering out into the corridor I summoned up my courage as the couple walked by my door. "I know this will sound weird, but do you have an extension cord I could borrow? I promise you'll have it back in an hour."

"Sorry, mate," the taller woman said as they paused.

Her cuddly girlfriend added, "We were sort of wishing we'd brought one along ourselves."

"Batteries just don't—"

"Got that right, mate—"

"I would have brought one if we'd—"

We all blushed because we all knew exactly what we meant. They drifted toward the stairwell, and I heard someone approaching from the other direction.

"Hi," I said cheerfully. "Do you have an extension cord I could borrow for about an hour?"

"Sure," the little redhead said. "I was ironing something earlier, but now I'm all done."

Whatever floats your boat, I wanted to say. I had other plans. I thanked her profusely, promised its prompt return, but she told me not to bother until the next day. My vibrator and I could have a long date.

I skipped back to my cabin, plugged everything in, pulled back the covers and spread myself on the bed.

What I needed was a naughty, hot fantasy. The rock band

party, there was a thought.

Muscles and tattoos, I mused, required a soft, pliable woman . . . perhaps one shared between the two musicians I'd encountered yesterday with Mel. They'd fuck her senseless, until her hair was in ruins, her body slicked with sweat, and she'd mewl with more need because the more she had, the more she wanted, and in my mind's eye, it was Tess wanting it like that, and there were no musicians, just me. Me and Tess, the way we'd been our first night together, and so many nights since.

A flick of my thumb brought the vibrator to life and the intensity of the sensation curled my toes into the bed. I knew I'd come, I always did with one and that was a very good reason to own one, I thought, but I didn't want to just come. I wanted the perfect moment in my head when I did.

My fingers going into Tess, feeling the quivering welcome of her luscious cunt, thick with want and the sound of my pushing in twining with her rising moan. The perfect moment, fuck, oh . . . The first time I'd fisted her and she'd reacted like nothing I'd ever felt before, oh . . . The last time she'd gone down on me, teasing me and teasing me, oh . . . The perfect moment, oh . . . The first kiss, the one after that, the last kiss, the next kiss when I got home, oh . . .

Oh. Oh, fuck.

There were so many perfect moments that about an hour later I selected a few more. In the morning, I mused sleepily afterward, I could have some more perfect moments before I had to give the extension cord back. There were so many to think about, so many that made my nerves jump, so many . . . all with Tess. And if I ran out of perfect moments, I could make more when I got home.

And then I slept, cradled against the pillow that was a poor substitute for Tess's shoulder.

Best Seats in the House
Radclyffe

"Have you ever been to an X-rated theater?" Chris Stanley whispered as she waited for the doors to the Sea Surge Video Lounge to open.

"This isn't an X-rated movie theater," her best friend Jacqui "Jac" Burns muttered back. "It's a film screening."

Chris snorted. "Yeah, of a porn film."

"Erotica."

"You didn't answer my question."

"Yeah, I've been. Once or twice."

"No, I mean the real deal—Triple X on the marquee, raincoat in the lap, questionable substances on the floor . . ." Chris grinned when Jac shoved her hands deep into the pockets of her black cargo pants and glowered. "Not one of those art-house soft focus, fade-to-black, pretend-sex movies."

"I know what you mean. And *yeah*, I've been."

"Not with Trish," Chris said with absolute certainty. Trish

was no prude, Chris knew, but she wasn't the type to frequent scrungy movie theaters on the wrong side of town, either. Trish was a lady, just like Chris's girlfriend Emily. Chris and Jac didn't talk about the details of their sex lives—that would be disrespectful to their girlfriends—but she got the feeling Jac was getting it regular, just like she was. Emily never let her go without. Nope. Emily—cute, curvy, sweet-tasting Emily—never said no when Chris was in the mood for fast, hard fucking or slow, easy teasing, and even better, Emily never hesitated to jump Chris when she was horny. Still, there was no way Emily, or Trish for that matter, would sit in a theater full of people getting off watching a dirty movie. Even if they were all women like tonight. "Trish would worry about getting something nasty on her shoes."

Jac smiled. "No. It wasn't with Trish."

"Who?"

"Tanika Phillips."

Chris flashed on the buff, black, All-American basketball player she and Jac had gone to college with, and she experienced a totally unexpected surge of jealousy. "Uh, I . . . uh . . . never realized you and Tan ever dated."

Jac looked at her like she'd grown two heads. "We didn't *date*. We were buds. We hung out together. You know she's not my type." Jac grinned. "I like my women rounder and curvier and . . . you know, softer."

"Sure, just like I do," Chris said. Which was true. Well, most of the time. Every now and then she'd look at some hard-bodied dude with a swagger and feel a twinge in her clit. But she didn't think about that too much. "So, uh, you and Tan never . . . got it on?"

The lounge in front of the theater was starting to fill up, and Jac shifted closer to Chris as the crowd pressed around them. "Not exactly."

"Not exactly?" Chris's clit jumped as she pictured Jac and Tan in a hot, sweaty embrace. Tight muscles straining, the two of them rolling around, fighting for the top position. She'd seen Jac naked in the gym plenty of times, so she didn't have any trouble envisioning her small firm breasts and tight pink nipples and long flat belly. She felt her clit thickening and tried to think of something else. "What does that mean? Exactly?"

"Well, sometimes we'd jerk off together afterward," Jac said in a low voice.

"You and Tan?" Chris was unable to keep the awe from her voice. "You jerked each other off?"

"Not each other, you twit." Jac shook her head and grinned, then tousled Chris's hair. "We just watched each other do it."

"Oh, right." Chris tried to sound nonchalant. She'd never jerked off in front of anyone except Emily, and even then, she usually got so self-conscious she couldn't come. She didn't have any trouble doing it when she was alone, thinking about Emily or sometimes . . . sometimes another face, another body, would fill her mind just before her clit exploded.

"Where?" Chris asked.

"Huh?"

"Where did you do it?" Chris got a flash of Tan and Jac shoulder to shoulder on a couch, their legs rubbing, groaning quietly while they . . . Her clit went *thump thump* and she banished the images. Jesus. What was wrong with her tonight?

"Where? Oh . . . in Tan's car, or sometimes in the alley out behind the bar. Remember that place?" Jac asked, fond nostalgia in her voice.

Chris nodded. They'd had some wild times, back before they got serious with their girlfriends. "Couldn't keep a lid on, huh?"

Jac laughed. "I might have been able to cool it, but when Tan had to get off there was no stopping her. And she liked company. Some nights I could hardly keep up."

The pictures were back—Tan and Jac leaning against the brick wall, heads back, eyes half-closed, hips dancing as they worked off their clits. Hoping to keep any more images out of her head, Chris scanned the crowd. Not far away she caught sight of a couple who had just joined the others waiting for the eight o'clock show. Both hot, both to her liking, in totally opposite ways. The taller one in the tight black leather pants reminded her of Jac—thick midnight hair, rangy build, slim hips—and she was packing and didn't care who knew it. The bulge behind her fly hung down like a sausage on the inside of her left leg. She had her arm draped over the shoulders of a smaller blonde in a short, *short* leather skirt and one of those satin corset-y things that pushed her tits up and made them look like they'd fall out if she took a deep breath. The blond femme seemed to like the package too, because every now and then she'd reach down and give her girlfriend's crotch a squeeze and a little jiggle.

"Jesus," Chris whispered. "Talk about getting some hand action."

"What?" Jac asked. "Where?"

"Over to your right. Some girl is jerking her girlfriend off in line."

Jac gave a little start and slowly turned. "Yeah. Sweet."

At that moment, the blonde caught them watching and smiled, the tip of her tongue snaking out to slick across her lush red lower lip. The muscles in her surprisingly buff arm tightened and she pumped a little harder. The girlfriend bucked her hips and closed her eyes for a second.

Chris hissed in a breath as the blonde's eyes brightened and slid down over Chris's body, lingering on her crotch. "We're busted."

"Yeah," Jac muttered, looking away. "And I'm hard as hell now too."

"Me too." Chris tried not to shiver as her clit twitched and she creamed in her jeans. The rough denim chafed her clit, and she regretted her decision not to wear underwear. "Hey, they're letting us in. Damn, we're gonna miss the rest of the floor show out here."

"Something tells me it's going to be a long, hard night."

Jac grinned and Chris laughed. As they moved toward the open double doors, Jac's upper arm and shoulder rubbed lightly against Chris's. It felt nice. Comfortable, but a little exciting too. A night out with Jac was always fun.

Jac stepped off to one side just inside the rectangular room. "Whoa."

"Whoa and how," Chris said, surveying the sofas and plush chairs arranged in semi-circular tiers in front of a large screen on the far wall. The whole arrangement looked oddly intimate. "No wonder we had to make reservations. This doesn't look like any theater I've ever seen."

"Must be why they said 'special viewing for the discerning audience.' I wondered what that meant."

"I don't know, what do you think?" Chris felt a little uneasy as women, some in pairs, others in groups, and some alone, filed past them. "Maybe we should catch up to Emily and Trish."

"At a fashion show?" Jac's voice rose, and her face suffused with horror. "Please." She grabbed Chris's shirt sleeve and pointed toward the far right side of the room. "Let's grab that couch up there in the corner. We'll be able to see okay, and if we don't like the movie, we can always sneak out to the bar."

"Okay." Chris threaded her way through the low tables scattered between the sofas and chairs to the second level and settled onto a short sofa next to Jac. Then she leaned back, her thigh just touching Jac's, and checked out the immediate area. "Catch who's down in front of us."

On the floor level to their left and perhaps ten feet away, the blonde and her girlfriend settled into a similar loveseat. The blonde immediately kicked her shoes off and curled her legs up on the sofa, snuggling into her girlfriend's left side. She glanced up and smiled at Chris and Jac.

"Busted again," Chris murmured, not looking away.

"Doesn't seem like she minds."

Within minutes, the doors at the back of the room closed and the lights went down, but not into total blackness the way Chris expected. Wall sconces provided enough light for her to see the people around her clearly, including the blonde and her girlfriend. She was determined not to watch them and focused on the screen. Next to her, Jac stretched her longer legs out in front of her and draped one arm along the top of the sofa behind Chris's back. The other hand she rested in her lap.

It wasn't an art-house film. Ten minutes in and the two main characters, hot chicks with tattoos and piercings in interesting places, arrived at a sex party. The camera panned from room to room, displaying a dizzying array of naked flesh and lust-filled faces. The quick cuts and crazy angles made Chris's head swim. The teasing, fleeting images of bare breasts and glistening cunts and orgasmic expressions made her already stiff clit throb.

"Jesus," she whispered, glancing quickly at Jac, who shifted restlessly beside her. "They're not fooling around in this thing."

Jac's eyes flicked from the screen toward the room. "Neither are they."

Chris followed Jac's gaze. The blonde had her girlfriend's cock out and was jacking it in long, slow strokes. It stood up through the fly of the leather pants, the pale head appearing and disappearing inside the blonde's fist. The girlfriend had both arms spread out along the top of the sofa, her fingers digging into the material while she stared straight ahead at the screen as if nothing was happening. The blonde was staring at Chris, her lips slightly parted, her eyes bright even in the dim room.

"Fuck," Chris whispered. She wanted to look away, but she felt hypnotized. Her clit jumped every time the blonde pumped the cock through her fingers. "You see that?"

"Oh yeah," Jac said hoarsely.

On the screen, someone screamed they were coming, and

Chris looked up in time to see a woman writhing in orgasm, her cunt grinding into another girl's face. Next to her, Jac grunted and slid her hand between her legs. The camera cut to a shot of a woman spread-eagled on a table, two or three women fondling her breasts while another stood between her thighs and methodically humped a thick black cock deep into her pussy.

The girl on the table whimpered and pleaded to come, and Chris wanted to do the same thing. If she'd been alone watching the movie, she'd already be jerking off. She moaned, not meaning to, but unable to stop. She heard a deep groan, and it wasn't coming from the screen.

Chris looked over just as the blonde slipped a hand inside her top and lifted out her breast. She pushed it against her girlfriend's face, and the girlfriend obediently sucked the nipple deep into her mouth. Chris could see the blonde's breast stretch out with the force of the suction as she arched her back in obvious pleasure. Through half-closed lids, she smiled at Chris and pulled her skimpy skirt up to reveal her naked cunt.

"Jac," Chris whispered, afraid to move. "*Jac*. Watch."

"I see," Jac grunted, her hand circling steadily in her crotch.

Her expression fiercely intent, the blonde shifted up, over her girlfriend's lap, and down—impaling her pussy on the cock. The girlfriend stiffened and arched off the seat, gripping the blonde's hips now instead of the sofa. Chris gasped and couldn't find enough air to even moan. She felt Jac's thigh quivering crazily against hers.

"I gotta go to the john," Chris finally blurted, struggling to get her legs under her and stand up.

Jac clamped her free hand onto Chris's thigh. "Why?"

Across from them, the blonde rode her girlfriend's cock in a frenzy—hard, swift thrusts of her hips—her breast still tethered in her girlfriend's teeth. She braced one hand on her girlfriend's shoulder and slapped the other one into her own cunt. Her lips parted in a tremulous, triumphant smile as she watched Chris.

Up on the screen, the girl on the table bucked and whined and gushed all over the stud who fucked her. Chris's pussy convulsed in time to her cries.

"I just . . . I just got to go. I'll be back."

"You're gonna go jerk off," Jac said, her voice rough. "Aren't you?"

"Oh man, I gotta. I need to come so bad." Chris sounded desperate even to herself. The blonde's girlfriend released her breast with a muffled shout, her body convulsing. The blonde's hand whipped between her legs.

"Shit, look at that," Chris groaned. "The girlfriend just blew her load."

The blonde continued her ride and mouthed, *Come with me*, to Chris. Chris squeezed her cunt through the soggy denim covering her crotch.

"I'm so fucking hot," Chris whimpered.

"Do it," Jac gasped. "You know you want to. It'll feel so good."

Chris popped the button on her fly. The blonde dropped her head down, her face contorted with pleasure. Jac moaned. Chris fingered her zipper, then yanked it down.

"I'm coming," Jac whispered. "Oh, fuck, Chris. I'm coming."

Chris shoved her hand into her pants as Jac twisted against her, hips jerking. Without thinking, Chris slid an arm around Jac's shoulders and held her as she finished getting off. Chris found her clit, hard and slick, and stripped it once from base to tip, feeling it fatten in her grip.

"Uh, uh," Chris moaned as she pumped her cunt.

Jac pressed her hand to Chris's stomach and circled her palm over the board-stiff muscles. "That's it, buddy. That's it, let it go."

The blonde's mouth formed a perfect O, her expression dazed, her eyes blank as her girlfriend clamped her teeth around her nipple again. Chris worked her clit faster. Jac rubbed the back of her neck and continued to massage the muscles in her belly.

"Yeah," Jac murmured. "You're almost there, aren't you? You're gonna come so sweet, Chris. So sweet."

The blonde let out a high, thin cry, and it was like a firecracker exploded inside Chris's cunt. Her come spilled out and she shouted in surprise and pleasure. She kept pumping until the last spasm released her, and then slumped back with a long, low groan.

"Sweet," Jac whispered, laughing softly. "Was that sweet, or what?"

Dazed, Chris turned her head and grinned at Jac. "Very sweet."

"Looks like she thought so too." Jac tilted her chin toward the row below them.

The blonde, curled up in her girlfriend's arms, slowly stroked the wet cock that now rested against her naked thigh. She had a dreamy, contented expression on her face. The leather of her girlfriend's pants was soaked with come. The girlfriend, still watching the action on the screen, absently fondled the blonde's breast.

"There's no way I'd let anyone watch Emily come like that," Chris said softly.

"No kidding," Jac said forcefully. "Me neither. When Trish comes, it's just for me."

"What about . . . you know, us getting off together?"

Jac gave Chris's belly a friendly pat, then moved back over to her side of the sofa. "What about it? You know we were both gonna jerk off the minute we could." She shrugged and grinned. "So we did it together. We're friends, right?"

"Right." Chris zipped her fly and got herself together. Her clit wasn't getting any softer, and she could still feel Jac trembling in her arms. She knew she'd be jerking off again before Emily got back to the cabin.

"So let's relax and watch the rest of this movie," Jac said.

"Yeah, good idea." Chris saw the blonde slip down to kneel on the floor between her girlfriend's spread thighs. She watched her unbutton the leather pants and work the cock free from the harness. As the blonde lowered her face to her girlfriend's cunt, Chris smiled. "Looks like we got the best seats in the house."

Quick-Change Artist
Radclyffe

"How does it look out there?" Cecilia "CC" Rhodes asked as she unhooked her bra, dropped it onto the makeup table, and then brushed her hands lightly over her firm B-cup breasts.

"Full house," I said, rescuing the bra and placing it with CC's street clothes on a shelf above the clothes rack. I loved being a gopher on the cruise ship. Actually, I was more like a "go to" than a "go for," because anytime somebody called in sick or someone needed an extra hand or any little thing needed doing, I got called. I used to think getting paid to sail around the Mediterranean with hundreds of gorgeous women was as good as it got. Tonight, after five minutes in CC's dressing room, I changed my mind. Being the official dresser for a fashion model was the ultimate dream job.

"Good," CC said, sliding her skimpy baby blue bikinis off and holding them out to me on the end of one finger. "I always perform better to an audience."

I held out my hand and she dropped her panties into my palm. I tried to look cool and hoped my face didn't show the way my clit tingled as I caught the barest whiff of sweetness and spice. She turned to the huge mirror behind the dressing table and cocked her hip, apparently appraising her naked body. She looked the way I imagined a model was supposed to look: 5 feet 10, an all-over tan with no hint of bathing suit lines, long, sleek legs, and high breasts above prominently arched ribs. Wild, red-gold curls fell to her shoulders, and a thin matching strip of the same red-gold ran down the center of her mons and ended at the top of her cleft. She was otherwise shaved clean—everywhere, as far as I could see, and I couldn't help but look. She was so fucking hot. I glanced up to see her eyes in the mirror watching me, her mouth curved into a knowing smile. I blushed, but grinned. She was a model, right? She must like people to look at her.

"Do you have the order of the changes?" She turned to face me, leaning her shapely ass against the edge of the long, narrow makeup table. Her breasts were the round, firm kind with small, dark pink, perfectly centered areolae. At the moment, her nipples were hard and tight.

I got that tingle again and forced myself to hold perfectly still, even though I felt the tiny muscles in my thighs quivering like the wings of a hummingbird. I licked my lips because my throat suddenly went so dry I was afraid my voice would crack. "I've got it."

I nodded my head toward the list on the wall that held the six changes she'd go through during the fashion show. There were two other models in adjacent cubicles, each with their own assistants to help with changes, and the three would alternate out on the runway. They were all gorgeous, each in her own way, but CC was the name-model among the group.

"Have you ever done this before?" she asked, pushing away from the table.

The room was small, maybe 10 x 10, and with the clothes

rack and the vanity and one chair, there wasn't much room to maneuver. If she stepped one inch closer, her breasts were going to brush the front of my T-shirt, and I wasn't wearing a bra either. And my nipples beneath my white T-shirt were as hard as hers and had been since the second she'd brushed her fingers over her breasts. I wore khaki shorts with no belt and I could tell my silk bikinis were wet.

"Not exactly," I said, refusing to back up. I kept my hands at my sides, but it took every ounce of willpower I had. I wanted to grab her hips, her beautiful, tan, curvaceous hips, and pull her against my crotch. I wanted to bend my head and put my mouth around her nipple and bite it until she screamed. "But I've undressed quite a few women before."

She smiled. "Have you?"

Up close, she smelled hot and tangy. Body lotion and perfume and sex. I hissed in a breath as her breasts touched mine for a heartbeat and then she stepped away.

"What about *dressing* them?" She opened a drawer in the vanity and removed a flesh-toned G-string. When she bent her knee and lifted her leg to slip the thin string over her ankle and draw it up her shapely calf, I could see the pale pink lips of her pussy and the shine of excitement clinging to them. Then she lowered her leg and the vision was gone.

"I catch on quickly."

"I'll bet you do." CC slowly bent her opposite knee, her toes pointing downward as if she were a ballerina. She slipped the other side of the G-string over the arch of her foot, her fingertips caressing her skin as she slowly inched the string upward. My clit jumped, and although I know I didn't move, she laughed. "Are you ready?"

I sucked in a shaky breath. "You're really beautiful."

For a second, she looked surprised and almost shy. "Thank you."

I turned and lifted the first number she'd be wearing that

evening and the only dress among the designer resort wear—a turquoise Sue Wong with halter top, beaded body and cut-away skirt that would open all the way up to that pale swatch of satin covering her pussy. I held the thin straps between my outstretched fingers as the dress swayed between us. "Ready."

She slipped the shimmering material over her head as I knelt with the high-heeled sandals I'd plucked from a row of them, each pair corresponding to an outfit. I couldn't help but flash on the image of Cinderella as CC slipped her foot into the sandal I cradled between my palms. Just as her foot slid home she leaned forward, her hand braced against the back of my shoulder, and eased her foot forward until her arch was crushed against my crotch. My cheek brushed her thigh just where the dress split, baring skin, and I let the corner of my mouth skim her flesh, so softly I doubted she could feel it.

"Sorry," she murmured, "I lost my balance for a second."

If you keep rubbing your foot right there, I thought, subtly pushing my hips forward until my clit squeezed against her ankle through my shorts, *I'm going to lose more than that*.

"No problem," I gasped. "I enjoy being a footstool."

She laughed, ran her toes along the seam of my shorts, and then pushed me away. I damn near fell on my ass, but it was hard to be angry with a beautiful woman for teasing your clit.

"Go check the runway. Make sure the girls aren't too close." She smoothed both hands up the inside of her thighs, over her belly, and cupped her breasts. The slightly dreamy expression on her face told me she liked the way her hands felt on her body. "Sometimes they like to touch."

"Don't blame them," I said hoarsely. "Do you mind?"

CC smiled. "Watching women watch me always makes me hot."

"You must be hot all the time."

"Mmm, you're right."

I heard a faint swell of music. "That's our cue. Let me check the stage."

The place was standing room only, and the atmosphere was more like a nightclub than a fashion show. The huge room was almost dark. Colorful strobes slashed through the air in intersecting patterns, and three spotlights roamed over the runway in wide, swooping circles. The faces I could see all appeared eager, and I smelled sex in the air. I ducked back into CC's dressing room.

"It looks like they're expecting you to take your clothes *off*."

"The trick is to make them *think* I might." She skimmed her fingers lightly along my fly as she eased by me and out of the room. Her voice floated back to me. "Make sure the red two-piece is ready next."

I stood with my mouth hanging open and my clit jangling for a full minute, then I double-checked that the Shay Todd bathing suit was in easy reaching distance and hurried after her. I wanted to see her in action. I hung back in the shadows just inside the curtain that opened onto the runway and watched her saunter down the ramp, limbs loose and hips swiveling seductively. She took her time making it to the far end of the runway where it turned into a T. I could tell she was making eye contact with women in the crowd along the way from the smiles on their faces. Maybe some of them came to see the newest styles, but from the way they watched her walk, I was pretty sure most of them came to ogle the models. When she turned and started back, it seemed as if her eyes searched the dark beyond the open curtains where I stood, and I swear she saw me. Smiling fleetingly, she drew her fingers up the center of her body and touched her lips, as if tasting some secret only the two of us shared.

I watched her draw closer, my feet nailed to the floor, my stomach growing tighter and tighter with anticipation. Then, to a round of hearty applause, she slipped between the folds of the curtain and joined me in the gloom backstage. The second model, obviously intent on her moment in the spotlight, passed us without a glance.

"You're supposed to be in the dressing room," CC whispered.

"I wanted to watch."

CC stroked her fingers along the edge of my jaw, down my throat and between my breasts. "Did you enjoy it?"

"Yes. You're amazing."

She hooked her fingers inside the waistband of my shorts and gave a little tug. "Four minutes and counting."

I jerked, as much from the realization that we had a timetable to keep as from the maddening pressure between my legs. "I guess we should go then."

She didn't wait for me, and I made it into the dressing room just in time to catch the dress as she pulled it over her head and tossed it in my direction. Then she slid the G-string off and threw that too. I caught it one-handed and slid it into my pocket. She caught the motion and her eyes widened.

"Souvenir?" she asked.

I quickly rehung the dress and took down the bathing suit. "Underwear fetish," I replied with a straight face and handed her the bottoms.

Laughing, she stepped into the minuscule bikini bottom. "Pervert." She turned to the mirror and checked her makeup. "God, those lights are hot out there. Make sure you have a towel ready for the next change."

"Okay." Her body was already misted with a fine sheen of moisture. It made her skin glow, and I seriously doubted that anyone in the audience would mind watching beads of sweat trickle down her tight abdomen and pool in the shallow indentation of her belly button. I had a quick flash of kneeling in front of her and dipping the tip of my tongue into that delicious . . .

"One minute," CC whispered.

I caught a glimpse of her bare breasts in the mirror. The shallow V between them was flushed, the way a woman's skin will get when she's aroused. CC lifted her arms, watching my reflection in the glass.

"You'd better finish dressing me, don't you think?"

I realized I still held the bikini top in my hand. It was really just a swatch of material that covered a tiny bit of her breasts and tied in the back. No straps, no clasps, no much of anything at all. I stepped behind her, my eyes meeting hers in the mirror. I reached around her and stretched the thin fabric across her breasts, molding my fingers to the soft undersides, my thumbs just grazing her nipples. She caught her breath sharply and I felt her body twitch against me.

"Hold that up," I instructed, my breath lifting the hair against the side of her neck, "while I tie it in the back." I kept my hands where they were until she reached for her breasts, our fingers gliding together as our hands changed places. I watched her unconsciously stroke her nipples as I tied the thin strand between her delicate shoulder blades. She leaned ever so slightly against me, the curve of her ass fitting perfectly against my crotch. I wanted to slide one hand down her taut stomach and dip my fingers beneath the tiny triangle of red that covered the red-gold beneath. When I looked down to where my fingers ached to explore, I saw the faint bulge of her clitoris tent the tight fabric that barely spanned the width of her cunt.

"Thirty seconds," I said. She still cupped her breasts and her eyes were heavy-lidded as her gaze met mine in the mirror.

"Thank you." Her voice was like warm whiskey, raw and intoxicating.

I stepped back and didn't touch her, because she had a show to do and I didn't trust myself to do more than look. I followed her out, watched her work the crowd, saw the lust in women's eyes as they fucked her in their minds. She didn't stop where I waited as she hurried backstage this time, and I rushed after her.

As soon as the door closed behind me, she practically tore off the suit. "I don't want to sweat this up. Wipe me down, will you?"

"Personally, I think any of those women in the audience would pay big bucks for a bathing suit with a little bit of your sweat on it," I said as I grabbed a soft hand towel and patted her neck and chest with it. "Hell, some of them would probably pay to lick it off."

She closed her eyes and let her head fall back, laughing softly. "Maybe you can sell the towels later. Get my stomach and legs, too."

It was easier to do it kneeling, so I did. I hoped she was watching the clock, because I wasn't. I was watching the way her breasts rose and fell with each slightly uneven breath and the ripple of muscles in her stomach as I brushed the towel over her skin. When the backs of my fingers grazed her mons, she moaned softly and shifted enough to open her legs. The shining tip of her clit protruded between the deep rose lips of her pussy. I pressed a knuckle very lightly to the swollen hood of her clit.

"You're wet here, too."

"I know," she breathed. "It always happens."

"Should I . . . do something?" What I wanted to do was fasten my lips around her clit and suck her until she came. She looked so hard I didn't think it would take more than a minute.

"Just pat me dry," she whispered. "Not too hard, you'll make me come."

"Jesus," I groaned, my vision going dim. My hands trembled as I took care of her, but I did as she asked and then stood up on shaky legs. "We better get you dressed."

Somehow, professional that she was, she knew exactly how much time she had and was back on the runway precisely on cue. This bathing suit had a circle of black material that looped around her neck and extended down her chest in two thin strands that covered an inch of the center of each breast before crossing in the middle of her abdomen and attaching to the thong bikini bottom at each hip. Her back was completely bare except for the bikini string circling her hips. I imagined the strand of the thong rubbing over her exposed clit with each step, her wet pussy swelling more and more with each passing second. There in the dark, with the scent of her arousal swirling through my mind and the image of her excitement burned on the surface of my brain, I squeezed a hand between my legs to ease the ache in my clit. It felt so good I closed my eyes and rubbed harder, a few strokes from coming—until fingers gripped my wrist and pulled my hand away.

"You can do that on your own time," CC said, a hint of throaty laughter in her voice. "You've still got a job to do."

"Right," I croaked. "Coming. I mean—"

"Oh, I know what you mean," CC called over her shoulder as she disappeared into her dressing room with me right behind her.

She stripped off her suit, flung it in my direction and braced her hips against her vanity table, her hands gripping the edges. "You've got three minutes to make me come."

I barely caught the bathing suit and had the presence of mind to drape it over the back of the chair before I dropped to my knees between her legs. Three minutes. Jesus. And then it hit me. I was going to make three minutes of my mouth on her cunt feel like eternity. I looked up and saw her staring down at me, her lips slightly parted, her eyes desperate.

"God," she gasped, "I'm so hot. Suck me, please."

Instead, I gently spread her open with my thumbs and kissed her, a series of kisses starting at her clit and skimming over her pussy. She was wet, sweet and thick, and I wanted to drink her dry. Her hands were in my hair already, trying to get my mouth where she needed it. I gave her my tongue instead, long slow sweeps, licking up her come as she creamed for me.

"Ohh," she breathed out. "Oh, that's so nice. I'm going to come with you doing that."

"Yeah," I whispered, leaning back just enough to see her face. Her eyes were closed, her hands on her breasts, her fingers plucking at her nipples. A tiny frown of concentration creased her perfect forehead. I massaged her clit with one fingertip.

"Don't stop licking me," she whimpered. "I need your mouth to come."

Two minutes. Somehow I knew, two minutes. I went back to licking, tracing the delicate furls and troughs with the tip of my tongue, tugging and sucking her lips until her hips writhed and jumped. She was open for me now, and I slid my hands around her backside and supported her thighs against the front of my shoulders while I circled her clit with my lips and sucked her for the first time.

"That's it, that's it," she muttered. "Nice nice nice."

Her clit bulged between my lips, hard and tense, and I knew she was a stroke or two away. I slowed just enough to keep her this side of bursting, counting the seconds in my mind. She twisted her fingers in my hair.

"Almost. Almost. Uh, uh, uh huh . . ."

Her breathing got frantic, her words lost in a jumble of incoherent pleas, her cunt pulsing against my face. With my time almost up, I tightened my lips and sucked her in, hard and deep. Her clit pounded between my lips and she came, drenching my face and neck. When her legs buckled, I held her up, cradling her cunt against my mouth while she moaned and shivered, until she was completely spent.

"One more minute," I whispered and got to my feet, swiping my mouth against the sleeve of my T-shirt. Her eyes were open but dazed. I handed her a towel, grabbed another and carefully dried her. By the time I was done, she'd regrouped. I pulled the next outfit from the rack as she checked her makeup.

"That was incredible," she said, touching my mouth with trembling fingers. "Incredible."

"Yeah." I held out the next suit. "And we've got three more runs to go."

CC smiled. "If we're quick, we might find a few extra minutes between changes to try that on you."

"Maybe we should wait until we're off the clock," I said, opening the door for her. "I just got this job and there's another show coming up tomorrow."

"Oh, don't worry." CC kissed me as she passed. "I intend to request your services for the rest of the cruise. Good dressers are very hard to find."

Group Rate Special
Radclyffe

When Angela heard the water shut off in the shower, she dropped her *Business Weekly* magazine onto the bedside table and padded nude across the cabin to knock on the door. "West? Honey? Let me dry your back."

The door immediately opened and a warm cloud of steam billowed out. A nicely tanned and muscled arm reached through the steam, grasped Angela's shoulder and tugged her inside.

West kissed her hard, as if she hadn't seen her for months. "You'll let all the heat out."

"We're in the Mediterranean, honey. It's warm," Angela said, indicating her own naked state. She hadn't bothered to get dressed yet because her plans consisted of spending the entire day on the deck in her bikini. After she completed one very important item on her agenda.

"It might be hot *outside*, but it isn't in here. I hate air-conditioning," West grumbled.

"I know. Turn around so I can take care of you before you freeze."

"Whatever you say."

"Since when?" Angela laughed and grabbed a towel off the rack before closing the bathroom door.

"I always do what you say," West protested.

"Sure you do. As long as it's what you were planning to do anyhow."

West peered over her shoulder. "Are you trying to tell me I'm failing obedience training?"

"I'm not sure you can fail if you don't volunteer for the class first."

"All right. I'm yours to command for the entire day." West gave Angela a long look. "I promise to do as I'm told."

"Oh, you're going to be so sorry."

"I hope so," West said, grinning. As Angela started working on her back, she leaned over, both hands on the vanity, and sighed. "I didn't realize how much I needed this vacation until we got out here on the ocean."

"Are you sure you're not mad about Jill sharing our cabin?" Angela blotted the droplets from West's back, pressing her mons to West's hard butt, partly out of necessity in the cramped space, but mostly because she loved West's ass, and running her hands over West's body was making her horny. Well, hornier. "I know you only met her that once at the office party."

West found Angela's eyes in the mirror. "I knew we'd be spending a lot of time with your friends from work. It is a group holiday thing, after all."

"That's not the same as having a near stranger sleeping in the same cabin." Abandoning the towel, Angela wrapped her arms around West's waist and rubbed her breasts over West's shoulder blades while she licked her neck. Just that little bit of rubbing made her nipples hard. She circled her palm over West's belly and combed her fingers through the sleek dark hair that shadowed the triangle between her legs. "And besides, I'm used to having you whenever I want."

"Did you wake up wet, baby?" West teased, twisting around to face Angela. She palmed her ass, squeezing the round, firm globes and rotating her crotch into Angela's.

"You know I did, because you teased my clit until I was dripping." Angela tugged on West's lower lip with her teeth. "And then you didn't let me come."

"Jill woke up." West nibbled on Angela's neck. "I couldn't do much more than play with you, not with the head of accounting in bed three feet away from us."

Angela sighed. "I didn't realize it was going to be such a problem, but if I hadn't volunteered for her to stay with us, she wouldn't have been able to come. Sheila getting sick at the last minute and bailing on her really screwed things up."

"It's not that much of an issue. We don't spend a lot of time in the cabin." West worked a hand between their bodies to clasp Angela's breast. "She seems nice enough."

"I think she thinks *you're* nice," Angela said playfully, spreading her legs so West would press her clit more directly as they worked their pussies together. She felt herself growing harder. "She watches you when she thinks I'm not looking."

West continued her explorations along Angela's neck to her ear. She sucked the fleshy lobe between her teeth and rolled it back and forth, imagining Angela's clit in her mouth. "I never noticed."

"Mmm, I saw her looking this morning when you got out of bed—*without* any clothes on." Angela pushed hard into West's crotch. "But since I like you sleeping naked, I guess I'm going to have to put up with Jill ogling you. She must have thought I was asleep, because she actually licked her lips like she was ready to go down on you right then and there."

"You aren't jealous, are you?"

"Unh-uh," Angela sighed, tilting her head back so that West

could reach more of the sensitive areas beneath her ear. Every time West licked one of those spots she felt it in her nipples and her clit—a sharp burning that flared for an instant and then settled into a steady pulse of heat. "I like it when other girls look at you and get hot."

"When they just look?"

"You're never going to forget I told you I got off watching you make it with Christie at the beach house before we got together, are you?"

"It's one of my favorite fantasies," West said. "You watching."

"Oh yeah?" Angela raked her nails up West's back. "Well, Jill being hot for you makes me wet."

"I'm not so sure all that lust is for me." West skated her teeth down Angela's neck and sucked the soft warm skin just above her collarbone. At the same time she rubbed her cunt in short, hard circles against Angela's, knowing the constant pressure would make Angela's clit swell, but it wouldn't be enough to make her come. "I think some of it was left over from the erotica film we went to see last night."

Angela laughed. "God, if I had known that everybody was going to be fucking instead of watching the damn movie, I wouldn't have suggested the *three* of us go together. At least I had you to get me off, even if we did have to do it standing up in that tiny bathroom stall. Poor Jill must have been suffering."

"Not for long. I heard her masturbating last night right after we all went to bed."

Angela gave a little jerk as her cunt flooded. "Really? How could you tell?"

"I was almost asleep, and then I heard her moving under the covers like she couldn't get comfortable. I didn't think anything of it at first, and then I heard her whimper. Just a little tiny sound like something hurt her."

"Could you see?" Angela asked breathlessly, rubbing her breasts over West's. "Pinch my nipples, honey."

West immediately caught both hard nubs between her finger-tips and rolled them. "It's really dark with the curtains closed over the porthole. I couldn't see her face, but I could hear this really steady swishing noise. It must have been her hand moving underneath the sheets, and she was breathing really fast. Little gasps and I could tell she was trying to be quiet."

"Oh God." Angela swept her fingers between West's legs and tugged on the swollen edges of her cunt. "Did you get wet like this listening to her make herself come?"

"Wouldn't you? I couldn't help it."

"What did you do about it?"

"I wanted to wake you up so you could do me," West lowered her head to suck Angela's nipple, "but I was afraid she would hear me if I moved and she might stop."

"Did you play with your clit?"

"Mmm," West replied, never letting up on Angela's nipple.

Angela cupped her palm over West's cunt and squeezed until West gasped. "Did you come listening to her get off while I was asleep?"

West raised her head, her expression totally innocent. "I would never come like that without you there to enjoy it."

"Good." Angela jiggled her hand until West was forced to close her eyes from the pleasure. "Let's go make out on the bed."

"Jill might come back," West pointed out.

"She might." Angela gave West's clit one quick stroke. "Will that be a problem?"

West grinned. "Nope."

"Good." Angela dragged West by the hand out of the bathroom and then tumbled onto one of the two slightly-larger-than-twin beds. Jill's bed was against the opposite wall, with two sets of built-in dressers just below the porthole between them. When West started to get under the covers, Angela stopped her. She propped pillows against the wall, pushed the sheets down and sat crosswise on the bed, her legs partly off the side. "Sit next to me like this."

When West joined her, Angela threw one leg over West's, pulled the sheet up to their thighs and leaned into West. "Now put that beautiful mouth to work before I scream."

"She's going to get quite a view if she walks in," West said, indicating the cabin door on the facing wall, just past the foot of Jill's bed. "I'm naked."

Angela looked down at her own full breasts and skimmed her fingers over both erect pink nipples. "Me, too."

"You're the one who has to work with her when we get home, not me," West whispered, moving in on Angela's neck.

"I wasn't the one jerking off to a fantasy of someone else's girlfriend," Angela whispered, holding both breasts in her hands and squeezing her nipples while West sucked on all the tender points in her neck. "She was."

"You don't know she was thinking of me," West said.

"Let's just say a woman knows."

"Uh huh." West flicked her tongue over Angela's lower lip.

"You have such a great mouth."

"I love kissing you."

"Good, because I—"

"Oh my God!" Jill stopped abruptly just inside the room, the cabin door closing behind her. "I am so so sorry."

"It's okay," Angela said as Jill swung around and fumbled with the door handle. "Don't go."

With her back still to them, Jill whispered, "I was just going to change into my bathing suit and go up to the sun deck."

"Go ahead and change then, but wait for us. We can all go together." Angela laughed softly, pulling West's head down to her breast. "We won't be long."

"Are you sure you don't mind?" Jill sidled through the narrow space between the beds to get to her dresser. She glanced down at Angela's and West's legs entwined on the bed and looked sharply away.

"No, it's fine," Angela said. "Right, West?"

"Sure." West smiled up at Jill, who blushed. "As long as you don't mind waiting."

"Oh, no. That's good . . . I mean. That's fine." Jill grabbed a two piece yellow bikini and rushed toward the bathroom.

"Oh, West just took a shower so you should probably leave the bathroom door open when you change. It'll be a sauna in there otherwise," Angela called. She tugged West's face up to hers and threaded her fingers through the thick dark hair at the base of West's neck. "Now kiss me like you fuck."

West played inside Angela's mouth like it was her cunt, circling the inner surface of her lips, probing with her tongue, plunging deep inside and slowly drawing out, tongue fucking her until Angela felt every stroke deep inside her pussy. When her chest and her cunt were so tight she couldn't catch her breath, Angela pulled her head back, gasping, and caught a flash of yellow out of the corner of her eye.

"Jill's watching us," Angela panted. West nodded, nibbling Angela's neck. Angela pressed a manicured fingertip to the hood of West's clit and rubbed it. "She looks like she's so excited she's about ready to masturbate any second."

"I know just how she feels," West said against Angela's throat, her voice husky. "Making out with you always gets me so turned on." She lifted her hips so that Angela's finger bore down harder against her clit. "And that's really getting me going."

"I don't want to hurry." Angela sucked on West's lower lip, easing off on her clit but keeping her finger on it. "I love the way you kiss too much to stop right now."

"Then don't." West dipped her tongue in and out of Angela's mouth, teasing her. "You know I can take a lot of clit play before I lose it." As if to prove it, West guided Angela's finger lower, coating it with the thick come that pooled between her legs, then guiding Angela's finger around her clit in lazy circles. The muscles in her inner thighs quivered as her clit lengthened and grew stiff. "I like it when you work me up."

Jill took two stumbling steps into the room before blurting, "I should go."

She didn't sound too convincing, and Angela saw that she had her hand in her bikini bottoms and was busy fingering her clit, the bulge of her knuckle making short, fast circles beneath the bright yellow material.

"I've got a better idea." Angela smiled at Jill's dazed expression. "Why don't you finish yourself off with West's clit in your mouth? Would you like that?"

"Oh yes," Jill murmured, staring with wide eyes at Angela's and West's fingers teasing West's clit simultaneously.

"Come suck her, then, but try not to make her come. Just make her feel nice for as long as you can."

When Jill hesitated, West inched closer to the side of the bed and spread her thighs wide. "It's okay. I'd really like it if you went down on me."

Jill rushed the last few feet and collapsed to her knees, her hands automatically clutching West's thighs. Their eyes met for a second before Jill delicately spread West's cunt open with both hands.

"What do you like?" Jill asked, wetting her lips with her tongue. Her eyes were fever bright and eager.

"She likes to be sucked pretty hard," Angela said before West could answer. "But stop and lick her for a minute every once in a while so she doesn't get off right away." She curled against West's side again and kissed her. "Okay, baby?"

Instead of answering, West tangled her fingers in Angela's hair and tugged her head back so that she could thrust her tongue deep into her mouth. She shuddered at the first hot brush of Jill's mouth over her clit and whispered against Angela's lips, "Whatever you want, remember?"

"I want to kiss you while you come in her mouth." Angela sucked West's tongue back into her mouth, teasing and playing with it, then darting her own into the warm inner recesses of West's mouth. The only sound other than their harsh breathing was Jill's quiet moaning as she sucked. Finally, Angela released West's tongue long enough to look down at Jill. Her eyes were closed, one hand kneading the swollen blood-flushed edges of West's cunt lips, the other rubbing her own pussy. Her mouth was shiny with pearly come.

"Doesn't she have a great clit?" Angela asked.

"Mmm. Mmm," Jill responded, shaking her head, her lips still fastened to West's clit.

The vibration shot through the core of West's clit and into her stomach. She jerked. "Jesus."

Laughing, Angela ran her tongue delicately along the inner surfaces of West's upper lip and then her lower. She rubbed West's tense stomach in small, light circles with one hand and started masturbating herself to the same rhythm with the other. "Mmm, you like this, don't you?"

"I like everything you do to me."

"Oh yeah?" Angela went back to stroking West's lips with the tip of her tongue, one hand still buried deep in her own wet cunt. "You like this?"

"You've got the greatest mouth." West fought to focus on Angela's dreamy eyes. She sucked the tip of Angela's tongue lightly, stiffening as Jill unintentionally pulled on her clit at just the same moment, mirroring the motion. "Oh fuck."

Angela smiled against her mouth. "Is she doing you nice, baby?"

"Yes," West gasped, gripping Angela's breast. It was heavy and hot, and when Jill swept the length of her clit with her tongue, she squeezed Angela harder than she intended.

Angela whimpered and pushed her cunt against West's leg, rubbing her crushed clit faster. "Tell me. Tell me what she's doing to you."

West worked Angela's nipple into a tight, hard ball between

her fingers, arching her neck as Angela sucked at her throat. "She's sucking me just like you told her to—slow and hard . . . uh . . . starting at the bottom and sliding all the way out to the head." As she spoke, Jill repeated the motions on her clit. West pumped her hips insistently, trying to get more of her clit into Jill's mouth.

"God it makes me hot." The bed rocked as Angela rode West's leg in short, hard thrusts, her fingers holding her clit. "I love to hear her suck you. What else? What else is she doing?"

"Uh . . . she's got the tip of her tongue under the hood and she's sucking . . . oh, Jesus . . ." West wrenched her head away as Angela bit her neck and Jill tongue-whipped her clit. "Fuck, she's good."

Angela dug her nails into West's stomach, and when West twisted her nipple sharply in response, she tried to pull free. "Stop it! You'll make me come."

West couldn't hear anything above the screaming ache in her clit. She kept tormenting Angela's nipple with one hand and grabbed the back of Jill's head with the other, forcing Jill's mouth tightly against her cunt. "Jesus, Jill, suck me harder. I want to get off."

"Me, too," Angela whimpered, thrusting her tongue into West's mouth as she thumbed her clit back and forth and drove her fingers in and out between the swollen folds of her pussy. West sucked Angela's tongue harder. Angela moaned into her mouth.

Jill abruptly stopped sucking and West yelled, "Oh man, don't quit now! I'm about ready to shoot like a rocket."

"I'm sorry, I'm sorry," Jill wailed against West's clit. "I can't help it. I'm going to come!" She writhed and rubbed her cheek frantically in West's cunt. "Oh. I'm coming. I'm coming!"

"God!" Angela cried, the sound of Jill coming setting her off.

West's thighs clenched as she stared down at Jill, her hard clit pounding as Jill ground her face into it while she came. "Fuck.

Fuck!" She let go of Angela's breast and grabbed Jill's head with both hands, trying to get Jill's mouth back around her clit. "Fuck, baby," she gasped, desperately searching Angela's hazy eyes. "I'm going to lose it if she keeps doing that."

"Come with me, honey," Angela pleaded. "Now, honey, now."

West howled and came in Jill's face. Angela whined and squeezed spasm after spasm from her gushing cunt. Jill found West's pulsing clit while it was still pumping and sucked it in, sending West off again with a hoarse shout.

When their last mingled cries of pleasure drifted off, Angela snuggled against West's shoulder. Wrapping an arm around West's middle, she gave a contented sigh. "Good, honey?"

"Better than good." West kissed Angela's forehead, one hand still tangled on Jill's hair. "You okay, Jill?"

Her face slack with pleasure, Jill pillowed her face against West's stomach and fondled West's still-hard clit. Drowsily, she sighed, "Oh yes. I'm really glad you invited me to share your cabin."

West and Angela covered Jill's hand with both of theirs and said simultaneously, "What else are friends for?"

Right Here, Right Now
Karin Kallmaker

"Did you think I was going to let you get away with that?"

My girlfriend's hoarse whisper in my ear as we hurried down the stairs to our stateroom was everything I could have wanted. The woman coming up the stairs gave us a strange look, probably because the words sounded threatening and my girlfriend did appear to be almost chasing me. I would have been moving even faster had I not been wearing white patent stilettos and managing my floor-sweeping toga.

Halfway down we got a completely different once-over from the butch lead guitarist of that rock band. She and my girlfriend must have exchanged split-second glances, too, because the guitarist looked at me again, and I was pretty sure if her eyes could have undone the single clip keeping my toga on one shoulder, they would have. It wasn't a come-on to me, but a compliment to my butch . . . just one of those things they do. When we'd booked the cruise she'd been afraid the femme-laden brochures meant she would be "odd boi out," but there were enough buzz cut butches for her comfort level. She looked smashing in a toga knotted on both shoulders, and with plain leather sandals, every inch a serious Roman senator. I'd decided to play the part of the very naughty Messalina.

We skittered around the final corner to our stateroom, and I could hear she had the key out already. A friend of mine thinks commitment means boredom. She'd pronounced that couples were guaranteeing themselves a life of predictable passion.

My butch was predictable all right, and I liked her that way. Frankly, I prefer *consistent* as a description of her.

She flattened me against the door to unlock it, her pelvis grinding against my ass. The door burst open and we stumbled inside. Her hands were pushing up the bed-sheet-cum-toga before the door even swung shut.

"You were showing off, weren't you? Waving your beautiful ass around?"

"That show was for you. I thought you'd like a courtesan's lap dance." I started to turn to face her, but she shoved me toward the tiny vanity area at the foot of the double bed. Leaning her weight into me, she parted and pulled up the fabric to expose my ass and back, then planted my hands on the edge of the narrow counter.

"Stay right there like that. God, I knew you weren't wearing panties."

I did as she told me and had no wish to do anything else. Grasping the edge of the vanity counter firmly, I bent into the same pose I'd adopted to pick up my napkin just before she'd told me we were going back to our room, right now.

"You wanted me to do you right there, in front of everyone. I know that's your fantasy." Her hands were all over my hips, my ass, grasping me firmly until I was where she wanted. "Oh, baby, look at you. You need it bad, don't you?"

"Like you weren't petting me so everyone could watch. We

both know what we want."

She draped herself over me and I realized she'd shed her own bedsheet. Her supple skin was slick against mine. I looked into the mirror and saw that look on her face, the one I loved, the one that was heavy with lust and determined to get completely lost in me.

With a yank at the clip at my shoulder, she released the toga, and the sheet whooshed to the floor. My breasts spilled free to our mutual moan.

"Did you think I didn't see these?" I met her gaze in the mirror and then watched her focus on the golden moons that hung from my nipples. "You wore our play gear in public—and that is going to get you fucked, just like this."

I shuddered and thrust back against her. "Are you just going to talk about it, or are you going to actually do something?"

She swatted my backside for an answer and let go of me. My laugh and wiggle in response to the swat turned into an arching, swelling groan as she pulled gently, persuasively on one of the moons. They stayed on with a simple loop that cinched around my nipples, and if she pulled too hard they'd slip right off. But she knew just how to twist it. Nearly invisible under my clothes, she loved it when I teased her with glimpses of body jewelry, and these were so comfortable I'd been wearing them all evening. She'd only realized as I'd ground myself on her lap that I might perhaps be wearing our very private jewelry. I'd have had a matching moon dangling from a soft clip that slipped behind and lifted my clit, but I hadn't been able to find it. I stared briefly at my reflection. The heavy, drunk look in my eyes told me I wouldn't care about the missing clip.

"You are the most incredible playmate. God, I could look at you all night."

"I'd rather you did something else to me all night."

"What about the midnight buffet?"

"Fuck the midnight buffet."

She laughed, as I had expected her to. The rustling of her suitcase stopped and then she was standing behind me again. "Nah. I'd rather fuck this."

Even braced, I nearly lost my footing at the force of her thrust. When she was in this mood, and I was in this mood, she always took me fast and so deeply that the leather of her harness pressed against my open, willing flesh. Her hands crept up my back as she rocked behind me, in and out, in and out, the slap of her cock keeping time with my panting grunts as she knocked the breath out of me.

She gripped my shoulders, first yanking me back against her even harder, then pushing me down until my head was on the little counter, cushioned against my arms. I loved this vulnerable position and letting her have me this way. There were no barriers between us. She took everything she needed and I had all that I wanted.

"You're so juicy, baby. I feel you on my legs." She twisted her fingers into my hair and pulled my head up. I gasped. "Look at those nipples of yours. So red and tight for me. You like getting fucked like this, don't you?"

The gold jewelry swayed and moved under me, adding the slight pull of gravity to my nipples. "You know I do, and you like having me this way."

"You know I do."

In the mirror I watched her chest gloss with perspiration as the temperature rose in the cabin and between us. Her own nipples were hard and I wanted them in my mouth. I didn't see her other hand slide under me, but I moaned loudly when she squeezed one encircled nipple. I shuddered and somehow kept my feet under me even as my knees threatened to give way.

"I'm gonna come, baby," I warned her hoarsely. "It's what you're doing to me. You fill me up. Your cock touches everything."

"Go ahead and come. Come all over me." She squeezed my

nipple again and I gave in to the sweet, welcome contractions that gripped at her cock and made my clit throb. The hours of teasing us both into this frenzy had been all for this moment, my strength balanced against hers, me pushing back, her holding on.

I shook under her, aware that her arm was holding me up even as she covered me with her body so she could continue to thrust into me after the strongest waves had subsided. Was it the position that woke up all the nerves inside me, or her forcefulness that made me so open and pliable? I had friends who wondered about such things, but all I knew was that she made me come like no one else ever had. I gave her all the right numbers and she unlocked the combination every time.

"More," she growled in my ear. She pulled out of me and swung me toward the bed. I stumbled, fell, bounced, and she was on top of me, spreading my legs as she claimed my mouth for a hot, wet kiss. "Right here, baby, right now."

"Please, please . . ." I seemed to know no other word. Everything inside me felt divine and now the harness was rhythmically pressing into my clit.

"Everything, you get it all tonight."

"So do you," I managed to say through my gritted teeth. I clung to her, rising to meet her, feeling the strength of her and the matching pulse of her passion.

"I don't care if you strut around in front of other women." She stopped, pushed inside me as far as she could go. Her hands clamped down on my shoulders, anchoring me to the bed. "Because I'm the one who gets to do this to you. I'm the one who gives it to you the way you want."

Subtle movements of her hips magnified the fullness of her cock and I resisted going limp. My mouth was watering. All of me was abruptly drenched. "Baby," I said weakly.

"I'm the one who knows how to fuck your brains out. Isn't this what you want?"

She was moving again, short thrusts that made my nipples

brush against her breasts. "Yes," I groaned. "This is exactly what I want."

Our gazes locked and her eyes were dark, the way they always were when she was very turned on. Time did not stop, but it lost all meaning to me. I didn't realize how long I'd been lost in her gaze while my body took her and took her and took her, not until she suddenly said, "Please, baby, come for me again. Don't make me wait for it—I can't stand it. Please."

I arched hard under her, and suddenly it was she who was clinging to me, trying to stay on while I writhed. She kept me on the bed somehow as I thrashed under her, abandoned and beyond words. She held me tight and encouraged me, begged me to give her more.

I gave her everything I had.

It was several minutes before I realized she was still quietly pleading with me for more. I smiled to myself. I never could resist her begging.

Turning onto my side I gave her a loving kiss. "You did very well."

"You make me so crazy. I love it when you are so slutty and I know I'm going to get to have you later."

I rolled on top of her and straddled her thighs. "You deserve a reward, don't you think?"

She was holding her breath as she nodded. I leaned down to whisper, "Breathe, darling," just before I kissed her. "We're just getting started. You did exactly what I wanted. Every bit was perfect."

My head on her shoulder as my hands undid the straps on her harness, I voiced the persistent truth that still amazed me. "You're the only one I can ever let see me that way. I trust you and I love you. You're the only woman who has ever made me come."

There was a slight smile of wonder on her lips when I straightened up to pull the harness free. "All I do is what you tell me, and I listen to you," she said.

"You make it sound so simple. You're the only one who ever got it right."

She whimpered as I slowly bent over her and licked her lips. "I love you."

"I know, darling. Slide your hands under your ass and don't close your eyes."

She did as I ordered and I watched her pupils dilate with anticipation. "Like this?"

"Yes, very good. Help me." She squirmed and lifted as I wove the short rope from under the pillow around her wrists. It wouldn't take much of a struggle to free herself, but it wasn't the restraint that worked for her, but the order behind it. "Keep your hands there or I'll stop and there'll be no more fucking tonight."

She relaxed under me, both of us knowing she would do as she was told, and I would make her obedience well worth her while. How could her response be predictable when the trust it demonstrated never failed to fill me with awe? I'd topped other women and truly enjoyed it, but my darling moved me like no other. Every woman before her had been part of my searching. Now there was only her.

I nibbled and kissed her neck, taking the time to smell the faint remnant of her cologne. This was a complicated dance, but only with her had I ceased to care if I touched her because I was giving my submissive what she wanted, or enjoying myself with her as my plaything, because that is what we both wanted. Whose needs came first, the chicken's or the egg's? With her they were inseparable. I bit down on her hard nipple and didn't care which of us that pleased more. She moaned just the way that made me deliciously dizzy. My own nipples swelled in response. I realized then that the steady pulse of the ship's engines were a match to her heartbeat, powerful and deep.

"You taste wonderful," I murmured. I trailed my tongue down her torso. "Sea air suits you."

When she didn't respond, I bit her nipple again, then said, "You have permission to talk, darling."

"Thank you," she said after a long moan.

"I want you to enjoy yourself. You fucked me. You made me come twice, plus all the little ones along the way." I arched so the body jewelry moons dangled across her nipples. "I haven't yet decided exactly how I'm going to make you come."

She shifted under me so the moons continued to dangle between us. "Anything you want."

"I love you in a frenzy like this," I mused. "Maybe I should have you wait another day so—"

"Please don't make me wait, please."

"Are you sure? Sometimes you're not sure."

"I really need to come, please, baby."

There had been a time she'd called me Mistress, but the years together had mellowed the need for the sharp dividing line between dominant and submissive. She was my lover, my partner. I adored taking care of her like this, of anticipating what she really needed even when she gave contradictory signs. Did she need to get higher before I gave her release? Her gaze had grown unfocused and her arms were stiff enough to induce cramping. If anything, she was too high and her body wouldn't quite know which pleasure center should respond. I needed to bring her down a little, then push her over the edge.

Freeing the heavy toy from the harness, I showed it to her. "In a while, I'm going to fuck you with your own cock."

She swallowed before saying, "I am so glad I'm a woman and that doesn't involve amputation."

I grinned at her, aware she was breaking the mood, but her eyes were focusing again and her breathing had slowed. "I am fond of all the things that are attached to you."

"Oh, good—oh fuck!"

I twisted one nipple, hard. "Like this. I like doing this to you because I know you just got very, very wet for me—"

"I'm already so wet, baby!"

"And I know your clit just turned into a rock."

"It is—"

I pressed my fingers to her lips. "No more words."

She shuddered and I felt her heart pounding deep and hard.

Slithering down her body I spread her legs, anticipating the feast of her thickly wet pussy. To my surprise a little moon winked at me. "What's this?"

She wisely said nothing.

"You're wearing my jewelry. You've got that little clip around your clit. You fucked me and got yourself off too, didn't you?"

Predictable? Hardly. She'd been a very naughty girl. I put my palm over her clit and pressed down. She immediately thrust back with a moan of need and distress.

"You look so pretty with my jewelry on, maybe I should leave it." I slid onto my stomach and parted her lips so I could marvel at the red, swollen beauty of her erect clit. I really ought to punish her, but her clit was so ripe and so tantalizing. I made a lover's choice, and covered it with my warm mouth.

She moaned so loudly that I couldn't hear the engines for a moment. And she kept on moaning while I used my tongue to work the clip upward until her clit was finally released. I knew exactly how good that felt, and enjoyed the helpless twitching of her clit against my tongue. I kept my mouth over it, just barely brushing it with my tongue as I slowly pushed her cock inside her.

Her moan became a half-cry, and I pushed a little faster. In my desire to be a good dominatrix I had studied what made the female body respond. I knew that her anterior nerve cluster was tightening against the stimulation while her clitoral nerves sent reciprocal sensations so that each area was equally pleasured. But my darling was no stranger I needed to study and safeguard, and the familiarity of her was so precious that I sometimes found my heart so tight in my chest I could not breathe.

The lover in me heard her choking, sobbing moans. She loved this. She loved what I gave her. I knew with her hands trapped under her she had no choice but to arch her hips up to meet me. She had no choice now but to come like this and I lifted my mouth from her to watch her gush around the cock. When she gasped for breath I pulled the cock out of her.

"More, baby." I tongued her clit hard this time, and the sharp sensation there unclenched the muscles inside her. She drenched my chest and the bed with a final, hoarse cry, then went limp.

I snatched a toga sheet from the floor to mop the bedclothes, then grabbed the other and covered us both just as she burst into tears. My arms were around her and I held her tight.

"Words now, darling, it's okay. I'm here, I've got you. It's okay."

She cried for only a minute, and I knew she was coming down when I heard a little ripple of laugher amongst the tears.

"What?"

She sniffed, then said, "We're going to have to tip the cabin steward big time, huh?"

"Won't be the first time. Won't be the last."

"God, you make me happy."

"Oh, darling, why would I not?" I curled into her arms as tears stung my eyes. I was coming down too. Sex was all about wet, and tears to me were a natural extension, a different and almost equally needed release.

She whispered a sweet nothing, but my eyelids were already drooping. I felt her fingers at my nipples and was confused for a moment, then realized she was taking off the jewelry moons.

"Thank you," I mumbled. She was so predictable, taking care of me in all the little ways as well as the big ones. Predictability meant trust, I thought hazily. No two nights with her were ever alike and yet they always ended the same way.

Her arms tightened around me. And I slept.

Pool Games
Karin Kallmaker

"This is the life."

"You got that right." Hana rolled her eyes as her friend Evie put her head back. Obviously Evie was referring to the sunshine and refreshing sea breezes.

Hana was busy admiring the scenery. The comic, Zelda, was organizing the next pool game, and so far there was no shortage of really fine looking women willing to play. "Check out the blondes. Over there, on the left. Asian chick, white chick, gorgeous long hair on both. Do you think they're going to play Pass the Orange?"

Evie struggled to get her eyes open. "If they do, wake me up."

Hana tipped a little of her drink onto Evie's stomach. After the expected yowl and protest, she said, "I don't know how you can sleep."

"I was up late. Later than I wanted to be."

"I'm sorry, she took longer than I thought she would. Wanted to cuddle and stuff."

"Well, if you're going to bag any more babes in our state-room, would you finish it up before midnight?"

"You're just pouting because I got her." Hana smiled at the memory. Simone? Samantha? Anyway, she'd been fun.

"Bro, I wasn't even trying."

"Bet I can bag one of those blondes before sunset."

"Sure, yeah, whatever." Evie closed her eyes for good, it seemed.

"It's your sunburn, bro." She glanced up at the overhang—with the sun shifting, Evie would be in the shade within a half hour. She'd leave her to sleep.

She studied the two blondes, oh so femme the pair of them. She'd noticed them at the singles' tables the last two nights during dinner. They both definitely looked up for fun or they wouldn't be wearing such revealing swimsuits and happily participating in the games.

Pass the Orange started, and sure enough, the cute twosome played along. As they and their teammates gamboled and splashed, they passed an orange from person to person without using their hands. Capturing it between chin and chest, a successful pass required full and complete body contact, and it was a show worth watching. Zelda added ribald commentary. Hana didn't know if the organizers had done it on purpose, but one team was mostly butch and the other all femme. She forgot to watch the butches with so many lovely and round female attributes rubbing up against each other, all wet and heaving.

This was one hell of a vacation.

The butch team was way ahead and would have won had not several of the femmes mysteriously lost their bikini tops all at the same time. The resulting consternation on the butch side of the pool resulted in a dropped orange that bobbed unnoticed. Meanwhile, the unleashed femme equipment seemed to help them make their passes even easier.

"Those are nipples, not oranges—be careful with the goodies!" Zelda was having a blast, and Hana was rapt counting all the bobbing bits.

She had one more thing to add to her homage at the shrine of Sappho, oh yes she did.

"Don't look now, but short, dark and cocky is headed this way." Felicia gave Zi a wry look. "I thought her eyes were going to fall out the way she was ogling you."

"Not me, you." Zi checked her bikini straps again to make sure they were firmly back in place.

"She is *so* not my type."

"Right—sure she isn't."

Felicia just shrugged, and Zi wondered what was bothering her friend. "I thought you came on this cruise to get laid. Repeatedly."

"I thought I did too, but I'm tired of being the one in the bin."

"Huh?"

Felicia tossed back her long hair in a gesture that wasn't quite her usual come hither signal. "Like I'm the one in a box with a bunch of other oranges getting picked over until someone decides to pick me up. I'd like to do the picking up for once."

The butch from the other side of the pool was nearly upon them, and Zi thought Felicia went on to say, "I'd like to be in charge for once," but she wasn't sure.

"Well, I'm damned well tired of being a good girl," Zi whispered. "Screw Yiyi and her good Asian girl crap."

"Be the blonde," Felicia said with a tease in her voice.

"You two looked like you were having a lot of fun," the new arrival said. Zi pulled up her feet from the foot of the chaise, and the butch readily accepted the invitation to sit. "Where you both from?"

"Santa Fe," Zi said. "How about you?"

"Denver. My friend and I both. She's asleep."

"Busy night for her?" Felicia's tone was cool, and Zi took that as a clear sign that Felicia wasn't interested in the butch, which was fine. She definitely was interested in the woman—she looked like she specialized in Quick, Hot and Seeyalaterbabe. Exactly what her inner therapist had ordered.

"She was screaming her head off at the heavy metal concert last night."

"You like metal?" Zi swept her hair off her back so it gathered over one shoulder, and hoped that her momentary puzzlement at its blond hue didn't show. It took getting used to.

"Sure. I'm Hana, by the way."

Zi introduced herself and Felicia, who nodded and returned her attention to the pool where a spirited game of Marco Polo was underway.

"Metal can be very liberating." Zi hoped Hana didn't hear Felicia's quiet snort. So fine, she hadn't ever heard heavy metal before last night, but Hana wasn't going to be around long enough to catch her in a few fibs. "Hey, your friend is looking for you."

Hana turned and waved, and the other butch headed around the pool toward them.

Felicia gathered up her towel and book. "I'm going to burn if I stay out anymore. Have fun, you two."

Zi watched her friend walk away and wondered again what was bothering her. Oh well, she'd tell her eventually. She always did.

"This is Evie," Hana said. "Evie—Zi. She lives in Santa Fe."

Evie nodded, seemed polite enough. "I was going to see if there was any ice cream left and then think about changing for dinner before I head to the casino for a while."

"Good idea. Go ahead and change for dinner. I'll, uh, find you."

Evie nodded and Zi pretended not to see the silent signal passed between the two friends. She and Felicia had a similar arrangement.

"She seems nice," Zi said after Evie left.

"We're peas in a pod." Hana stretched her legs out in front of her. She tanned easily, it looked like, but she was still several shades lighter than Zi was. "When we were eight we were the only two tomboys in our neighborhood, and we've been butch brothers ever since."

"Bet you were both cute little girls."

Hana gave her a sidelong look. "But we wanted to be boys. A lot. No dresses to begin with. And we both had brothers and they didn't have to do any housework. My brother got taught how to drive when he was eleven. Why wouldn't I want to be a boy?"

Zi grinned. "Okay, I can get that. Believe me, I'm well-schooled in what good little girls can and can't do."

"My folks tried." Hana gave her a lopsided smile that Zi knew brought women running for miles. "I was the kind of girl who liked to do the other girls, and from the time I was fifteen I was a terror. Evie and I—we both *adore* girls."

Yes, that smile was devastating and, before Yiyi, Zi might have tried to resist it. But now she had some major time to make up, and a fast-talking butch who wanted an hour or two of fun was exactly what she needed. Cheap sex, and lots of it. "All sorts of girls, or a certain kind?"

Hana ran one finger along the curve of Zi's calf. "I like all sorts of girls. I'm especially fond of those who like me to be very much in charge."

Zi tucked her toes under Hana's thigh and stretched. "So you like telling a girl what to do?"

"Only in private."

"But this isn't very private." Zi tossed back her hair, aware that Hana was enjoying the view.

"So I'm not telling you what to do, am I?"

Zi drained the last of her frothy drink. "Why don't you give it a try?"

Hana gave her a long, smoldering look. "I've got vodka and orange juice in my room."

Zi rose to her feet, trying to make the most of all her five feet. The high-heeled sandals helped. As always when she stood up, she had to pause to catch the ship's motion. Hana steadied her with a firm hand at her elbow. "Thank you."

Hana kept her hand where it was, even tightened it a little. "Have a drink with me."

"Yes." She let the next swell under the ship shift her weight toward Hana. Practically in her arms, she whispered, "There, that wasn't so hard, was it? You told me what to do and I said yes."

If Evie had had any idea how easy it would be to talk this particular babe into their cabin, she wouldn't have given up, Hana thought. She kept the pace slow as they chatted and laughed on their way down two flights of external stairs. They went indoors at the rear lounge and the frigid air hit their overheated bodies.

"I always feel like I need a sweater inside." Zi caught Hana checking out her nipples. "Like what you see?"

"Oh, yes," Hana said with all the fervor she could muster. "I'd like to see more of it."

"You could get your wish in just a few short minutes."

"I knew rubbing that lamp would pay off." Well, Zi was certainly eager. The ol' Hana charm really worked aboard ship. If she was one of the officers all decked out in their white uniforms she'd never get any sleep on a week like this one. "This is the stairwell closest to my room," she said, guiding Zi toward it.

Zi was a little more serious when she said, "I get the impression you do this often."

"Often enough to make me and a number of other women very happy."

"Don't oversell yourself—I could be disappointed if my expectations are too high."

After Hana stopped laughing, she managed to say, "And do you do this often?"

"As a matter of fact, no." Zi paused on the landing between decks. "I just got out of a relationship and I'm ready to kick it over."

"I'll be happy to help you forget all about her. Anything you'd like." Sometimes being a butch with a sincere desire to make a woman happy had its rewards.

"Believe me, she's easy to forget." Zi resumed their downward journey, one hand gracefully sliding along the handrail. "It's her endless crap I want to be sure is out of my head."

"Like what? One more floor down I think." The lower they descended, the narrower the stairwell became and the more rhythmic and noticeable the engines were.

"She never could reconcile being gay and being Asian. Being gay brought shame and dishonor on her family, so she made up for it by practicing being gay as little as possible."

"I don't get it."

"We had good sex for two months, then it was more important to be good girls. She actually thought that her family would accept us as a couple if she told them we were more or less celibate."

"Oh, I get it now. Like some religious nuts say it's okay to be gay as long as you don't have gay sex."

"Bingo. Except her shit was all family stuff."

"Right here," Hana said, pointing at her cabin door. She had the key ready. "So you didn't have much sex, I take it."

Zi looked her right in the eye. "I haven't had sex in thirteen months and eleven days."

Hana spared one last pitying thought for Evie. "So, I guess

you'd like me to scratch a few itches for you?"

Standing right there in the hallway, her back to Hana's door, Zi reached up and undid her bikini top. She had really beautiful tits and her nipples were begging for attention. Hana didn't see the need for any further talk.

"That's right, baby," Zi moaned. Hana was all over her, seemingly intent on devouring every inch of Zi in as little time as possible. The kisses almost bruised, and the teeth at her breasts were almost too rough, but she was certain she was about to get very, very fucked and every part of her body was in favor of that. Damn Yiyi and her constant lectures about being above the base carnality that plagued gay society. Damn Yiyi for getting Zi's heart all caught up before announcing that the sex had to stop. Damn Yiyi for making her ashamed that she really liked lesbian sex, and ashamed for all the nights she'd rolled over looking for a cuddle and maybe a fond caress only to be pushed away and, in the morning, scolded for her nymphomania.

A middle of the night fuck—what was wrong with that between lovers? If she was some kind of nympho she'd have not lasted thirteen days without sex, let alone thirteen months. All that Yiyi had fucked was her mind, and right now, with a hot butch on top of her, she wanted the rest of her to get fucked so her mind could let Yiyi go.

"Tell me what you want." Hana was kissing her ribs, her stomach.

"I want lesbian sex," Zi said with a laugh. "Lots of it, and right now."

"How about we start with the basics?"

Zi yanked on a handful of Hana's hair, which made Hana grin. "Like what?"

"I lick your clit until you scream."

"Okay." Zi felt slightly dizzy. Yiyi, shut up, she thought,

annoyed she could hear the remnant of that judgmental, scolding voice.

Then, courtesy of the sinuous touch of Hana's tongue between her legs, Yiyi shut up for good.

Zi dug her nails into Hana's scalp, drawing a groan and a hard tap on her clit from Hana's tongue. She wanted to hold Hana's head still and rub her clit back and forth across Hana's mouth. It felt fabulous and incredibly real and good and lesbian and queer and female and downright raunchy in the very best way possible.

She arched into Hana's mouth, all of her alive and wanting to go as far as she could feeling just the physical delight of being with another woman. Her writhing brought her quickly to the edge of the narrow bed, her head hanging over the edge while Hana continued to feast on her. I'm gonna pull a muscle or something when I come, she thought distantly, but by then it was all academic—she was coming, and hard, one leg twined around Hana's shoulders and one hand still yanking on Hana's hair.

She was still gasping when Hana dragged her back on top of the bed. Zi made a show of trying to evade her.

"Vixen." Hana flattened Zi with her body. "Am I going to have to tie you up to keep you where I want you?"

"You wish. You travel with that kind of gear?"

Hana got a very sexy, very cocky grin and Zi wanted to swoon. In her experience there wasn't a butch walking who didn't fancy herself a top, and if Hana wanted to play, Zi wasn't going to resist. The first two weeks with what's-her-name had been full of all sorts of fun. Then the guilt had arrived and the toys had disappeared.

She was unceremoniously rolled over onto her tummy as Hana pushed her arms over her head and wrapped something silky and strong around her wrists. Once again, Hana used her body to flatten Zi into the bed.

"I'm guessing you can probably rip that open, vixen, but it's your own bikini you'll be ruining if you do." Hana began a slow grinding motion on Zi's ass. "You want to party like this?"

Being small, most people underestimated her in a number of ways. Zi hooked one foot behind Hana's knee, then quickly flexed up with her shoulders as she rolled to her hip. Hana practically bounced off the wall as Zi settled onto her back. Varsity wrestling had proven useful in more than just the ring.

"You're a tiger," Hana said appreciatively.

Zi planted her high heels into the low footboard and extended her arms over her head. "Now I'm ready to party."

Hana ran a lazy hand down Zi's torso, smoothing her skin and tweaking her nipples. A light massage of her neck followed, and when a finger wandered too near her mouth, Zi bit it, drawing a laugh from Hana. "Okay, you want to get fucked. I get the message. You don't have to mark me."

"Meow," Zi said, wrinkling her nose.

Hana got off the bed to fumble in the bottom dresser drawer. Drawing out a small black bag, she unzipped it and smiled at the contents. "Based on my examination, you're a medium girl." She held up a sleek, ungrooved toy. "Pink suits you."

"And who says butches don't care about fashion?"

Hana was stepping into a harness mainly comprised of thin straps that made her ass look fantastic. "I think you're going to look great with your hair in that just-fucked style."

"Talk, talk, talk."

"You are really asking for it, baby."

"Are you finally figuring that out?"

Hana unhooked Zi's sandals and tossed them aside. "I don't want a stiletto in my back, thank you."

Zi stretched her bound wrists over her head again, not laughing anymore, and neither was Hana. There wasn't anything but lust between them, and Zi's focus narrowed to the feeling of Hana fitting the head of her cock right where Zi wanted it so badly.

"Damn, you're hot," Hana whispered as she pushed forward,

opening Zi with a long, steady glide inside. "Feel that, baby? It's just the beginning. Want it so bad you going to stop giving me attitude?"

"If you want me to moan, give me something to moan about—oh yeah, that's better."

Hana moved faster as she wrapped her hands around Zi's upper arms. "There you go. You feel it now. You wanted it, you got it."

"I want it bad," Zi managed to say. "You're right, I do want it bad. Fuck me with that thing, and don't stop."

"That *thing* is my cock, baby, just your size, just what you want."

Zi arched up to nip at Hana's lower lip. "You're right, that's what I want. I want you to fuck me until you can't breathe."

Hana said something, but Zi heard it as gibberish. The words didn't matter when Hana's intent was so clear. Her arms kept Zi pinned to the bed while her hips pushed that wonderful cock into her hard, steady, fast, and nothing in Hana's face said she planned to stop. Ever.

When she came the first time, Hana didn't even pause. With a shared groan, it was on to the next climb, the next plateau, then the next surge to another climax, then another. At some point Zi knew she'd never been done like this before. She'd wanted some hot, no strings sex, and that was just exactly what she was getting.

"I'm not going to stop, baby," Hana kept saying, and then Zi realized she had been begging Hana not to stop. Thirteen months since she'd felt so alive. For a little while she'd almost believed she ought to be ashamed for enjoying everything her body could feel, but no more.

She wasn't sure who actually stopped first. Hana was panting, and their sweat-slicked bodies were burning hot from the friction. Zi was too high to feel it yet, but she knew tomorrow her thighs would be very, very sore. She was going to feel this for days. Oh yeah.

Somewhere she found a half smile. She hoped she sounded less sex-fogged than she felt. "Is that . . . Is that all you got?"

Never let the woman get out of bed still hungry. That was Hana's cardinal rule, and if Zi wasn't done, then Hana wasn't either. Her shoulders were screaming, and she felt a not-good trembling in her hips. She couldn't ask for a rest. What if Zi implied to Evie that she had wanted more and Hana had been too wiped out to oblige? Evie would never let her forget it. Bag the babe and make her happy. She couldn't admit she'd met a babe she couldn't satisfy.

"Nah, baby, that was just foreplay."

She poured more lube over Zi's red, luscious cunt. Damn, the lube practically steamed on contact. The pink cock looked tired.

"Let's go baby," Zi said. "Let's set a record."

"I have a surprise for you then." Hana eased the pink toy out of the O-ring and reached for the next largest, which wasn't just wider, but also heavier. Lube, lots of lube, and she got back on top of Zi, who gave an appreciative wiggle.

"Oh, did you get out the big gun for me?"

Hana gave a little push and really liked the way Zi's eyes glazed slightly. "Put your legs around my waist."

Okay, that turned out to be a mistake, because as they found a rhythm again, the weight of Zi's legs just added to the trembling muscles in her ass and back. She wished in the worst way she'd looked at the clock when they'd begun because she had no idea if it had been thirty minutes or an hour. All she knew was that Zi was coming for like the twentieth time. The bed was getting soaked and her arms were getting tired.

Hang on, she told herself. Hang on, maybe this will be the last. Fuck her harder, she wants it. Oh yeah, big bad butch that you are . . . give it to her.

Even as she told herself to go faster, she felt herself slowing.

She felt like she had the last time she'd tried a 10K run. The wall. She'd never hit the wall during sex before. Was she getting old? Damn, Hana, idiot! Fuck the girl. Don't stop.

She summoned what strength she had left for a half-dozen more plunges. Sappho, she pleaded, Sappho, please be the patron goddess of butches and make her come.

Zi gave a funny little cry and Hana didn't dare hope this meant something different. But maybe it did, because she was shaking all over and then went a very satisfying kind of limp.

Hana collapsed on top of her, breathing hard and praying for a rest. She could do more. She could try. Damn, she felt drained.

Zi said something into Hana's hair, but Hana didn't catch it.

"Huh, baby? Want some more? Plenty more where that came from."

"No," Zi said. "I just want you to get off of me for a minute so I can breathe."

"Oh." Hana flopped over onto her back in the small space between Zi and the wall. "Only for a minute, then I'm really going to fuck you silly."

Zi laughed and sat up. Her wrists were free and she held up her bikini top. "No damage."

"You're not going to put it on, are you?"

"Not yet. Five minutes."

"That all?"

"I'm meeting Felicia for dinner."

"Well, we have five minutes, then." Hana started to move, but Zi was suddenly on top of her, weight spread out.

"I think that'll be enough."

"You want to ride me for a while?" I could just lay here and play with her tits, Hana thought. She wouldn't have to know I'm totally wasted.

"No," Zi said. Then Hana felt Zi's hand sliding past the harness. "I want to fuck you."

"Oh—it's okay—oh hot damn."

"Damn hot is more like it. Baby, your pussy is on fire."

Zi was going inside her and it felt really, really good. Hana usually didn't go for this, preferring to hold on to the high in a kind of Tantric sort of thing, but Zi was doing something very right. Being held down like this wasn't at all a bad thing. She couldn't have pushed Zi off if she'd wanted to, but that was beside the point. Zi was a totally aggressive femme type who still liked a butch on top most of the time. She was a secure enough butch to let Zi think she was running things for a little while.

The itch inside, where Zi was fucking her, got stronger, and Hana found herself spreading her legs even more, even arching her hips to really feel every stroke. Smooth, steady, even, but deep. Bracing one foot, Hana arched to meet the thrusts.

"That's right, baby, you fucked me just about senseless, and it's time for you to get some back. You like that?"

The next push was particularly deep and Hana used the last of her energy to lift her hips again. "Yeah, I like it. Just the way I liked shoving my cock into you for an hour."

"Did you like me coming for you, over and over, getting you all wet and hot?"

"Oh, damn . . . damn, baby . . ." She had thought her muscles too weak to spasm the way they did, but Zi held on until their rocking had slowed.

"I'm glad you liked that," Zi said after a minute. She gave Hana a kiss, then stood up next to the bed to on put her swim-suit. "God, I'm starved. Free champagne at dinner, too. Do you have a T-shirt I could borrow? It's freezing out there."

"Top drawer, mine are on the left."

"White one okay?"

"Sure." Trying not to look numb, Hana watched Zi pull the shirt over her head. "Five minutes up?"

"Only needed three. See you around, babe. It's been a hell of a lot of fun."

With that, Zi was gone and Hana slumped back on the bed.

She nearly fell asleep, but her growling stomach made her feebly work the straps of the harness loose. She didn't know why Zi had run off so quickly. They could have talked for a bit.

Evie was waiting at the dining room entrance. "Fun time?"

"You bet. I left her a broken woman."

Evie arched one eyebrow. "She and her friend went in just a bit ago. She looked like she had fun. You look like you're going to fall over."

"No way." I can't let Evie know, Hana thought desperately. When she'd gotten up to put the harness and toys in the bathroom for cleaning while she took her shower, she'd realized the pink one they'd started with wasn't on the vanity where she'd set it after deciding to switch to the larger one. It had been moved to the bed. And left on the bed where she'd been laying while Zi had fucked her. No way could Evie know that she'd been fucked by her own toy. "In fact, check out the brunette over there. The short one with the short hair and the tight little body. Bet I can bag her by ten."

Evie rolled her eyes. "Don't you ever get enough?"

"No." Things might be a little off-kilter at the moment, but that fact remained constant. "I'll never get enough."

Chained Melody
Radclyffe

"Great set, Reo."

"Yeah, we rocked," I said, grinning at our drummer, Lila.

"You coming back to Sophie's to party?"

"Gotta pass tonight," I said, upending the bottle of Evian and draining it before securing my Stratocaster in its case.

"If you don't get what you need," Lila said, giving me a come-fuck-me look, "stop by later. We'll be up until whenever, and I promise to take good care of you."

"I dream of it."

She was teasing, so was I, and we both knew it. I handed my guitar off to our equipment tech, the only person who ever handled her except me, and climbed down from the stage. I managed to sidestep the four obviously drunk girls who were waiting for me in their crotch-high skirts and skimpy stretch tops that showed every pucker in their nipples. I deflected one's hand just before she grabbed my crotch, tossed another one a quick grin, and called to the third over my shoulder, "I'll catch you later, babe, promise," as I fled to the darkest section of the bar that ran along one entire side of the nightclub.

I don't drink while I'm performing, not anymore. As I slid onto the barstool, I reflected on how things had changed. I didn't need to get high any longer to settle my nerves or get in touch with the sound. Five years ago I wouldn't have believed how sharp and clean the beat could feel inside me when there was nothing to blunt the edges, the music slicing through me, drawing blood so effortlessly I didn't feel the pain through the pleasure. Five years ago there were a lot of things I wouldn't have believed.

"Hey, Reo. Vodka rocks?" Marcia asked.

"Yeah, and the sooner the better," I told the bartender, a petite blonde with a punk haircut and a mouth I couldn't look at without thinking of her lips locked around my clit. Big surprise, my clit twitched right on cue—I had so much adrenaline running through my system after a gig I usually needed to drink myself down or fuck off the energy, with or without help. Fortunately, being a band member in a roomful of dykes is like being a hunk of red meat tossed into the lion's cage at the zoo. Everyone wants a piece and is happy to fight for it, which is why I woke up a lot of mornings with bite marks on my neck and scratches down my back and no memory of who put them there. Once upon a time, anyhow.

While I waited for my drink, I checked out the few people still hanging at the bar—most had headed off to party or fuck or both—and tried not to stare at Marcia's ass. I met Marcia the first time Chain Maille, the band where I played lead guitar, worked a cruise. At the time, spending a week or so stuck on a ship had seemed like a crazy idea, especially not knowing what kind of audience we'd get. We're a rock band—lots of raw guitar, angsty lyrics and angry sex. When I thought of a cruise ship crowd, I pictured a bunch of married-with-children couples who had finally managed to squeak out enough time and money for a vacation, singing along to Anne Murray and slow-dancing—not exactly our kind of audience. Turned out, Marcia wasn't the only pleasant surprise on the first cruise. There were some of those couples, sure, and who would've guessed how wild and crazy married-with-children lesbians could be *without* the kids, but there were plenty of single, or not-so-single, hot and hungry dykes looking to get laid, too. After the first set we played, I'd walked backstage and Marcia had been waiting. She'd said, "Sexy guitar," and I'd said, "Sexy body," and yanked her in for a deep-throat kiss. Then she'd gone down on her knees and blown me right there.

That first trip, the club was packed for every one of our shows, and that blow job was the first of many memorable back-stage moments. Now, five years later, the cruise was a regular twice-a-year gig. Marcia was still tending bar, but she wasn't blowing me anymore. Only thing was, my clit—hard and aching and totally mindless—hadn't gotten the message, which was why I never stayed for more than one drink after a set.

"Here," Marcia said, handing me a clean white bar towel. "You're dripping on my bar."

"Sorry." I glanced in the mirror across from me and saw that my hair was plastered to my forehead and the back of my neck in thick, black strands. Rivulets of sweat streamed down under the neck of my black, fine-mesh metal T-shirt. I whipped a hand through my hair and mopped my face with the towel. When I checked the mirror again, Darla, the cruise director, was stand-ing so close behind me I could feel the stiff balls of her nipples rubbing my shoulders. My nipples tightened in response, the tips scraping the inside of the metal shirt and sending a shock to my clit with every breath. Like my clit needed any more encourage-ment. *Fuck.*

"Hi, Reo," she purred, sliding her arms around my middle and raking her fingernails up and down my bare belly. My shirt stopped just at the bottom of my ribs so the metal wouldn't scratch the back of the Strat when I played. Good for the guitar, bad for me at the moment. Fuck, I was wired.

"Hi, Darla. Careful, I'm sweating up a storm."

"You can drip on *me* anytime," Darla said, scraping a nail along the rim of my navel.

I grinned into her green eyes in the mirror and tried to hold still while my stomach muscles writhed beneath her fingers. This was the third night in a row she'd let me know she'd like to work me over. The tip of her moist pink tongue skimmed her pouty lower lip, and I imagined sucking on that tongue while I palmed her breasts and rolled her pebbly nipples between my fingers. She skimmed her fingers under my shirt and over the bottom of my breasts. I must have jerked, because she got a hungry look and leaned closer, her full, round tits flattening against my back, her breath hot on my neck.

"I bet you'd taste sweet." She rimmed my ear, and I felt it between my legs, felt the flat of her firm, hot tongue lapping up my come and whipping the underside of my clit. "Going to let me find out tonight?"

"Can't," I said, stopping the hand that was wandering toward my crotch. I grabbed the vodka that Marcia handed me and gulped gratefully, hoping the alcohol would do its job and take just enough edge off my hard-on so I didn't explode in my pants. That's not quite how I planned to end the evening. "But I appreciate the offer."

Darla sighed good-naturedly and looked around the rapidly emptying bar. "I don't see anyone waiting for you, and I've been sooo patient." She ground her crotch against my ass and whispered, "There's only so many times I can make myself come wishing you were fucking me before I just have to have some of the real thing."

"*My* real thing isn't available," I said, "but I'm sure you won't have any trouble finding some that is. Maybe like that tour guide

I noticed swallowing your tongue while I was playing?"

"You're *so* not fun," Darla complained, mercifully abandoning my stomach and moving her hands up to my shoulders. She dug her thumbs into the tight muscles there and rubbed her body against my back like a cat. "You're really not going to go to bed with me?"

I sighed at how good her hands felt and shook my head. "I'm really not."

Marcia wiped down the bar, watching us with an amused expression. "Got a hot date waiting, Reo?"

"As a matter of fact," I made a show of checking the time in the neon pink clock over the bar as I finished my drink, but I knew exactly what time it was. "I do."

I stood, kissed Darla on the cheek as she slid onto the stool in my place, and headed back to my cabin. My clit was still stiff, but now it ached not with frustration, but with sweet anticipation.

Road trips are hell, on both of us. Five years and it still hasn't gotten any easier leaving her for even a few days—let alone a few weeks. I never thought I needed order in my life until I met her. Until her, I thrived on playing guitar until three a.m., partying until six, fucking whoever I stumbled out with, and sleeping until two. Then getting up and starting all over again. My life had been an inferno of music and sex and I'd been burning fast.

Funny, I didn't meet her on the road. I met her in a business meeting right after the first cruise, five years ago tonight. The band had finally gotten a contract offer, and we needed an entertainment lawyer. Alana was the attorney. Ten years older, sophisticated, beautiful and smart. I sat in her office staring at her full, ripe mouth and her sleek legs crossed oh-so-casually—and showing just a hint of thigh. While trying to catch a peek at her cleavage beneath the expensive silk blouse, I didn't hear a thing she said about percentages, rights or agents. All I wanted to do was push her back into her posh leather chair, shove her Armani skirt up to her hips and fuck her until she screamed. I left the office with the rest of the band, walked around the block by myself after begging off a victory drink or ten, and went back.

"Did you forget something?" Alana asked when she answered the door herself.

I looked past her and saw that her secretary was gone and most of the lights were turned off. She was closing up.

"Yeah." My voice—the voice me and my three best friends were betting our futures on—came out hoarse and thick.

"What's that?" she asked, reaching back to release the clasp that held her midnight black hair coiled at the back of her neck. It dropped in thick waves around her shoulders as she reached out and flicked a short polished nail over my nipple. I grabbed her wrist and pushed through the door.

"I forgot to tell you how much I want to fuck you."

"If you do," she gasped, her teeth already on my neck as she dragged me to the floor, "you'll have to get another lawyer."

"You can give me a referral later," I groaned, sliding my hand up her skirt to cup her hot, silky sex. I shoved the flimsy barrier away and the next second I was in her.

And that's when everything changed. I fucked her, and she fucked me back, and when I came to my senses—sprawled in the middle of her thick Persian carpet, her mouth sucking my breast and her fingers still twitching inside my pulsing cunt—I knew I wouldn't be fucking anyone else, ever again.

She had a high-powered job she loved, and I needed the music like air. I needed to travel, and she couldn't always get away. I needed to rock, and when I did, I needed her.

I let myself into the cabin, poured myself another inch of vodka and sprawled on the sofa in the sitting area. Then, whispering a prayer to whatever genius figured out wireless ship-to-shore satellite transmission, I called Alana.

"Happy anniversary, baby," I said when she answered.

"Happy anniversary, lover," she replied in her rich, creamy voice. "Are you back in your cabin?"

"Uh huh. You in bed?"

"Mmm. I took a nice long bath and then slipped between our nice cool sheets. I've been lying here thinking about you up on stage, hot and sweaty and dripping with sex."

"The hot and sweaty part is right, at least," I laughed, absently rubbing my free hand over my belly.

"I've seen you perform, remember?" she whispered. "How hard is your clit right now?"

"Hard enough to cut glass."

"Mmm, I'll bet. Did you come after your set?"

"No," I said through gritted teeth, because just the sound of her voice had my cunt pounding like mad.

"How many girls were waiting to get you off?"

"Only a dozen or so."

She laughed, the warm, throaty sound she made when she was about to take my clit in her mouth. "And you waited, with a hard-on that bad?"

Her voice had gotten just a little bit breathy, her words a little slower. "Are you fingering your cunt?" I asked.

"Not yet," she sighed. "I'm just holding myself, squeezing my lips a little to make my clit nice and fat. Was Marcia there?"

"Uh huh." I loved to watch Alana masturbate, stroking and massaging her smooth cunt until it was red and swollen and shining with come.

"Did you think about her . . . sucking you off? About . . . her soft, wet . . . mouth around your clit?"

"Maybe." I gripped the crotch of my leathers and rubbed my thumb over the bulge of my clit. Alana had met Marcia on one of the cruises and had figured out instantly we had a history. She'd made me tell her all about it while I fucked her one night, coming all over my hand when I described me leaning against the wall and blowing my load in Marcia's mouth. "Maybe for just a second I thought about riding her face until my clit exploded."

"But you didn't, did you?"

"You know the answer," I said roughly, rubbing the leather over my brutally, relentlessly hard clit. "You're fingering yourself now, aren't you?"

"A little." She already sounded half-gone. "Oh lover, it feels good."

I leaned back and closed my eyes, listening to her breathing become more and more ragged, watching in my mind's eye as she swept the tip of her smooth, shiny nail back and forth underneath the hood of her clit, teasing it until her clit stood up stiff and purple. She liked me to lick the head of her clit while she played with it. She'd want to come soon. "Do you need me to suck you, baby?"

"No," she gasped. "I need you to . . . fuck me . . . until I . . . oh God . . . I want to come all over you."

"There's plenty of time for that."

"Oh," she whispered, a small, broken sound. "I really need to come, lover. Don't make me wait tonight."

I could faintly hear the slick sound of her hand circling in her cunt, faster and faster as her hips pumped higher. "Is your clit swollen?"

"Oh, God, yes."

"Is it wet?"

"Mmm, slippery. Slippery and hot." A shaky breath . . . a tremulous sigh. "Oh, and it's so hard now."

"Are you playing with it?"

"Uh huh. I have to. I want to come, lover, please. Can I?"

"Yes . . . but not just yet."

A whimper. "But I'm so close."

"Then you better stop touching."

"Ooo, no," she wailed. "I can't. I'm going to come so hard. So hard."

She was panting, every breath a little cry.

"But you're a good girl, aren't you? You won't come unless I let you, will you?"

"No, uh uh uh . . . oh God. Oh God, baby. Oh, I'm going to come. Oh. Oh!"

"Damn it, stop! Stop it right now."

"Oh, please," she screamed, before ending with a choked sob.

"That's it, baby, just breathe." I sat forward, my eyes tightly closed, and willed her to hold on. "That's it," I said soothingly. "Breathe until you slide away from the edge." I waited, listening to her pant. "Ready to try again?"

"Yes. Yes."

"Don't touch your clit yet."

"I'll be good. I won't come," she begged desperately. "Please. Please let me touch. I won't come."

"One finger."

"Where?" A tremulous plea.

"On top of your clit. Slide the hood back and forth with just your fingertip."

Incoherent sounds. I thought she might be crying.

"Feel good, baby?" I asked tenderly.

"Uh huh. Uh huh. I need to jerk off. I won't come. I won't come. I promise. Please. Let me jerk off just a little. Oh, God, my clit aches . . ."

I laughed. "You'll come. I know you."

"No. No. I promise. I won't. I won't. Oh . . . oh that's good."

"I didn't say you could squeeze it."

"Don't you want to hear me come? Can I . . . for you? Don't you . . . oh, I'm going to come so hard . . . come for you . . . you like that . . . when I . . . don't you . . ."

She was babbling. I knew she was losing it and I knew what she needed. "Rub it faster."

"Oh that's making me come," she blurted.

"Keep going. Do it harder."

"It's starting . . . big, so big . . . oh! Oh! God! Oh I'm . . ."

A high, faint whine rose into a screaming wail that went on forever. Then . . . nothing but rasping breaths and plaintive little cries. I sagged back, listening to her moan, and pictured her curled up on her side, stroking her swollen cunt with trembling fingers. She'd keep at it, plucking and rubbing her clit until she came again, but I couldn't wait for her encore. I yanked open my pants and grabbed my clit, strumming the stiff shaft between my fingers while her sharp, sweet pleasure notes shimmered through my cunt, an electric riff that fattened my clit and set me up to burn. My heels beat out a jittery rhythm on the carpet while I shot off in tense, heart-stopping silence.

Finally I expelled a long breath and groaned with relief.

"I came when you did that time," she sighed. "God that was nice."

"Yeah."

She laughed. "Are you falling asleep?"

"Yeah, maybe." Eyes still closed, my clit still in my hand, I kicked off my boots and rolled up on the couch. "I love fucking you."

"Are you playing tomorrow night?"

"Uh huh." My clit twitched and started to get hard again. Music and sex and her—each part of the other, forever linked.

"Then I'll see you after the last set, lover."

"I'll be rockin' for you, baby."

Gonna be another cruise to remember.

Invitation Only
Radclyffe

I know a lot of chicks get off on guitar players, but me, I like the drummers. Especially when they look like this one did— slinky and sexy in some kind of clingy white top that showed every pucker in her neat little nipples, and hip huggers that were so low they barely covered her pussy. The stretch of bare, tight belly in between was nice too. But mostly, it was her hands. Watching the way she fingered the wood and beat the rhythm out on the hot skins cradled between her thighs gave me some wood of my own, in addition to what I was already packing.

I'd skipped the talent show to catch this band, because I'd rather sit in a dark club like Medusa shooting tequila and watching girls wail and sweat and hump on stage than do most anything else. Except fuck one of them. Which was what I was hoping to do very soon.

"Hey," I said, squeezing my way through the maze of little, round tables that ringed the stage to where she was breaking down her gear. "Nice show."

"Thanks," she said brightly without looking at me.

I could tell she was used to fans trying to get a little piece of her attention, and probably other things, too. So I stepped up onto the stage and crowded her just a little. "What are you drinking?"

She looked at my face for the first time, and she didn't hurry as she took stock of the rest of me either. I knew I'd pass inspection in a tight white tee and black jeans. Nothing fancy, but then, I wasn't offering fancy. We were about the same height, except I was heavier and darker, which made me feel bigger than I was. She had spiky blond hair and a tiny little waist and those round, half-shell tits that made my mouth water. I hooked my thumbs over the waistband of my jeans and let the fingers of my left hand rest on the dick in my pants. It was eight inches long and two inches thick, and it made a big bulge. I don't usually load up quite so heavy for a night out, since after an hour or two with something that big crammed in my jeans my clit feels like someone's been kicking it with steel-toed boots. But every now and then, like tonight, I like to be reminded just how righteously sweet it feels to finally get off under that big tool. When her gaze wandered down to my crotch and she smiled, my clit hammered against the backside of the dick like it was trying to bang its way out of my pants.

"Vodka rocks," she said, still checking out my package. "And my name's Lila."

"AJ. Let me get you that drink."

"Sorry." Lila shook her head. "*Really* sorry. Maybe next time. I've got someplace to be."

I pulled her against me so my dick settled in the dip of her pussy. "How much time could it take to get wherever? We're on a ship."

"Maybe I'm in a big hurry." She rolled her hips a little and rubbed herself on the rod in my jeans, giving my clit a healthy workout at the same time. Her smile got a little loose and her eyes the tiniest bit hazy as she tilted her head back and shot me an "I'm *soo* horny" look. "Maybe I've got a hot date."

I snaked an arm around her waist and gripped her tight little ass. "You do. Right here."

"I'm going to a party," Lila whispered, riding me a little faster while she rubbed her tits back and forth against my chest. "It's invitation only."

"So invite me." I caught her earlobe between my teeth and sucked on it, wrapping my other arm around her and backing her against the wall. She whimpered a little, like I had hurt her, but I knew that wasn't it. She was just hot as hell, and I knew exactly what she wanted.

"Take me to the party so I can fuck you like you want to be fucked."

"My girlfriend will be there. We like to share." She was panting.

"I don't mind playmates." I licked her neck and shifted one hand to her breast. I thumbed her nipple and she dropped her head against the wall and moaned. "But the first time you come, it's going to be on my dick. Okay?"

She closed her eyes and rocked her head from side to side. She was into it, *too* into it, and I was afraid she might get herself off. I tweaked her nipple hard. "*Okay?*"

"Fuck," she said through clenched teeth, jerking upright. "Okay. Let's just go."

I stepped back, grabbed her hand and crushed it against my crotch. "I'm ready."

"Aren't you tough." Quicker than a grace note, Lila fisted my wood with her strong drummer's hand and beat me off so fast her wrist was a blur. I thought my legs were going to drop out from under me it felt so good. I've never had a girl jerk me to the finish line in my jeans, but she was ten seconds away from doing it. My clit was on the edge of blast off and flames ate away at my insides.

Determined to keep my cool, I twisted out of her grip. "And the first time *I* come, it's gonna be inside *you*. Now take me to the party."

"Keep up." She let go of my dick, clamped onto my wrist and dragged me off the stage and out into a service corridor. An elevator stood open and Lila jumped in, keyed a floor with her room card and climbed back onto me. She dug her fingers into my shoulders and wrapped one slender thigh around my hips so she could rub the length of her pussy over my dick. Then she buried her tongue in my mouth, and she felt so good everywhere, I almost let her steal the scene. But I knew if I let her, we'd both go off like Roman candles, and that wasn't what I had in mind. I grabbed her ass and swung her around so her back was to the wall and held her there with the weight of my hips and dick jammed between her thighs. Then I forced her head back with one hand under her chin, bit down on the side of her neck and palmed her breast at the same time. Lila shoved her fingers into my hair.

"Suck my neck," she gasped, bucking underneath me, both legs scissored around my thighs. "Fuck, I wish we could fuck right here."

"Slow down," I murmured, raising a small love bite just below her ear. "I promise I'll make you come so hard you'll cry." I licked her lips with my tongue and softly sucked on her lower lip. "But first I want to make out. So just forget about getting off for a while."

"God." Lila groaned and sucked on my tongue. "I'm so horny, I don't think I can wait very long."

I laughed. "You don't have anything to say about it."

The elevator slid smoothly to a stop and deposited us on the highest passenger deck where the big expensive suites were located. It figures that the band would have one. We were both a little wobbly-legged from being so turned on, and we half staggered through a door into the main part of a huge cabin. Through an open doorway just off to the right I could see two naked girls sprawled on a bed, but I only got a glimpse of a very nice pair of breasts before Lila dragged me into another room as big as my whole stateroom. A naked redhead with a lush, full body who I recognized as the bass player in the band perched on the edge of a sunken tub, deep-throating a blond butch I remembered from the audience. The butch was a shorthaired muscular stud with tattoos on both forearms. The redhead's legs were spread so a third chick, half submerged in the tub, could lick her pussy. I caught a glimpse of a flat pink tongue snaking over the redhead's cunt and mine clenched with envy.

"Hey, JoJo," Lila called, leading me by the hand to a sofa in one corner where we'd have a nice view of the threesome. "Having fun, babe?"

The redhead looked our way. "Hi, sweetheart. I was wondering where you were." She glanced down at the face moving between her thighs and half smiled, half grimaced the way you do when something feels so good it almost hurts. "I invited some friends."

"That's okay, baby." Lila dropped her hand to my crotch and stroked my dick. "Me too."

The blond gave me a quick look, then lifted one of JoJo's heavy, ripe breasts and dragged the nipple into her mouth. JoJo jerked and her lips formed a surprised circle as she said, "Ooo, Lila, I wish you could feel her mouth. So fucking hot."

"Lila's busy," I said and pulled Lila down next to me on the sofa.

"A little toppy, isn't she?" JoJo said, but she was smiling. Then the one between her legs did something to catch her attention and JoJo moaned, grabbed the woman's head and pushed her pussy up and down like she was air-humping her Strat. "Oh yeah. Suck me."

I leaned over Lila and stuck my tongue in her mouth, plundering her hot cavern while she clawed at my back. I could feel her twisting to watch what was going on by the tub, but I didn't care. She bit my tongue and I grabbed her breast, squeezing until she whimpered. I felt her hand in my crotch, pulling and jerking, and the next thing I knew, she had my dick out in her fist.

"Oh yeah, Lila," her girlfriend crowed. "Pump that big dick. Make her shoot that load."

Lila worked me like a jackhammer and I shoved her top up over her breasts so I could get at them. I grabbed one nipple with my fingers and sucked the other into my mouth. Lila tightened like a bowstring and I got the message. She'd come if I tortured her nipples much more. I eased off and put my mouth against her ear. "Remember where I said you were going to come. You want to sit on my dick now?"

"Oh yeah. Oh yeah. God yeah."

"Stand up, baby." I rolled off her and helped her to stand. Then I slowly skimmed her top over her head and kissed her breasts. When she sagged against me, I wrapped both arms around her waist and worked on her tits until she was whimpering again. Out of the corner of my eye I saw JoJo stretch out on a towel, turning her head to keep kissing the woman in the tub while the blond butch knelt between her thighs. A half-naked girl with long dark hair I hadn't seen before wandered in and mumbled something about lube. The butch tipped her chin toward a couple of tubes on the floor. I opened Lila's pants, and she helped me push them down.

"You going to be okay with this?" I asked, fisting the big dick that was sticking out of my jeans.

"More than okay." Lila kicked off her high heeled boots and left her jeans in a tangle on the floor. Before I knew what was happening, she'd dropped to her knees between my legs and I looked down just in time to see my dick disappear into her mouth.

"Oh fuck," I whispered. She wrapped her fingers around my

dick and pumped it while she sucked. Lightly, I cupped the back of her head because feeling her move up and down on me was a turn on. Then I heard someone say, "Bend your knees up for me, baby," and I looked over Lila's head to the trio by the tub. JoJo was on her back with her legs pulled up tight to her belly while the little blond butch drizzled lube all over her hand and forearm. The one in the tub was staring at JoJo's cunt, and from the look on her face and the way her shoulder was shaking, I could tell she was masturbating like crazy. The butch slid all four fingers inside JoJo, and then all I could see was her thumb rubbing a bright pink clit. I figured in another minute or two, she'd have her fist in JoJo's cunt.

JoJo lay with her eyes scrunched closed, mauling her own tits and groaning, "Do me honey fuck me deep. Do me honey fuck me deep. Do me honey . . ."

"Lila," I groaned, feeling myself getting close again, "you're missing the show. Get up here, baby."

Lila gave me a couple more good tugs and my ass clenched, and I thought for sure I was going to lose it, but she eased up just in time. My belly felt like a board someone had been pounding with a hammer. "Here," I said, digging a safe out of the front pocket of my jeans. "Put this on, and for Christ's sake, climb up on my dick."

JoJo had the blonde's whole fist in her cunt and was whining and pulling on her nipples, the butch was grunting, and someone in the other room screamed she was coming. Lila ripped the foil open with her teeth, snugged the condom on my dick, and rolled it down with two fingers like a pro. She started to sit down facing me, but I shook my head and guided her around the other way. "Let's watch your girlfriend get fucked."

I steadied my dick in one hand and Lila braced herself on my thighs and eased down onto it. It was big, and she was small, but she swallowed it in one long, slow glide, moaning as the head seated deep inside her. I reached both hands around her and cupped her breasts. She dropped her head against my shoulder and I rested my chin in the curve of her neck so I could see the floor show.

"Ride me, baby," I murmured, holding still so she could move the way she needed to. I fingered her nipples and tilted my hips up so the dick had the right angle to hit her clit. "Is your clit hard, honey?"

"Uh huh," she gasped, nodding vigorously. She made a little mewling noise, and I knew she was playing with it.

"Your girlfriend's gonna spill it any second," I said, pumping my hips just a little. The stud's fist moved inside JoJo's belly, an undulating wave that made her toss her head and cry. As the butch slowly rotated her arm, JoJo shoved both hands down to her pussy and rubbed at her clit. JoJo bucked and strained, and sweat dripped from the butch's face onto her belly.

"There goes the babe in the tub," I said as the one masturbating screwed up her face and let loose with a long, wavering cry. The sound must have flipped Lila's switch because she lost her rhythm and her hips started jumping around.

"Oh I want to come, I want to come," Lila said anxiously, as if I wasn't going to let her.

"I know, baby, I know," I said, sliding my hands under her butt. I lifted her to give myself a little room and started to fuck her for real. Her arm was vibrating the way it did when she was beating her drums, and I knew she was working herself off. She got her beat back and circled her hips in my lap, grinding the dick into my clit. It hurt so fucking good I almost cried.

"Oooo, God!" JoJo yelled, jerking her shoulders off the floor and staring wide-eyed at the fist buried in her belly. "Oh my God I'm coming so hard." She screamed and bucked and thrashed, and Lila started shaking and making gasping sounds

I heaved her all the way to the end of my dick, then wrapped my arms around her middle and pulled her back down while I jammed myself in to the hilt. She gushed like a fire hydrant with me buried high inside of her, jerking on the dick so hard I was afraid she'd throw herself off.

"JoJo," she screamed. "Baby, it's so fucking good!"

Then she collapsed like a rag doll in my arms. I needed to come so bad I couldn't breathe, but I couldn't get a hand between us to get at my clit and I couldn't move enough to jerk myself off on the cock. Tears leaked out of my eyes.

"Lila, baby. Lila," I gasped. "Baby, I gotta jerk off. I'm dying, baby. Can you slide up—"

And just like that she came to life, raised her ass, and my dick slipped out. Then she was on the floor between my legs, popping my fly and dragging my jeans and harness down my thighs.

"In my mouth," she said urgently, and licked my clit. "Let it go in my mouth."

I pushed my clit up at her and she latched on to it, sucking like it was a Tootsie Pop. And that's what it did. *Pop.* Ten seconds of her lips sliding up and down while she sucked, and I went from rock to rocket in a heartbeat. My clit blew into a million pieces and I levitated off the sofa like I'd been electrocuted. When I came back down, my insides still twisting, she kept right on licking.

"Oh man, Lila," I gasped. "I'm done, baby. I'm done."

She made some kind of noise like *Mmm mmm good* and circled a fingertip around the rim of my ass and my clit shot up hard as concrete again. Out of the corner of my eye I saw JoJo half-crawl toward us, her eyes so big she looked like she was stoned, but I knew it was just the sex. She crouched behind Lila.

"Did she get you ready for me, sweetheart?" JoJo murmured, licking the side of Lila's neck where I'd left the love bite.

Lila nodded her head vigorously with my clit still clamped between her lips.

"Fuck," I yelled and grabbed her head to hold her still. "Jesus Christ, take it easy—"

JoJo shoved her hand between Lila's legs from behind and

Lila pushed one finger deep into my ass and I cannoned right up to the edge again. My legs jerked out straight and Lila started whimpering and sucking harder. I locked eyes with JoJo. Hers were glazed and triumphant.

"Doesn't she give the best head?" JoJo purred.

I opened my mouth, but all that came out were groans and broken bits of words because I was coming in Lila's mouth, coming from my toes to the top of my head, coming so hard I felt like my skin was going to turn inside out. JoJo pumped away in Lila's pussy the whole time I was creaming all over her girl-friend's face, and then, as if she knew exactly when my orgasm quit, she pulled Lila off me. Lila fell back into JoJo's arms and they locked lips instantly. JoJo reached around Lila's middle, stuck her hand between her legs and jerked her off while they kissed. Lila shuddered and cried in JoJo's arms.

The girl from the tub and the butch were reverse spooning on the same towel where the butch had fisted JoJo, noisily licking each other off. I lightly fondled my clit, my dick drooping between my legs, while Lila came a couple more times. By then, my clit was showing wood again. With any luck, the invitation was still open, and I could get the drummer and her girl to play me another set or two.

Next-Door Neighbors
Karin Kallmaker

"Have fun, Mom." Tammi waved cheerfully as they parted near the Piazza Casanova, her beach bag slung casually over one shoulder.

Alice resisted issuing warnings about sunburn even though she knew the skimpy bikini top wouldn't be on for long either. Tammi was the free spirit her mother never had been. As always, Alice consoled herself with the knowledge that had she figured out earlier in life what she knew now, there would likely be no Tammi to worry over skin cancer.

She took a very deep breath, counted to ten, then assumed an air of confidence and experience before she walked through the open door to the Piazza.

As she followed the long curving marble path that led toward the clusters around the gleaming brass bar, she was first struck by how many women there were close to her own age. As a fifty-plus, shorts and tank top kind of woman, she would fit in okay.

There were younger, swimsuit-clad and thinner girls to be sure, but she spotted enough silver-haired, crow's-feet-and-laugh-line women in the room for her comfort level. Perhaps, like her, they were hoping to meet up with someone interested in the same excursions throughout the week. Yes, a friend for the ports of call, that was why she was here. And she'd just keep telling herself that in the hopes that her libido started believing it.

She'd gone back to the cabin for a light sweater, ostensibly because the ship kept the common spaces frigid. The embarrassing truth was that her nipples got hard every time she went to one of the public gatherings. It had to be chemicals floating in the air or something. Her nipples weren't the only things staying hard, either. Feeling like an adolescent was a new—and mostly unwelcome—sensation. Just here for companionship, she repeated. Just here to . . . She averted her gaze from a really attractive thirty-something with muscles like iron. Since when had she been attracted to muscles? Was it the muscles or the woman who happened to have muscles? Was it any woman?

Her head said *of course not*. Other parts of her said *of course*.

Fleeting eye contact with a grinning shorts- and polo-shirted gal about her age left her with high color. She consciously shifted her tank top a bit lower and held her head a bit higher. She wanted everyone to assume she was experienced at lesbian mingling.

After all, she was an expert in lesbian erotica. If it had been put into book form, she had read it. There wasn't a position, pose, power play, accessory or scene she hadn't read about. Even though most of the women in the lounge looked cuddly as teddy bears, they were all no doubt conversant in brands of lubricant, sizes of O-rings and uses of ordinary household items for bondage.

She'd also read just about anything there was to find on the Internet. The stories written by men to titillate themselves she could easily spot. She was far more interested in stories written by women, as they almost always told their tale from the inside out, from the inside of the woman's heart and mind to the outside of her body where the physical and the emotional unified.

All of which sounded quite intellectual, but there was nothing intellectual about the sensations between her legs. It was embarrassing, and she was glad no one could tell.

Drifting slowly toward several clusters in the hope of picking up a phrase or making eye contact that would allow her to join the conversation—just like at PTA meetings, except these were all lesbians very likely looking for a different kind of play date—Alice found herself again glancing at the woman in the polo shirt. From her short gray hair to her sensible sandals, she was comfortably familiar, except now Alice was considering that the sense of recognition wasn't just the overall similar attire she shared with other women in the room.

She *was* familiar. Something about her eyes and the smile. Alice could picture her with much darker hair and a coffee mug in one hand, laughing about something. A noisy crash of glassware at the bar had everyone else turning their heads to investigate, but Alice's gaze stayed glued to the other woman's face. She'd seen her turn her head sharply like that, more than once . . .

Candace. It was her next-door neighbor Candace, from what, twenty-five years ago? Candace with the twins who were always knocking something over. With the laugh, and the walk, and it had been such a shame when her husband had been transferred and they'd moved away. For nearly two years they'd traded babysitting and shared a lot of morning cups of coffee at the park across the street.

Candace—it had to be—looked back in her direction, and Alice started to blush. It was a sign of her lesbian adolescence that she had the irrational but unavoidable thought: *If Candace sees me here she'll know I'm gay.*

❧

Candace ground to a halt, mid-sentence, as she realized the redhead on the other side of the room was staring—and blushing. She tried to pick up her train of thought on the evaluative merits of gear for hiking, snorkeling and other adventures, but the woman's total fixation on her was too distracting.

"Excuse me," she said to the others in the little cluster. They were all newly met, and she'd been enjoying the conversation, but the woman looked like she might explode. Ginny would have been amused, and claimed that Candace had that effect on most women, but it wasn't true. That would have just been Ginny being Ginny, being kind.

The woman's mouth dropped open as Candace approached and there was something very endearing about her lack of composure. Even obviously embarrassed, there was humor dancing in her eyes—green eyes—and the crimson hue that spread down her chest served to highlight the generous curves framed by the scalloped edge of her royal blue tank top. She wore sleek, form-fitting shorts and skimpy leather sandals that wrapped up her ankle and calf with Roman elegance. Casual, but turned out, a look that Candace had always admired and never achieved herself. Ginny—now Ginny had always looked that good.

Ginny had never minded that Candace liked to watch the ladies. She'd enjoyed hearing what Candace admired and enjoyed in the appearance of other women. "As long as it's me you're looking at when we turn out the lights at night, you look all you want," she'd always said.

Swallowing down the still vivid memory of the last night they'd turned out the lights together, she came within a polite distance of the crimson-flushed woman. Even as she said, "Are you okay?" she felt a thrill of recognition.

"Yes. I'm sorry. I—Candace? Candace McNamara?"

"Yeah, how do you . . . ?" Candace studied the woman even more closely, subtracted some laugh lines and put more red in the hair before she hazarded, "Alice? Hayes?"

Alice nodded fervently. "Amazing!"

"Now *that* is a small world. What have you been doing with yourself all these years? How's Bill? How's . . . Tamera?"

"She prefers Tammi now." Alice's high color began to fade. "How are your twins?"

Stupid question about Alice's husband, Candace told herself. She's *here*, you dummy—hubby must be out of the picture. Berating her lack of brain, Candace answered, "They're fine, I presume. I haven't heard from them much since they left for college. That was nine—ten years ago, so I've given up thinking they'll forgive me for the sin of divorcing their father before they went into middle school."

"That must hurt," Alice said. "I don't know what I'd do without Tammi. She was great. I mean—Bill passed away a few years ago. And since Tammi was already out, she was cool when I came out to her."

"Oh, that's wonderful. Tammi, I mean, not Bill." Now she was going to blush. "Hey—would you like a drink? I'm told they're not often free, and they've still got a tray of those blended daiquiris."

They walked together to the bar and each got one of the small frozen drinks. Alice also picked up a skewer of melon, lifted an eyebrow at Candace, and when Candace nodded, handed it to her, before picking up a second one for herself.

The simplicity of the gesture reminded Candace vividly of the mornings they'd shared coffee and watched their kids gambol about on the grass. That easy generosity and elegant economy with actions had been a very attractive quality. But at the time Candace hadn't had a clue that maybe she found her next-door neighbor so fascinating for more than just her ease as a loving parent, a seemingly content housewife and a sympathetic friend. It had been a pity when their sporadic correspondence had petered out altogether.

They continued along the bar, without speaking, toward an

out-of-the-way table that looked out on the pool deck. Once they were settled Candace said, "I'm sorry to hear about Bill."

Alice lifted one shoulder, but it was a shrug. "He was quite ill. He had congenital heart disease and it got very bad when Tammi was in high school. She, thankfully, appears to have inherited my heart. He couldn't work but did what he could to get Tammi places she needed to be. I went back to accounting."

"That's right—you were an auditor before you had Tammi." Candace watched Alice take an appreciative sip of the cold drink, studying the way she pressed her lips together, then licked them to catch all the ice.

"I'm in private accounting now. It pays well and I get plenty of vacation time. A good company."

"So you decided on a lesbian cruise?" Candace grinned broadly. "This is my first one."

"Mine too. Tammi has been before, and convinced me to come along on this one. Look." Alice pointed at the long line of bodies surrounding the pool below them. "She's the strawberry redhead in the cluster of exhibitionists. She has not one ounce of shy. Yesterday at the scavenger hunt when they asked for a pink triangle, my Tammi dropped her shorts."

Laughing, Candace admired the vista on the lido, taking note of the topless women gathered halfway down the near side of the pool. She'd wondered if the cluster was bravado or affinity. It didn't matter. It looked dandy. "The redhead—oh. Well. Oh my."

"She *is* a looker. And there's a brain to go with it."

"Like mother, like daughter." The words were said before Candace thought better of them, and what the hell, why not? Alice was attractive and Tammi looked much the way Alice had all those years ago. Well, she would look like her mother had back then if she was wearing a chic twinset and capri slacks. As it was, Candace found herself thinking that Alice of twenty-five years ago had darned well been shaped just like her daughter was now. Alice of today was still damned sexy.

Alice blushed the way only a redhead could, and Candace tried not to delight in it. It wasn't nice to make the poor woman blush just because it was easy . . . oh hell, it was fun. She wondered how long Alice had suspected her longing for women, and how hard it had been to be a caregiver instead of a partner with Bill. Still, Tammi had turned out okay, it seemed. Unlike life with her own ex, their home must have been peaceful and loving enough.

After another sip of her drink, Alice said, "So you divorced?"

"Yes, it was impossible to stay. Not just because I'd figured out I was gay, but Larry's alcoholism was destroying the kids and our finances. I scraped together some capital and started my own transcription business."

"You got custody?"

"Yes, and that lasted through high school. But the day after their eighteenth birthday, I introduced them to Ginny, the woman I'd been seeing for a while, and after that . . ." She shrugged. "They chose to believe their father's version of events, that I'd driven him to drink and had stolen the kids and the money out from under him to finance my deviant lifestyle."

Alice's expression was laden with sympathy. "How awful. It must have been terrible for you."

With someone else Candace might have made light of it, but already she could remember the worries they had shared as young mothers. "It was. Thank goodness for Ginny, though. She helped fill the void. I mean—I expected them to go away to college of course. But not with such bitterness. Ginny was very good for me."

"Are you still together?" Alice abruptly put down the skewer of melon she'd been nibbling. "I'm sorry, that's a silly question. You're here. Mingling with the singles."

"She died. Two years ago, nearly." Seeing that Alice had that oh-what-to-say look, Candace went on, "We booked this cruise, and a couple of days later during her annual check-up the doctor found a lump on her ovary. It was the bad kind and moved really fast. Just a few months."

"Oh my." Alice dabbed the gleaming corner of one eye, and Candace remembered all at once how easily Alice showed her emotions. "Candace, I'm so sorry."

"I was going to cash in the ticket and then I thought I'd honor her by coming anyway. And as the last year went by, I realized she'd really hate it if I put on widow's weeds and stopped living." She wasn't going to admit that she thought of Ginny as an angel on her shoulder these days, a second set of eyes and a kind voice to get her through some bleak times.

"I can't imagine you wasting away. I used to marvel at your energy. You had that long list of things you wanted to do. You were always adding to it."

"Italy and Greece—I get to cross both of those off. Though I didn't see nearly enough of Italy for my liking. I want to go back."

"Me too. Venice was beautiful. I want to see Rome and get out into the countryside. Have real Italian food."

This time Candace's brain engaged before she suggested they do that together sometime, even though her Ginny angel was loudly cheering her on. It had been twenty-five years, but why did it feel as if it had only been twenty-five weeks? Or twenty-five days? The past had been painful for them both, but abruptly Candace no longer felt weighed down by it. The present was quite diverting.

"Outside the restaurant at six fifteen, then." Alice waved a good-bye to Candace and headed back to her cabin. Where had the last two hours gone? She was supposed to meet Tammi by the pool to watch the pool games, but instead she and Candace had kept an eye on them from their table in the lounge. Now she had to tell Tammi she was ditching her for dinner. Not that Tammi would mind. She'd been in deep conversation with a brunette most of the afternoon. She suspected she might not see her daughter until morning.

"Sure, Mom, whatever," was the reply she got as she explained the situation. Tammi turned from the mirror where she was brushing out her long hair. "I don't remember her, though."

"You were only three when they moved, so of course you don't." Relieved that Tammi was taking their change of plans in stride, she was half out of her clothes in anticipation of a shower when Tammi suddenly laughed.

"Hey, wait a minute—you have a date! Way to go, Mom!"

"Stop that—"

"Oh no, you don't." She turned from the mirror grinning ear-to-ear. "It's *my* turn. Alice and Candy, sittin' in a tree, K-I-S-S—"

"Don't be childish." Alice put her hands over her ears. Considering the serviceable Tevas and many-pocketed shorts Candace had been wearing, she added, "And I don't think she'd like being called Candy. It was always Candace, way back when."

"Now, Mom, I don't want you to get serious about the first girl you meet. You should take your time." Tammi was obviously relishing her role. "Do you have protection? You know that you don't have to say yes to be popular, right?"

She lobbed a handful of water from the shower toward Tammi, managing to spatter her midriff. "Zip it, kid!"

Alone in the shower she relaxed into the steam with a groan that she hoped Tammi didn't hear. Adolescent didn't even begin to describe her physical response to Candace. The longer they'd talked, the more she couldn't tear her gaze away from Candace's strong, flexible hands. She couldn't remember where she'd read that if men had to wear pants then lesbians should wear mittens, but for goodness sake, what was she supposed to do? Okay, so she was vibrating like a bowstring and just about anybody could play her at this point, but two hours with Candace had brought back all the ease of their conversations. Had their closeness been based on something neither of them had been able to interpret?

Her skin felt unreal, as if there were a layer of electricity on every inch. But you don't do this, Alice, she told herself. You don't just get into bed with someone you just met. And you did just meet her, really, for the first time. What about all the speeches you made to Tammi about respecting herself and the mind being mightier than the sex drive? Right, that's a laugh.

She toweled her hair and then wiped the mirror to regard her anxious face. You don't know that Candace even wants to, she pronounced firmly, hoping her libido was listening.

Except she did know. Candace was obviously a more practiced woman, and she'd been mingling with the singles for a reason. Alice knew when she was being appraised, especially after those long stints at the hospital when other men assumed she might have unmet needs. She knew how to deliver a firm brush-off to the kind of look Candace had given her, but the thought had not crossed her mind. She hoped her flirtatious manner, though rusty, conveyed confidence to match Candace's.

Tammi made various *ooo la la* noises when Alice got out the little black dress she'd acquired just for the cruise. A wonder of synthetic science, it didn't look wrinkled and could be rinsed out with shampoo to be worn over and over. With the sheer emerald green wrap over her shoulders, it also managed to look like she'd fussed, just a little.

"I thought that dress was for the formal night."

Alice patted a last hint of blush on her cheeks, then surveyed her lipstick for creases. "I just don't want to look dowdy, that's all."

"As if." Tammi put her hands on her hips and regarded her in the mirror. "If she's not panting to have you, she doesn't have eyes."

"Thank you, dear." Alice wondered, with parents who had been practically celibate for a decade, how Tammi had become so openly sex positive. Rebellion?

"I think that dress looks terrific on you."

On her way out the door, she looked over her shoulder to say, "Don't wait up."

She was halfway to the stairs when Tammi called from behind her, "In fact, I think that dress would look terrific on the floor of her cabin, too."

So, Ginny Angel, what do you think? Candace studied her reflection in the highly polished brass of the Degli Argentieri Restaurant portico. No matter what Alice wore it would look elegant, and you didn't take a woman like that into dinner not dressed to match. It was too early in the week for her tux, but the cabin steward had gotten her tan slacks pressed in a matter of minutes and she could only hope that the white button-up, string bolo, and black suede over shirt—sleeves not rolled up— would pass muster.

It was a damned good thing she saw Alice before Alice saw her. Oh Ginny Angel, she thought, that is one gorgeous woman, and I am the luckiest gal on this ship to get to look at her all night. Then Alice saw her and smiled and Candace felt like a million bucks. She hadn't felt quite like that since Ginny had slipped away. Don't feel guilty, she told herself. Ginny wouldn't want you to feel guilty for thinking Alice is . . . special.

"You look fantastic," Candace said sincerely. Without thinking better of it, she gave Alice a hearty peck on the cheek.

A little flushed, Alice said, "You are looking very spiffy yourself."

Was spiffy good? Or was it code for *nice try but no cigar*? Candace had to trust the look in Alice's eyes, then, which said spiffy meant maybe even better than good. She proffered her arm and they went into the dining room together.

She'd already spoken to the maitre d' and they were escorted to the second level, which was quieter and less brightly lit than the larger tables of more raucous groups on the main floor. Once seated, she accepted the daily menu and had to hide a smile. *Roma means Romance* was emblazoned across the top, and offerings included oysters on the half shell, chilled champagne soup, antipasto for two and a choice between lamb in rosemary or lobster Corfu.

They discussed the selections, told the waiter what they wanted and Candace was pleased to ask the wine steward to open the bottle of wine her travel agent had provided as a thank you for booking the cruise. They were just confronting the half dozen oysters when he returned and displayed the bottle for Candace's approval. Just like that, with smooth efficiency, they had oysters, wine and only each other.

"The trick," Alice said after she tossed back her first oyster, "is not to chew. Just swallow."

"This isn't my best thing."

But the oyster went down, and stayed down, and a glass of wine and bowl of champagne soup later, Candace found herself smiling nonstop at Alice, who was smiling back.

"I've read that anthology," Alice was saying. "It was one of Tammi's hand-me-downs. She does like the more outré stories."

"I enjoyed it," Candace admitted.

"I have to admit," Alice said after she sipped her wine, "that I didn't initially think you were a *Raw Divas and Ready Dykes* kind of reader."

"Ginny liked—sorry."

"Don't be. It's okay, she's still part of your life." Alice reached across the table to briefly cover Candace's hand. "I truly understand."

"Of course you do. Anyway, Ginny liked adventurous . . . reading." No need to tell Alice that reading about power scenes and accessory-laden sex was the closest she and Ginny had gotten to it. They'd certainly found it inspiring.

Alice flushed beautifully. "So do I."

They shared a long look over the top of their wineglasses, and Candace wondered why it felt as if they'd settled something. She certainly found Alice attractive, and the thought of skin-to-skin contact after such a long hiatus was quite appealing. Alice seemed to be agreeable, but on the other hand, well . . . on the other hand . . .

She could hear her Ginny Angel telling her not to get cold feet with such a warm and lovely woman, one who was adventurous and fun-loving. She wasn't a Ginny, Candace thought with a flash of insight. But she was an Alice, an interesting, intelligent Alice.

Their evening couldn't have been more romantic, really. By the time they finished the strawberries and cream and strolled the deck under the bowl of star-studded sky, they were holding hands. The talent show by volunteer passengers had them laughing together, and it was Candace's decided opinion that shared laughter was nearly the same thing as sex, except you could do it in public all you wanted.

"Another turn around the deck?"

"I'd love to." Alice linked her arm with Candace's as they slowly walked, agreeing again that they didn't know the constellations as well as they'd like. The warmth of Alice's skin had Candace revising her opinion about laughter and sex. Sex was better.

In a small nook off the quiet pool deck, she confessed that she didn't want their evening to end and Alice, whose dress in the warm wind left little to Candace's imagination, agreed.

"Perhaps a nightcap?" She indicated the sign to the Tivoli bar and Candace opened the access door for her. The first thing that hit them was the noise and she saw the same dismay on Alice's face.

"We could bring the drinks back outside," Candace hollered over the din. But the line at the bar was long, and she decided to accept that she only had one choice to offer. She led Alice back outside and said, "I have brandy in my cabin, if that appeals."

Alice's lips parted, then she said very quietly, "It appeals."

"We can sit on the veranda and sip, if you'd like." Candace smiled reassuringly at Alice. There would be time to get mellow and then see what happened.

Alice looked quite calm. She'd certainly been perfectly comfortable talking about erotica over dinner, and had used words like *orgasm* and *cock play* with the same casualness she'd once used to discuss diapers and baby bowel movements. She'd talked about sex so casually that Candace wondered what it would take to create a memorable encounter for Alice. She didn't have any toys or bags of tricks. Nothing up her sleeve or down her pants.

They left the wide, carpeted stairwell and encountered two women, one with a hand out of sight between the other's legs, making out against the wall next to one of the suite doors. They didn't even take notice of the two of them passing by.

The suite door was open, too, and a glance inside reminded Candace that this was the suite the rock band was sharing. The heavy metal musicians—and some friends, it seemed—were entertaining, and various stages of nudity had already been reached. More than nudity. Body parts were already in contact.

She took Alice's arm and finished escorting her to her own suite, two doors down. Once the door was unlocked she said, "Excuse me, I'll be right back. Make yourself at home," and left a surprised Alice on the other side of the door.

Quickly, trying not to lose her nerve, she dashed down the hallway and walked through the open suite door. The twosome sprawled on the couch had progressed to loud groans, and interrupting them was more than Candace could contemplate. She was about to back out of the suite when she heard voices coming from the bedroom.

On tiptoe she got close enough to peek in. A threesome was getting quite involved in the bathroom beyond, but closer was a couple not yet in the throes and a dark-haired girl perhaps looking for someplace to get involved herself.

Catching the dark-haired girl's eye, she said something she never in a million years thought she ever would. "Can I borrow some lube?"

The girl, looking more than a little out of it, wandered over to the threesome. Gestures ensued, then she made her way a bit unsteadily to a table where little bottles were scattered. Candace tried to keep her gaze at the level of the girl's eyes, but her breasts were hard to ignore. She took one little bottle gratefully. "Thanks."

"Yeah, whatever. Enjoy."

Now she had a bottle of something called Elbow Grease. She was in the hallway before Ginny Angel pointed out that Elbow Grease must be useful stuff because, yes, one woman's hand had been easily sliding inside the other woman and maybe they should go back and watch—sometimes, Ginny Angel was a Ginny Devil.

She took a moment to catch her breath at her cabin door, hoping she didn't look like she'd just walked in and out of a sex-soaked room. It was for the best, she thought, because Alice was comfortable with that kind of action and her own pulse was now quite elevated.

When she let herself back into her suite, Alice was already on the veranda. That beautiful green wrap—the precise shade of her eyes—draped around her shoulders but looked as if it might slip off at any moment. One sexy sandal dangled from the tips of her toes, also threatening to leave Alice more naked. Candace hurried into the bedroom to stash the little bottle under the mattress and then made herself useful at the bar, pouring two brandies into the ship's lovely stemware. She told herself that regardless of all the fun she'd just witnessed among the younger generation, she would still be able to show Alice a good time without all the goodies. She'd proven time and again with Ginny that passion, and a little bit of lube, made many good things possible.

And if Alice wanted something more, well, maybe she could borrow other accoutrements as well.

Alice turned as she heard Candace join her on the veranda. She hoped the low light hid the flush that she could feel burning her chest and neck. She knew perfectly well why she was flushed and sweating at the small of her back, why the hair on her neck felt like electrical wires. In the moonlight Candace looked like Cary Grant, except she was a woman, most definitely a woman, unquestionably, desirably, wonderfully a woman.

"What was that all about?"

"Something I needed to do. Tell you later." Candace looked a little flushed too as she took off the suede overshirt and relaxed into the chaise lounge next to Alice's deck chair. "There's quite a party going on just down the hall."

"So I noticed." Alice sipped the brandy, not sure if she would care for it, but found the heat on her lips and tongue, followed by a sweet smoky flavor, quite pleasing. Let's face it, she told herself, anything would please you right now.

Wrong, an inner voice corrected. Right now, a man isn't going to please you. You don't want Cary Grant, you want Carrie Grant. You want Candace.

What if she's stone? What if she only tops or only bottoms or only likes things one way, and as soon as you get going you realize that is exactly the one way you don't like it? What if . . . How was she supposed to explain she'd had a C-section because her pelvis was too narrow, and if Candace was hoping to get out some big toys it just wasn't going to work?

Candace was saying something about the moon, and Alice

tried to settle her fears and worries and let her body take over. Her head might not know what to do, but her body seemed quite focused on what it liked. She sipped the brandy again as they chatted, and after a few minutes her pulse steadied to a more manageable level.

"I'd love to see Lesbos with you," Candace said. "We can maybe swap our departure times around to get into the same group."

"I'd like that." She took one more sip, decided she liked brandy very much, then put the glass down on the deck. She was trembling. She didn't know what part of her was in control as she transferred herself from her chair to perch on Candace's chaise. The veranda was private in the moonlight, and it seemed quite natural to lean down to find Candace's mouth.

Just before their lips touched she felt Candace's hand slipping around her waist. The kiss was completely mutual, soft and sweet.

"I was wondering what it would be like when I kissed you," Candace whispered. Her hand tightened its grip and she pulled Alice to her more firmly.

For a few minutes, at least, Alice was lost in the wonderful pleasure of another woman's mouth. There was none of the harsh possessiveness or raging haste she had been used to while dating and in the early years of her marriage, and she realized she could kiss a woman for hours. This alone was the best sex she'd ever had.

But after a few minutes of whispered reassurances and shifting positions until she was stretched out on top of Candace, she was aware that Candace's tongue was dancing with hers more and more deliberately, with teases and flicks. All at once Alice felt her nerves burst into flames at the thought of Candace using that sensuous, sensitive tongue to tease her nipples or flick at her clit. She didn't know if Candace could tell what Alice was now considering, but Candace's body shuddered under her and their pelvises began to move in an unmistakable rhythm.

It was unreal, the way she felt, the waves of tingles along her ribs, up her back, across the soles of her feet. She was the one who unzipped her dress, until Candace finished the job, and she was the one who pulled the dress over her head as she straddled Candace's lap.

"Alice," Candace whispered, "you're a beautiful woman."

The dress fell from her fingertips as Candace slipped the bra straps off her shoulders. "Thank you."

"It's not flattery. God, woman, you're gorgeous." Candace massaged her shoulders lightly.

"You're certainly making me feel beautiful." Feeling a sensual allure that blossomed from the inside out, she unhooked her bra so that it fell into Candace's hands.

The noise Candace made was gratifying, and it was with heat that Candace pulled her down for more of those incredible kisses. Between kisses she unbuttoned Candace's shirt and encountered a smooth cotton bra, oddly endearing and reassuring. Candace made no protest when Alice unhooked it.

A moment later her breasts touched another woman's for the first time, and again Alice thought that this alone was the best sex she'd ever had. Skin against her skin that was both similar and different. When Candace's nipples hardened she could feel the tight peaks against her own. Could Candace possibly feel this excited, this transported, at the sensation of Alice's body against hers? The idea that she could be having the same effect on Candace that Candace was having on her filled her with a sense of wonder.

When the chaise creaked alarmingly, Alice sat up with a laugh. "Perhaps we should go inside."

Candace ran one finger down Alice's chest to the tip of one nipple. "If you insist."

"I do." She drew Candace up to her feet and they held hands until they were in the bedroom, bathed in the low golden light from the bedside lamp. Alice's fingers went to the button on Candace's trousers. "May I?"

"Be my guest." Candace pulled Alice to her for a long, wet, demanding kiss as the trousers were undone and there were more kisses as shoes and socks joined the heap of clothing on the floor.

Alice hadn't meant to be so bold as to pull Candace's underwear off with the trousers, but now Candace was naked and she would not listen to the little voice that kept repeating "What if you don't know what to do?"

Stepping back, Candace pulled down the covers on the bed, then sat on the edge. Alice moved naturally between Candace's knees, leaning down to resume the wonderful kisses. She wanted to say she couldn't believe this was happening to her, that for the first time in her life her desires made sense, but kissing was too good to stop for mere words.

She wiggled her hips as Candace hooked her thumbs into her pantyhose, helping the process along. She wanted to be naked too. Candace's hands were warm and firm as they massaged and squeezed her hips. Alice already felt as if Candace had touched her body more than anyone else ever had before, and this was, she thought with a shiver, only the beginning.

When Candace's hands moved from her hips to her breasts, Alice moaned into their kiss.

"Is this all right?"

"Yes, it's very all right." She nuzzled along Candace's neck and gently pushed her back on the bed. "And I hope this is all right too."

"A gorgeous woman wants to rub her body all over mine? Hmm, let me think."

Alice tickled lightly under Candace's chin. The shared grin further relaxed her, and some part of her that she'd never felt before knew it would be okay to take Candace's straining nipple into her mouth.

She knew her own body and the feel of the rough, erect flesh but had never felt it with her tongue. She played with it, along the flat of her tongue and against the edges of her teeth, loving the responsive textures and feeling drunk on the sound of Candace's moans. She remembered all at once that the last woman to touch Candace had probably been Ginny, and she had loved Ginny. Ginny had known what to do.

She nearly stopped, feeling abruptly lost, but Candace's hand came around her head with a loving, encouraging gesture. The encouragement continued as she moved to the other breast, rubbing her lips in delight along the underside. The soft, yielding slope of Candace's stomach was equally delightful, and all at once she was sliding down to her knees and there it was, another woman's sex.

She had to close her eyes for a moment. It was too beautiful to take in, too sacred and too sexual. She had eagerly studied all the pages of Tammi's *Femalia*, astonished at the infinite variety of the hundreds of photographed cunts. They were as different as snowflakes, and as beautiful. She opened her eyes to look at Candace again, studying the curls and twists of hair that parted to reveal gleaming red that gave way to pink. She fluffed the kinks of hair that obscured what she most wanted to study, but shuddered as her fingertips came away wet and slick.

She licked her fingers. It was instinctive. This was what sex tasted like, she thought, and she could not stop herself from bringing her mouth directly to the source of the sweetness. Candace groaned. The folds of Candace's cunt were soaked and slippery, and Alice's tongue found its way farther in.

They had made her giggle, references to honey and nectar in erotica, but what else could this be called? Her chin and cheeks were smeared with wetness. By any name, she wanted to bathe in it.

When the firm bump of Candace's clit jumped under her tongue, it was unexpected. She lifted her head for a moment to marvel at the flared hood and what it revealed. It *did* look like a pearl, but it didn't feel like one. She kissed it wetly, eagerly, and explored the yielding nerves with her tongue. She pressed and it slid away, delightful to chase and kiss. She played it under her tongue, back and forth, until she caught it briefly between her lips and heard Candace groan, long and loud.

After that her head swam with an overload of sensations. Her mouth and Candace's cunt were equally wet. The sounds Candace made were echoes of the ecstasy Alice felt inside. Candace's hands were suddenly in her hair, around her head, then grappling for her wrists until their fingers entwined and Alice found herself pulled up onto the bed, rolling over it into Candace's embrace, their legs tangling as Candace kissed her. Now both their faces were wet, and Alice wondered if Candace was crying too.

"God, woman, are you trying to kill me?" Candace kissed her way down Alice's throat. "That was fantastic."

Alice felt light as air. "I'm glad you liked it."

"*Like* is for a pair of shoes. If I'd known all those years ago you could do that to me, I'd have run away with you on the spot. I *loved* that."

"It felt fantastic to me too."

"Oh, I think I can make you feel even better than that." Candace licked around one of Alice's nipples, then blew on it softly. "Much, much better."

"Okay," Alice said weakly.

After reaching under the mattress, Candace held up a small bottle. "I really want to make you feel wonderful, and we've got some of this, if it's needed. I'm sorry, I don't have any of the usual toys and goodies—"

Alice pressed her fingers to Candace's mouth. "It's okay."

Candace leaned up to kiss her again. "I want you to feel fantastic. I'll take care of you any way you want. I just don't have those—"

"Honestly," Alice said. "It's okay. I don't . . . I didn't expect . . ."

Candace's smile stiffened a little bit. "I'm really not all that adventurous. I've read lots, but what you did, just now, is pretty much my favorite thing. But I can do anything you want. I want to do anything that you need."

Alice saw the insecurity in Candace's eyes and realized she'd played her part too well. "I think I gave you the wrong impression earlier. Maybe on purpose."

"About what?"

"I've never done this before."

"Gone home—sort of—with someone you just met?"

"Well, that too. No, I mean . . . *this*." She indicated the two of them. "I'm a virgin."

Candace froze.

"I mean, I'm not a virgin, Tammi was conceived the usual way, and I dated some before I got married. But with a woman, I mean . . . I've never . . ."

A tender smile eased the stiffness of Candace's face. "You're right, I got a different impression."

"I've read about—oh dear heaven."

Candace's mouth closed around her nipple and at the same time one hand was between her legs. "We're not going to need the lube, at least not at first."

"Candace," Alice said softly, reeling from the intimate brush of fingers near and around places that seemed to throb in time with their heartbeats.

"I'm not going to hurt you," Candace whispered.

"I know, I know. I'm worried I'm going to hurt you somehow."

"I'm tough, darling." Candace straddled one thigh and ground down slightly.

Alice felt the lush cunt she had been making love to with her mouth wet and hot on her skin. She wanted to go back to doing that again. She couldn't do anything about the urge because

Candace was leaning down to kiss her, and the heat of their bodies, once again pressed close and soft, made thought almost impossible.

Candace said very softly, "I want to feel the inside of you, before I taste you."

"God," Alice said explosively. "Yes." Don't cry, she told herself, don't cry.

But she did cry. Everything felt too good and too real and too intense not to cry. Just a few of the tears were for the years she hadn't let herself experience this kind of love, and all the rest were the wonder of a woman's sure and sensitive fingers touching places that had been there all along, in theory, but now she knew were definitely real. Like being a lesbian, she thought irrelevantly. I've been one all along, but now I know it. *Now I feel real.*

"Don't worry," Candace said. "Just let it happen. My first time I didn't understand, but it'll happen and it's really, really fun."

The touches were insistent, but gentle. If Candace added lube, Alice wasn't aware of it. Steady strokes all along the wall, just inside her, were melting years of ice and clearing away cobwebs—she had clarity about sex for the first time.

She liked it. She enjoyed it. Damn and dear heaven, she really loved sex with a woman.

When Candace's tongue teased and licked its way through every fold between her legs, when tongue and fingers worked together to open Alice for a kind of exploration she'd never felt before, Alice understood what Candace had been saying. Just let it happen—you don't have to understand. Just feel it.

She felt it, long minutes of red lightning behind her eyes and roaring thunder in her ears. She felt it until the dancing fire eased and tears turned into laughter.

Candace was holding her close and tight, kissing her smiling mouth. "You are a very responsive woman."

"I didn't know that. Thank you—that was . . . You were right.

I didn't know. It's not like I had bad sex before, but I didn't know."

Candace pulled the covers up until they were swathed and curled into each other's arms. "Stay the night?"

Alice regarded the drooping eyes and wondered what it would take to wake Candace up in the morning. She slipped one hand over Candace's hip and felt a reflexive response.

"Of course I'll stay the night." She walked her fingers down the length of Candace's hip. "You may have trouble getting rid of me in the morning."

Candace rolled on top of her with a lazy grin. "You say that like it's a bad thing. I'm pretty sure if I went back down the hall to the neighbor's I could borrow some restraints and you wouldn't be able to leave."

"It's okay," Alice murmured. Candace's warm skin was reawakening all the nerves that ought to have been quite, quite satisfied. Candace's little gasp as Alice's fingers found their way between her thighs was very pleasing. "I'm quite content with everything you have right here."

Luxury Options
Radclyffe

"I don't know, honey," Erin Carmichael whispered, leaning close to her partner on one of the butter-soft leather sofas in the spacious health club reception area as she studied the choices on the reservation form. "Maybe we should just go for the basics."

"Remember what we said when we planned this trip," Valerie Tyler chided affectionately. "If we can only splurge on a vacation like this once every ten years, then we're going to be adventurous."

"I know, but don't you think a couples' massage is daring enough for two thirty-something, happily-married-with-children dykes? We don't even know what 'luxury options' means."

"So we'll find out when we get in there." Valerie's gray-blue eyes took on a smoky tint as she brushed Erin's unruly curls away from her face. She traced the curve of Erin's ear with a fingertip and smiled with satisfaction as Erin's lips parted with a small gasp. "By the way, we're signing up for a double, but I'm really just going to watch."

"But I thought—" Erin glanced sideways toward the desk where one of the attendants entered information into a computer. Like all the women who worked at the spa, or anywhere on the ship for that matter, her buff body was displayed discreetly but enticingly in a white polo shirt with the cruise ship's logo over her nicely-shaped left breast. Black Lycra workout shorts came to the middle of her toned thighs. She wasn't looking in their direction, and neither was the dark-haired woman in the tight white T-shirt and faded jeans who leaned against the counter with her back to them. All Erin could see of her were broad shoulders, tapered waist and a tight, hard-looking ass. A bit of smooth, tanned skin peeked through a rip in the denim just below the curve of her butt. Even though she knew no one was listening, Erin dropped her voice so low it was barely audible. "Does this have something to do with your secret fantasy?"

"Sweetheart," Valerie murmured, her eyes drifting down over Erin's curvy, petite body and then back to her face. "It's the first time in years it's just been the two of us—no work, no worries, no after-school soccer or ballet. *Everything* about this trip is a fantasy."

Erin pretended to glare. "I'm talking about the one where you get to play director, and I'm the star of your private film."

"What if I said yes?"

Erin searched Valerie's face and saw the plea in her eyes beneath the unmistakable flush of desire. She drew a shaky breath, feeling heat suffuse her face and neck, and curled her hand beneath the lower edge of Valerie's shorts. As she fingered the hard muscles on the inside of Valerie's thigh in slow, firm strokes, she pressed close until her breasts brushed against Valerie's arm. Her nipples hardened, and she felt a tingle between her legs as if Valerie had lightly brushed her fingertips over her sex. "Just remember. I told you that massages always turn me on a little."

Valerie stiffened, imagining Erin's pale smooth skin gleaming with oil, the delicate scent of spice and sex saturating the air. A stranger's hand gliding over her lover's body. Erin's fingers moved higher, and Valerie had to struggle not to lift her hips and push out for more contact. She was wet, throbbing and hard. "I hope you like it more than a little."

"You're sure?" Erin glanced quickly across the room again, saw that everyone was still occupied elsewhere, and pressed her fingertips quickly and unerringly down on the exact spot where Valerie's clitoris pulsed beneath the thin cotton of her shorts.

"Unh," Valerie gasped, jerking back on the sofa to escape. If the mental pictures and a little bit of finger pressure almost made her come, she was going to be in deep trouble very soon. "I'm . . . sure. Stop, sweetheart." She shivered, a knot of pleasure tightening her pussy. "Don't get *too* adventurous out here. God."

Erin laughed softly and moved her hand back to the top of Valerie's leg. "You've forgotten *I* was the one who made the first move, all those years ago."

"I remember you teasing me for weeks before you'd let me do more than feel you up." Valerie shivered. "I was so horny all the time. I never spent so much time masturbating in my life."

"Mmm," Erin said. "Now that's something I wouldn't mind watching while I'm getting my massage."

"Really?"

"Really."

Valerie covered Erin's hand where it lay on her thigh, twining her fingers through Erin's smaller ones. "You'll be okay? With someone else touching y—"

"As long as you're there." Erin wet her lips with the tip of her tongue. "I have fantasies, too, you know."

Valerie stared, her heart racing.

"Ladies! Ready?" the spa attendant called to them.

Valerie took Erin's hand and they hurried to the counter, just as the woman in the white T-shirt was signing a voucher.

"Thanks, Ryan," the attendant said. "How about you two? Made a decision?"

"Yes," Valerie said, "I think so. We're just not sure about the luxury options part."

"Definitely worth it," Ryan said as she passed the pen and voucher back to the attendant. "I highly recommend it."

The attendant chimed in. "That part of the service is personalized for each customer. Our goal is to make the experience *everything* you want it to be."

Valerie caught a glimpse of what looked like a very satisfied smile on the woman in the T-shirt before she turned to Erin. "Okay?"

Erin squeezed her hand. "Let's go for it."

Valerie put a checkmark in the box next to *Luxury Options*.

Since the room was on the interior of the ship, it had no windows, but warm yellow light from multiple wall sconces created a sense of intimacy. The relaxed ambience was further enhanced by the pale blue textured fabric that covered the walls and the music drifting from hidden speakers. Two tables covered by crisp sheets stood side by side. The four feet of plush carpeted expanse between them left enough space for two masseuses to work on two clients in tandem. Thick white terry cloth towels sporting the familiar cruise line logo were folded neatly in the center of each.

"Do you think we should undress?" Erin whispered.

"Let's wai—"

A knock sounded and then a second later the door opened to admit a petite young woman in loose black cotton pants and a white wraparound blouse that crisscrossed over her ample breasts and tied low on the left side of her waist. Her shimmering, shoulder length blond hair fell free around her face.

"Hi, I'm Stephanie. I'll be one of your massage therapists this afternoon."

"Hello," Valerie and Erin said simultaneously.

"I see you opted for the double luxury package." Stephanie's expression softened, her eyes flickering from Erin to Valerie. "That's great. We'll have fun."

"I know we scheduled a double," Valerie said quickly, "but only Erin is getting a massage. I . . . I'd really rather just watch."

"Anything you want," Stephanie said immediately as the door opened again after a soft knock and a similarly dressed African American woman entered. "This is Anka. Since we're both scheduled to be with you, why don't we both work on Erin?"

"That sounds wonderful." Erin glanced at her lover. "Honey?"

"Yes," Valerie replied. "Wonderful."

"It gets warm in here," Anka said in a rich, melodious voice, "so perhaps you should both remove your clothing." She lifted the soft, white bath sheets from the tables and handed them to Erin and Valerie. "Erin, stretch out on the table and cover up with one of these." She smiled at Valerie. "Perhaps you'd like to sit on the opposite table where you can see us."

"That would be perfect," Valerie said, her fingers digging into the luxurious cotton, her voice husky.

"We'll be back in a few minutes then," Stephanie said.

The instant the door closed behind the two masseuses, Valerie dropped the towel on the table behind her and pulled Erin into her arms. She kissed her hard, her tongue delving deep into her mouth, one hand skimming between their bodies. She cupped Erin's breast, squeezing rhythmically as she breathed her in. Erin's fingers dug into her shoulders and Valerie backed her against the opposite table, never breaking the kiss as she wedged her pelvis between Erin's thighs. She couldn't remember the last time she'd been so nearly out of her mind with lust.

"Valerie, honey!" Erin jerked her head back, her lips swollen from kisses. "Honey, stop! They'll be back in a second."

Valerie groaned. "Oh, my God, I'm so turned on. Maybe we should forget—"

Erin laughed shakily. "Oh, no. We're going to have an adventure." Gently, she pushed Valerie away. "You stay over there now. Take your clothes off and just . . . watch."

"They're both gorgeous," Valerie muttered, glancing across the room as if the two women still stood there. "It's going to make me crazy watching them touch you."

"I know." Erin unbuttoned her blouse and slid it off her shoulders. She opened the clasp on her bra and brushed her hands over her breasts, her eyes on Valerie's face. "And I'm going to be crazy knowing it's making *you* crazy."

Her attention riveted to Erin's breasts, Valerie unbuttoned her pants and pulled them off along with her underwear. "How far do you want them to go?"

Erin skimmed her fingers down her stomach, then unzipped her slacks and stepped out of them. Her pale blue silk panties were dark between her thighs, soaked through already. She touched her fingertip to the slight swell of her clitoris beneath the silk and drew a sharp breath. "As far as you want."

"I want to see you come."

"It's going to be hard for me *not* to," Erin gasped, adding another finger and circling her clitoris beneath her panties, dragging the slick fabric back and forth, spreading her wetness where she needed it. "You got me so ready with that kiss. God, that feels so good."

"Stop touching yourself before you come," Valerie said, removing the last of her clothes. She wrapped the large towel around her torso and secured it under her arm. "Lie down on your belly, and I'll cover you up."

Erin tilted her head back and closed her eyes. Her fingers moved faster. "Just a little more—"

Laughing, Valerie caught Erin's hand and lifted it to her mouth. She kissed Erin's fingertips. "You won't last with much more of that. Be good, sweetheart."

With a faint sigh, Erin stretched out on the table on her stomach, rocking her pelvis in short, quick motions against the soft surface. Valerie slapped her playfully on the butt.

"I said stop. I want you to enjoy this for as long as you can." Valerie covered her with a towel from mid-thigh to shoulders and leaned down to brush a kiss over her ear. "Try not to come, no matter what. Not until I say."

"That's going to be so hard, honey," Erin protested. "You know when I'm this far along I just need a little touch to make me—"

A knock sounded and Stephanie reentered, followed by Anka.

"All set?" Stephanie said.

"Yes," Valerie replied, easing away from Erin and climbing up on the edge of the adjacent table. She sat with her legs over the side, her hands curled lightly around the edge. The towel parted in a long narrow vee that ended just below her crotch. If she spread her legs even a little, Erin would be able to see all the way up. She did.

"We're going to start on your legs and back," Anka said, reaching out for the bottle of massage oil that Stephanie extracted from a warmer on a nearby counter. "If there's anything you want us to do, or don't want us to do, just tell us." She glanced from Erin, who lay with her head pillowed on her folded arms facing Valerie, to Valerie. "Either of you."

"She likes it hard, as deep and hard as you can get," Valerie murmured, her eyes on Erin's. "Is there anything else you want, sweetheart?"

Erin smiled lazily. "Why don't the three of you surprise me?"

"That sounds like a great plan." Stephanie folded down the towel so that it covered the crest of Erin's ass, leaving her shoulders, back and legs bare. She slipped to the head of the bed, and Anka moved to the far side away from Valerie. Each poured warm oil into their hands.

"Ready?" Anka murmured.

"Oh, yes," Erin whispered.

Minutes passed in silence, Valerie watching Erin's face as two sets of hands, one light, one dark, worked the oil over her body. Erin's lips parted into a soft curve and her eyelids opened and closed slowly. Valerie knew that look. She'd seen it hundreds of times as she'd stroked Erin's clitoris, teasing her until she was full and wet and trembling. Of course, that expression might just be because she was enjoying the long, firm glide of fingers and palms down the backs of her thighs, around her calves, and into the arches of her feet. It might just be due to the strong hands kneading the muscles in her shoulders and the base of her neck. But Valerie didn't think so.

Erin groaned and arched under Stephanie's palms. Her hips rocked ever so subtly beneath the white towel. The fine muscles on the inside of her thighs, high up in the soft delicate delta adjoining her pussy, trembled visibly. Valerie felt a sympathetic twinge shoot down the inside of her legs, and she unconsciously parted her thighs farther. The air in the room was thick with scent and promise. It wafted over her exposed clitoris like a lover's kiss. Wetness coated her thighs, and she fought not to slide her hand beneath the towel.

"Take off her towel," Valerie said hoarsely. "Work on her ass. She likes that."

Erin caught her lip between her teeth and moaned softly as Stephanie poured oil into the cleft between her cheeks and Anka smeared it in firm circles over her clenched muscles. She spread her legs on the table and lifted her ass, opening herself. A trickle of oil ran down between her pussy lips, warm and slick. Her clitoris twitched. She felt the pressure of Anka's hands massaging her ass all the way inside her pussy and she moaned.

"Is it good, baby?" Valerie asked.

Erin opened her eyes and sought Valerie's. "I want to come," she whispered, as if they were alone.

Valerie smiled at the dazed look of need on her lover's face. "Not yet, sweetheart. Just enjoy."

"Feels so good."

Valerie's nipples tightened painfully beneath the towel wrapped around her chest, and without thinking, she flicked it open and let it fall. Her breasts stood out, full nipples aching. Her stomach quivered with the effort to hold back her excitement.

"Squeeze her pussy," Valerie said roughly, groaning as Anka's fingers disappeared between Erin's legs. When Erin jerked and cried out, Valerie's cunt spasmed. She thrust her hand between her legs and pressed her palm hard against her clit, forestalling the surge of orgasm. "Not her clit. She'll come right away. Don't touch her there yet."

Erin writhed, her hips pumping erratically. Anka kept one hand in the center of her back, fingers spread wide, while the other circled between her legs. As Anka worked Erin's pussy, Stephanie slid her hands beneath Erin's chest and massaged her breasts.

"Oh, please," Erin whimpered, "tell them to let me come. I'm almost there."

Stephanie glanced toward Valerie. Valerie shook her head no.

"Turn her over," Valerie said. "Her nipples are very sensitive."

Gently, Anka and Stephanie guided Erin over onto her back. Valerie climbed down from her perch and strode to the foot of Erin's table. Stephanie and Anka moved, one to each side. Valerie leaned forward and skimmed her hands up the inside of Erin's thighs, her thumbs tracing the wet, swollen lips.

"Play with her breasts." Valerie pressed her mons against the lower edge of the table, riding her distended clitoris over the padded surface. She flicked Erin's clit with a fingernail as she worked herself close to coming. Erin bucked and twisted, her face and neck flushed with impending orgasm, her breasts taut beneath the hands that teased them.

"Fuck me," Erin pleaded, raising her head to meet to Valerie's gaze, her expression beseeching. "Oh, please, baby, *fuck me*."

"Oh, Erin, baby." Valerie grabbed Erin's knees and pulled her down the table, then pushed her legs apart. Erin's pussy was red and glistening. Her swollen clit looked ready to explode. "I'm going to make you come, baby. I'm going to make you come."

"Wait." Anka grasped Valerie's wrist before she could plunge her fingers into Erin's pussy. "I have something for you."

Valerie could barely focus, but she held back. She heard a drawer slide open, then looked down as a hand caressed her thigh. Anka knelt beside her, a leather harness anchoring a long, thick cock in her hand.

"Part of the luxury option," Anka whispered. "One time use only. Let me help you get ready."

"Hurry," Valerie said through gritted teeth, her clitoris pounding, her head threatening to burst. Moving almost without volition, she let Anka strap her up while watching Stephanie lower her mouth to Erin's breast and lick her nipple. Whimpering, Erin grabbed a handful of Stephanie's hair and pressed her breast deeper into Stephanie's mouth. Erin's pussy contracted, and Valerie saw her clit spring up as if pulled by invisible fingers.

"Jesus, hurry," Valerie gasped. "She's going to come with Stephanie doing that to her nipples."

"Then fuck her," Anka whispered, one hand on Valerie's hips and the other on her cock, guiding her forward and into Erin.

Valerie sank in, and Erin heaved up to take her deep, wrapping her legs around Valerie's waist. Suddenly Valerie was buried. Her thighs trembled and she gripped Erin's hips to steady herself. Slowly, she eased out, almost all the way, and then in again. Deep, she was so deep.

Erin shook and uttered a string of pleas. "Do it. Do it hard, baby. I waited . . . waited . . . oh, going to come soon."

"Like it, baby?" Valerie gasped. "Like it? Are you going to come for me?"

"Oh, yes," Erin wailed. "Soon soon soon oh please do it to me harder. I need it hard."

Valerie fucked her, long full strokes while Stephanie bit and sucked at her breasts. Anka's hands came around Valerie's torso and fondled her breasts, fingers plucking at her nipples. Valerie's clit pounded beneath the base of the phallus, but it wasn't enough to get her off. Ignoring the screaming pressure in her cunt, she concentrated on Erin instead. She gripped Erin's clit and squeezed.

Erin creamed all over the cock. "It's good. So good. Oh, honey, honey, you're making me *come*."

"That's it, baby, that's it. You go ahead." Valerie wanted to cry her clit ached so much.

With her pussy clenched on Valerie's cock, Erin forced herself up on her elbows and stared through wild eyes at Anka. "Make Valerie come too," Erin gasped. "Make her come inside me."

Anka slid a hand from Valerie's breast down her body, spread two fingers into a vee, and drove them beneath the base of the cock. She captured Valerie's clit and jerked, fast and hard.

"Oh, God, baby," Valerie shouted, her clit on fire. "Oh, sweetheart, I'm coming."

Valerie exploded a second after Erin and fell forward, catching herself with her arms on either side of Erin's body. She rested her damp cheek between Erin's breasts and struggled for breath, the cock still buried inside her. Erin's heart beat wildly as she made soft whimpering sounds in the back of her throat. Someone unsnapped her harness.

"You can come out now," a gentle voice whispered in Valerie's ear. Stephanie? Anka? "If you want to."

"Sweetheart?" Valerie murmured, her eyes still closed. She felt Erin's fingers running through her hair. "You done?"

Erin laughed unevenly. "Oh, my God, I am so so done. That was . . . you were . . . God."

Valerie slipped her hand between their bodies, grasped the base of the cock and very carefully drew it out. Someone took it from her.

The same gentle voice said, "We moved the table over so you can lie down next to Erin. We've still got forty-five minutes."

Somehow, Valerie managed to straighten up and with help, climbed up and stretched out on the second table. She turned her head and met Erin's gaze. She imagined that her eyes looked as soft and satisfied as Erin's. She smiled as Stephanie smoothed warm oil over her breasts and down her belly.

"I could get used to these luxury options," Valerie whispered.

"So could I," Erin said, stretching languorously as Anka stroked her legs. "Good thing we've got plenty of time to schedule another session or two before the cruise ends."

First Time for Everything
Karin Kallmaker

"Fine, so you got the babe again." Evie was growing tired of Hana's strut. After all the boasting of her prowess, this morning Hana had been utterly zonked, looking like she'd crawled to their cabin with her last ounce of strength. "I still say that Zi wore you out."

"Like I said last night, she was all over me. Putty in my hands."

The woman sitting next to Evie at the blackjack table said, "That's not what I heard."

Evie did a double-take, then remembered the leggy blonde leaving poolside just as she had strolled up to see how Hana was faring with Zi.

Hana leaned in aggressively. "Oh yeah? What did your friend say about me?"

"Zi implied that if there was putty it was very, very mutual."

"I gave her a good time."

Evie raised a placating hand, knowing all too well that once Hana got her dander up, there would be no peace. "I'm sure you did, but I don't think it's very nice for you to be talking about it where anyone can hear you."

"Just tell her I want my T-shirt back," Hana snapped before stalking off.

"Why do you hang out with that Neanderthal?" The other woman was playing two hands and set chips on each queen she'd just been dealt.

"Good cards," Evie said, avoiding the question. "Two ladies are always lucky."

She laughed and brushed luxuriant blond hair over her shoulder before extending a hand. "I'm Felicia, by the way. Zi and I are roomies. She did say she and your friend had a good time yesterday afternoon, then parted ways."

Charmed by the engaging smile, Evie nevertheless didn't want to gossip in detail about her best friend. "Hana is not the type to be around for breakfast."

Felicia's eyebrows arched in what could have been exaggerated agreement or skepticism. Evie was going to have to ask Hana for more details of her tryst with Zi, but in private.

Two women crossed the casino to buy chips. Evie had seen them before—the tall brunette was extremely eye-catching. Heads turned as they passed.

Felicia whispered, "Isn't that . . . ?"

Evie shook her head. "No, but she certainly looks like it in profile. There—see?"

"Oh, you're right. Wow, though. She could play her sister. What a gorgeous body."

The brunette grinned down at her girlfriend, who gave back a megawatt smile that left Evie feeling envious. Belatedly she realized the dealer was waiting on her, so she scratched the table to get another card. Her luck at cards held when she busted with twenty-four. "They look happy."

Felicia gave her an odd look, just long enough for Evie to appreciate the purple-tinged blue eyes. "You know," she said slowly, "if you hang around with someone like Hana, no one's ever going to know you're a romantic at heart."

Startled, Evie tried not to frown. She was used to being in the shadow Hana cast, but she hadn't realized women might think she was like Hana. She was unlike Hana in a number of ways, some of which she just couldn't admit. She changed the subject. "How come you look familiar?"

Felicia's smile was a mix of pride and chagrin. "Do you watch much TV?" She was dealt a five on the first queen, hit again and busted with an eight. The second queen drew a nine, but the dealer revealed twenty and swept up all the chips.

"Not a lot, no."

"Well, I was on *Survivor* last season. One of the ones voted off in the middle as Most Likely to Be Forgotten. On the reunion show even Jeff Probst couldn't recall my name."

"How could anyone forget you?" Lovely eyes, Evie thought, and that smile. Hair that would be wonderful on your stomach, and satiny, long arms.

Felicia shrugged. "They just do. I'm the girl that cashiers look right past when they ask who's next in line."

"They're all fools." Realizing she was about to blush, Evie indicated the blackjack table and said, "I'm about tapped out for today."

"Lunch buffet ought to be underway," Felicia said. She gave Evie a direct look of invitation.

"That sounds great."

A few short minutes later Evie found herself speculating that Felicia might be vegetarian based on her choices of greens, lots of edamame beans and tofu chunks while passing up lightly grilled fish and chicken. She herself couldn't resist the sea bass with lemon and basil. "I am already overeating."

"Why not? Next week we can get back to the grind."

That Felicia worked out was evident in the muscles in her upper arms and firm shoulders that peeked out past the lace trim on her tank top. She was an attractive woman, Evie had to admit, and she wondered if there was any chance she was as available as her roommate had been for Hana. Not that Evie had that kind of move and confidence, but maybe if they got to know each other, by the end of the week maybe . . .

They drifted toward a cluster of tables for two some distance from the piano player and were greeted by a server offering to bring them water, coffee or tea, or anything they liked from the bar. They both opted for water and settled in.

"I hope this isn't a boring question, but what was it like being on *Survivor*?"

Felicia's face crinkled into a smile. "It was really fun. Frustrating to find out about two hours in I'd been excluded from all the burgeoning alliances. As usual, everyone just looked past me. The best I could hope for was being the expendable fifth wheel. I was cooked by day two and decided to enjoy the experience. If I had to do it over again, I'd take control of my own fate, at least. I lasted as long as I did because I could climb up for coconuts."

They chatted about wilderness living and their hometowns— Felicia lived in Santa Fe, not far from Zi—then turned briefly to their work. A long day's drive from Denver, Evie thought, not that she was thinking about any future or anything like that, it was just that when you meet someone and think they're attractive the mind does some basic math. After laughing agreement that talking about work really sucked, they drifted to movies and concerts.

"I know it's almost a cliché, but I love the Indigo Girls," Felicia admitted. "They don't often come through Santa Fe. You're lucky. They get to Denver nearly every year. They make me feel embraced, you know? The music keeps me close." She shrugged. "I don't know how else to describe it."

"I'm a bit of a Joan Jett kind of girl." Evie couldn't imagine listening to an entire recording of folk music, not when there was rock and roll.

"No!" Felicia feigned surprise. "Weren't you in the mosh pit at the Chain Maille concert?"

Evie blushed. "That was likely me, yeah. What did you think?"

"That sometimes heavy metal is pretentious, but those girls live had me from the first note. Raw dyke energy—gotta love it."

Evie's attention was distracted by the couple just to their left and slightly offset so she saw them more directly than Felicia. The very femme woman wore form-fitting shorts and a halter top that covered everything but somehow suggested it could fall off at any moment to reveal two really lovely breasts. The butch across from her appeared mesmerized by the ice cube the femme was trailing along the curve of her neck. She rolled one shoulder suggestively, and Evie thought she detected the outline of nipple rings.

Felicia had been saying something but, Evie realized belatedly, had paused to see what had Evie distracted. She followed Evie's line of sight just as the femme leaned forward to say, perfectly audibly, "I'll let you touch me tonight, but you have to wait until then. I'm going to make it very hard for you to wait."

The butch visibly gulped and at the same time Evie thought fervently, "Lucky her!"

For a moment she thought she'd said it aloud, but was certain she hadn't. She just as well might have for the knowing look Felicia gave her.

"They seem to have a fun dynamic working for them," she said in a low voice. "Is that what you like?"

"Uh, no, not really, I . . ."

"Are you sure?" Felicia suddenly seemed very cool and appraising, her expression a match to that of the femme at the next table, who was looking at her butch like she was going to eat her whole, one orgasm at a time. "Have you explored that?"

"No . . . I'm kinda butch. It's not . . ."

"Oh, please." Felicia rested back in her chair, her color rising. "Your Neanderthal friend puts out that air too—butches don't get on their backs. But she apparently liked it just fine."

"Well, yeah. Hana isn't stone. But she's not a . . . you know."

"A bottom? And you are?"

"Butches aren't—"

"Why not?"

"Because. They're just not."

With a flick of her gaze at the couple next to them, Felicia said, "That one is. And she seems to be really happy."

"Well, um . . . Hana always says . . ."

Felicia gave her a long, steady look. Evie broke into a sweat. She couldn't speak and her heart was pounding so hard she couldn't hear the piano anymore. Finally, Felicia said, "Drink the water. You're going to need it."

Evie gulped down the remainder of the glass. What did Felicia mean? The temperatures outside were hot and they'd all been warned about dehydration, but she didn't think that's what Felicia meant at all. But she couldn't mean . . . *that*.

As she set the glass down, Felicia leaned forward and whispered, "If you're good I will let you do more than touch me."

"Damn," Evie exhaled. She felt vulnerable and confused, but her crotch was suddenly so tight she couldn't quite think. "Don't play with me."

"Oh, honey, playing with you is exactly what I'm going to do."

Felicia resumed eating her salad as if she hadn't just knocked the breath out of Evie. The other couple left and Evie hardly noticed. She managed to swallow more of her lunch and they resumed their conversation about music. She had just begun to feel more normal again, and had decided her mind had just been playing tricks, when Felicia asked casually, "What's your safe word?"

Evie choked on a mouthful of citrus rice. When she was able, she said, "I don't have one."

"We'll have to see about that."

She said it, just like that, as if planning some kind of power sex date was something one did over blue cheese and water crackers.

The server cleared their plates and offered dessert wine from the bar, but they both demurred.

"Zi is doing rehearsals for the talent show at the end of the week." Felicia paused in the broad hallway that led to the shops. "Our cabin is empty all afternoon. And we have a signal worked out."

"I don't know what to say." It was the literal truth. Evie wasn't indifferent to some casual sex, but there was nothing casual about how she felt.

"Say 'Yes, Felicia.'" She moved closer and Evie realized her neck and shoulders were mottled red and her mouth looked swollen, as if it ached to be kissed. "Say 'Yes, Felicia, take me back to your cabin and do anything you want to me.'"

Yes was trembling on the tip of Evie's tongue. She could taste it, all the slick, sweet, salt of that yes, the heaviness and ecstasy of that yes. It seemed stupid to think at that moment about what Hana would say if she knew her best buddy wanted in the worst way to get topped by an anything-but-forgettable femme, but she worried about it as she always had, and it was the one thing that had never let her get this close to *yes* before.

Felicia moved close enough that a deep breath would have brushed her breasts against Evie's bare arm. "I would really like to explore you, explore us. Besides, what happens on the high seas, stays on the high seas."

It was the little joke, the sudden humor in Felicia's eyes that decided Evie. She didn't want a cold, detached experience with a woman intent on servicing or breaking her. Humor was warm, and making a joke, even a light one, was a gesture of vulnerability.

"Yes, Felicia," Evie said, her tone thankfully even.

Felicia slipped an arm around her waist. The rest of the world became a blur of gold and beige. Into Evie's ear she whispered, "Say the rest of it."

Evie's tone was no longer steady as she added, "Take me back to your cabin and do anything you want to me." Her body flushed cold.

Felicia exhaled noisily and let go, but not before Evie felt her shiver. This wasn't one-sided, she realized, and that, too, was important.

Felicia's cabin was on the deck above the one she shared with Hana, but still an exact replica except for the small porthole between the two narrow beds. It let in filtered light that shifted as the ship rolled over the waves. Felicia closed the door then turned Evie to face her.

"I really think we should have a safe word."

Felicia's hands were hot on Evie's cold shoulders. She was scared but she didn't want to stop. All her fantasies had been nothing like this. "I don't have one. Really. I've never done this . . ."

"I promise we're not going to do anything you don't want to. If things go well we can play harder or differently another day. But today . . ." She brushed her lips against Evie's. "Today I'm going to enjoy your body. But there must be a safe word."

"Honest," Evie said. "It's not that I want you to hurt me or anything. If I say *ouch* or *wait* or *stop* I mean it. I don't want to play like I'm not liking what you're doing."

Felicia nodded, and if anything, she seemed relieved. She ran her hands over Evie's arms as if to warm them. "Then for right now, I think those are excellent safe words. I will listen. If you say *don't* or *not that* or *stop* or anything like that I will hear you. I will stop. We might not be able to start again. And you must understand that if you don't say any of those things, I will assume you like what I'm doing. And I won't stop."

Her heart pounding and her hands feeling like ice, Evie said, "I understand."

Felicia's hands moved quickly to her shoulders and she pushed Evie downward. For just a moment Evie resisted, not understanding.

"Get on your knees." Felicia's voice had gone throaty and deep.

She decides. Evie sank quickly down. She didn't anticipate Felicia's next move, but she was deeply pleased when Felicia pulled her face into the crotch of her shorts, the seam rubbing against her lips. Felicia smelled hot and wet, and the cold flush turned to molten desire as Evie imagined the shorts out of the way and Felicia rubbing her cunt all over Evie's face.

"Oh, I like your greedy mouth already." Felicia worked her fingers into Evie's short hair and pulled her head back. She looked down into Evie's eyes and said softly, "Are you okay with this?"

"Yes," Evie gasped. "I've always wanted this. Like this."

"Pull down my shorts and panties."

She found a side zipper and eagerly slipped her hands in to bare the lush, powerful hips. Felicia stepped out of the clothes, and Evie appreciated for the first time how lovely Felicia's legs were in sandals, especially naked. Curved lines of muscle swept up her calves to the firm fullness of parted thighs. Felicia lowered herself to the edge of the cabin's only chair and spread her legs wider. Evie had a scant moment to take in the beauty of Felicia's sex before the hand in her hair tightened and she found her mouth full of wet, luscious cunt.

"Lick me," Felicia ordered.

She didn't need to say it, Evie realized, but being told added to her soaring pulse. She pushed her tongue in, parted the ripples of skin, and sought out the delicious, slippery wetness inside. Felicia tasted wonderful, and she was very obviously aroused. At the first touch of Evie's tongue to her clit, Felicia's legs jerked, but the hand in Evie's hair was unrelenting.

Felicia rubbed her cunt over Evie's face, and Evie again realized that this moment was nothing like her fantasy. Felicia was in control, which Evie realized meant she, Evie, had permission not to be. Permission to like whatever Felicia would do. Permission to enjoy sex this way. All the other labels of who she was became irrelevant while Felicia controlled the moment.

To move lower and stay with the grinding rise and fall of Felicia's hips, Evie had to spread her knees apart and that, too, excited her. If not for her own shorts she thought she might have dripped on the floor. Sucking and licking, worshipping Felicia's cunt was the sexiest, most erotic thing she'd ever done. Her whole life until now seemed like foreplay. This was what she wanted to do and how she wanted to do it. If her knees ached, she didn't feel it. When Felicia began to hump and moan, jerking upward toward Evie's mouth, Evie wanted to push fingers inside her, but she didn't have permission. She would have to earn that permission, and that idea turned her on further. Her tongue circled and circled Felicia's clit, and swirled lower and harder when Felicia arched.

"That's right, make me come with your tongue. Don't you dare stop until I come on your face."

Evie hadn't foreseen that while submission had her heart pounding and clit throbbing, it was also strangely quiet. There was no other noise in her mind but that of her mouth making contact with Felicia's cunt, and the crooning lilt of Felicia's voice. There was no moment in time before this one and she could not anticipate a future. Now was what mattered, and for the first time in her life the word *ecstasy* made sense. She felt it, deep and quiet, powerfully contained in a place she had always controlled. She wanted to teach Felicia—or someone like her—the secret pathway into that part of her.

Felicia came against her mouth with an earthy cry of delight.

There was luscious dripping wet on her chin and chest as she panted against Felicia's thigh. She'd gone down on women before and not felt like this. Her head spun as if she were high and the disbelieving thought persisted: *You are this turned on, this hot, and all she did was order you onto your knees.*

The grip on her hair had eased slightly, but was still strong enough to turn her face into Felicia's thigh. Evie laughed as she realized Felicia was wiping her chin for her. She couldn't remember which comic had pointed out how good the thigh was as a napkin.

Felicia laughed too, rich and easy. "For a first timer, you have the hang of this."

"I'm trying," Evie said quietly.

Felicia met her gaze and the world narrowed again. "Goddess help me, Evie. You give me such ideas when you look like that."

"Like what?"

"Like you'll let me do anything."

Evie nodded. Her head was clearer so she said, wanting to be certain of it, and honest, "Well, not everything. Whips scare me—not in a good way."

"I don't own any," Felicia said. "Not my thing. I'm quite comfortable with *ouch* as your safe word."

Evie laughed a little and finally felt her knees protesting the position. She said nothing, but it might have shown in her face because Felicia ran a hand down her T-shirt to cup one breast.

"Stand up."

Trying not to move stiffly, Evie still appreciated Felicia's helping hand.

"I'm sorry," Felicia said abruptly. "I should have thought of a pillow for you."

"It's okay."

"No, it's not. If I'm the top, I should be thinking of those things."

"There's no question that you're the top," Evie said. Blood

rushed to her knees and she instantly felt better. "But I really am okay."

Felicia's fingers tightened on Evie's hard nipple as she pulled Evie close. "I have a confession to make." After Evie's inquiring look, she went on, "You're not the only one having a first time. I've never topped anyone before."

Surprise made Evie's jaw drop. "You could have fooled me."

"I'd thought about it, believe me. A lot. But I didn't know if I could pull it off. When I saw that other couple and the look on your face I got all . . . inspired, I guess."

"Am I that readable?"

"You were to me. That look got me hotter than anything I've ever felt in my life." Her fingers twisted Evie's nipple. "Is this okay with you, my responsive butch bottom?"

It *was* okay, suddenly, Evie thought. She finally made sense to herself and that was all that mattered. If Hana had a problem with it, that was Hana's problem, not hers.

"Yes," Evie said easily. There wasn't a quaver in her voice or in her mind. "This is okay with me."

Gladiators
Karin Kallmaker

"Half the women on board are going to think you're her at first." Marissa surveyed Linda's gladiator costume, complete with breastplate and rubber sword.

Linda shrugged with a smile. "It doesn't bother me anymore. Besides . . ." Without warning, she pushed Marissa flat on the bed. "You are most definitely not some featherweight sidekick everyone wishes was really my girlfriend."

"Got that right. I am most definitely your girlfriend, and I'm no featherweight."

Linda kissed her and Marissa happily took note that it was not a light, bouncy I-love-you kiss, and not a later-let's-do-more kiss. It was a let's-turn-on-all-the-lights-and-take-off-all-our-clothes kiss.

When she was able, Marissa said, "I just got into these stockings."

"Are you really going to make me wait?" She was treated to

another kiss and one of those patented dark-eyed looks where Marissa could see herself in the depths.

"Our seating begins in fifteen minutes."

"Why did we go for the early seating?" Linda planted little kisses all around Marissa's collarbone.

"We wanted to be sure to have time for a nightly walk on the deck before going to bed."

"Mmm. Bed." Linda continued with the little kisses, moving down the deep cleavage of Marissa's servant-of-the-temple costume.

"And so far, my dear Ms. Bartok, we've gone to bed every night without taking a walk."

"And, my dear Ms. Chabot, we achieved highly aerobic activity with sustained target heart rates."

Marissa giggled. "Brown-eyed woman."

"Are you saying I'm full of shit?"

Marissa's quip died on her lips as she touched Linda's hair where it brushed her shoulders. The dark strands moved like silk against her fingertips, and for just a moment she was back in the bungalow where they had first made love, experiencing the magic of Linda's touch, feeling wanted and sensual for the first time in her life.

"Hey." Linda's gaze was gentle and open. "Where'd you go?"

"I was thinking about Tahiti." The pain of all that had happened after that night had been washed over with the promise of their future. Where she had once dreaded each new day without Linda, now she welcomed every sunrise. "Thank you for loving me."

"Are you kidding?" Linda moved off of Marissa, settling along her side. "That was the best night of my life."

Marissa could have spent the next hour like this, quietly talking about whatever came to mind, and reveling in the little sensations, like the warmth of Linda's cheek against her fingertips. They both worked too hard and rarely had time like this to waste together. "The *first* best night of your life, you mean."

Linda grinned again. "I stand corrected." She leaned in for a kiss, but the breastplate got in the way. When a strap popped and a point dug into Marissa's forearm, Linda acknowledged defeat.

"Okay, we'll wait. But I am going to liberate you from your days as a temple slave." She clambered off the bed to fix her breastplate strap.

"And I'll be just your slave after that?"

"Of course." Linda wiggled in a circle as she tried to adjust the pleated leather skirt. "I plan to have my way with you."

"Let me." Marissa slipped both hands up Linda's skirt and found the hem of the undershirt. With a little tug she got rid of the rumple. Then, just for good measure, she gave Linda's backside a very friendly squeeze.

"Liking your slave duties already?"

Marissa answered with a sharp swat. "You have to help me get my bra on correctly."

"Gladly." Linda posed in the narrow mirror with her sword. "The skirt looks just right now. Thanks."

Marissa slipped the gathered straps of the diaphanous gown off her shoulders.

Linda made a show of tossing her sword to one side. "How can I help with the presentation of your boobages?"

Marissa gave Linda a dour look, which Linda ignored as usual, and then turned her back. "Tighten the hooks and then when I've got everything lifted, you're going to tighten these silly clear straps so everything stays. You know, the package says it's for the full-figured gal, but not one with shoulders."

Linda adjusted the hooks as Marissa asked, then kissed Marissa between the shoulder blades. "And have you got shoulders. Free weight heaven."

Marissa looked at Linda's reflection in the mirror. "I could care less about the weights. But it felt really good to heave my own carryon into the overhead bin." She lifted the bra cups so the straps had more slack. "Tighten please."

Just as they were leaving, Linda reached into the small refrigerator in the suite's tiny bar area. "For my beautiful slave girl. A slave no more."

"Oh, Linda." Touched, Marissa took the simple crown of laurel leaves wrapped around florist wire. She snipped off the little tag from the ship's florist. "It makes the costume perfect."

"Allow me," Linda said. Marissa bent her head and felt the cool touch of the leaves all around her scalp. "My divine lady."

She blushed. Sometimes she still caught herself not believing that Linda saw her as beautiful. When Linda made it clear with such romantic gestures, she still felt surprised. Linda pulled her close and they shared a soft, very tender kiss. It was a few minutes before they made their way out of their cabin.

"Okay, so we're in the minority for costumes." Marissa held Linda's hand as they approached the dining room. There was a smattering of women in similar white-gowned garb to her own, but most of the other women were in casual evening clothes. Linda, in her full gladiator regalia, was attracting quite a lot of attention, but that was nothing new. Linda took it in stride, and Marissa wanted to tell Linda how proud she was that the attention no longer sent Linda running to the ends of the earth. The warm hand she held reflected none of the tension that had been present when they'd first met, when a remark about Linda's resemblance to glamorous heroines of stage and screen caused Linda a great deal of anguish.

"That sword should be a Chakram," a petite blonde observed as they waited for the maitre d's attention.

Linda patted the breastplate. "Chakram's under here."

Stepping well into Linda's personal space, the blonde said coquettishly, "Can I see?"

Marissa arched one eyebrow. Blondie didn't see that Linda

was holding hands with someone already?

"Sorry," Linda said easily. "I've already got a Gabrielle."

With a flutter of eyelashes the blonde moved on.

"Oh, the travails of fame and fortune," Marissa said. She nodded at the maitre d' and followed him across the main floor of the restaurant.

Linda pulled out Marissa's chair and they greeted the other three couples at their table. The day spent cruising and lounging was evident in a number of near sunburns, but one couple had had some success in the casino.

"We tried yesterday," Linda said. "Blew our budget in about two hours."

"Cat's lucky with cards." Marissa could not remember the speaker's name. "Now we can buy more souvenirs for the grand-kids."

Cat gave her partner a mock scolding glance. "Jessica, we're not grandmothers, remember?"

"Yes, dear."

Marissa chuckled appreciatively. Someday she hoped to be just as comfortable and indulgently affectionate with Linda as Cat and Jessica were with each other. They'd even had a child together and now were grandparents. Kids weren't in her and Linda's plans, not yet anyway, even if her mother was agitating in the worst possible fashion.

An uproar at the door brought all conversation to a halt. With a stamp of feet and clash of very real looking swords, female crew members in full gladiatorial regalia marched into the dining room, flushed and giggling. Their breastplates bore the colors of the Italian flag, and many had a face more red than her costume.

"They never get to do the march," Cat yelled over the din. "This week the cruise organizers made them make an exception. Woo!" She began swinging her napkin over her head, and soon everyone followed suit.

The cheering screams as the gladiators circled the room were deafening. Linda stamped her feet as Marissa tried to yell herself hoarse. Impossibly, the bedlam escalated at the promised presentation of Bacchus. A chaise appeared carried on the shoulders of toga-clad men, but instead of the god Bacchus, it was the woman who owned the touring company, wrapped scantily in a toga and bearing the sign, *Sappho*.

After the chaise made a circuit, "Sappho" stepped off to thank her bearers and made a little speech ending with "More wine!"

The cheering resumed as the gladiators exited the dining room and calmed somewhat as the pianist launched into "That's Amore!"

"Sounds like plenty of wine has already been had," Linda said as other diners began singing along with the music.

Jessica grinned. "It's high spirits. It's been such a great week so far and we all get to be who we are."

"It's been a real reminder to me that not everybody gets to live where we live." Marissa recalled that Jessica and Cat also lived in the Bay Area. "We're very lucky there."

"I met this adorable couple from Topeka and they are on Cloud Nine. One woman doesn't know how they'll be able to go back to the so-called real world."

The waiter offered them their daily menu and she and Linda quickly agreed on what they'd split and share. By then the pianist had segued to "It's a Small World," and the singers quickly adapted the lyrics.

Linda chortled and joined in. "It's a gay, gay world!"

Dinner was a blur to Marissa. There were so many good pheromones in the room and the wine was so wonderful that it all felt like something out of a dream. But most wonderful was the way she felt about Linda. The last year had been as heavenly as the first year had not. They both worked hard but every day, at least once a day, they said I love you and found a way to make the other laugh. They made love sometimes in quick little bursts of release and other times set aside a long afternoon to explore each other.

By dessert, though she'd only had one glass of wine, she felt tipsy. But when Linda tried to guide them down the stairs to their suite, she instead insisted on a walk around the deck. "Come on, the dessert was decadent. There's later, sweetheart."

Linda indulged her and they walked toward the bow, sheltered from the wind until they reached the foredeck. A good-sized barrier prevented them from going into the bow, but the wind was refreshing and it cleared Marissa's head. By the time they'd made a complete circuit, she felt much more focused, but the tingles of wonder and awe everytime she looked at Linda were just as strong.

Out of the wind on the aft deck above the pool, she leaned into Linda and pointed out the moon rising. "Remember that beautiful moon in Tahiti? The sea was so still that it looked like a magical pathway over the surface would let us walk right to it."

"I have to say I'm really happy to be on a ship that has stayed afloat."

Marissa squeezed Linda's arm. "Me too, even though I got what I wanted and needed out of that experience."

"Yeah?" Linda gazed down at her, and Marissa recognized the only shadow that ever existed in Linda's eyes.

"Don't," Marissa said. No matter how often she told Linda she forgave her for that long, painful year when Linda had dropped out of her life without a word, Linda sometimes needed to be reassured. "It's okay."

"I could have sent a postcard from New Zealand, or an e-mail from any Internet café in Boston. I could have told you the truth before we left Tahiti, even."

"It's okay," Marissa repeated. "The hurt is long gone."

The shadow lessened, but it hadn't entirely left Linda's eyes. "I want to spend the rest of my life making it up to you."

"Okay," Marissa said easily. "Sounds like you want to get

married."

"I do."

A little silence fell and Marissa's heart was suddenly beating like she had just finished a half-hour on a stair-stepper. Linda reached into the little waist pouch that Marissa had thought purely decorative and extracted something very thin.

"I'm not perfect, Marissa."

"I don't care if you're perfect or not. All that matters is that you're perfect for me and you think I'm perfect for you."

"Marry me. Please."

"Yes." Marissa's chin quivered and she looked down at what Linda had in the palm of her hand.

"When we get home we'll pick out real rings. But for now . . ."

She gently pushed a woven ring of blue fabric onto Marissa's ring finger. It was a little thick, but even through a veil of tears, Marissa thought it was beautiful.

"I made it out of what was left of that scrap I carried to remind me of you. A real ring will replace it, I promise."

She threw herself into Linda's arms. "Yes, darling, yes. I want forever with you."

Linda swung her in a circle, setting her down to kiss her hungrily. "Let's go back to our room."

"We'll miss the jazz trio."

"Don't care."

Marissa was already leading Linda into the atrium. "Neither do I."

Her reflection, the woman she was, was bright and clear in Linda's eyes. The lights were on, all of them.

Linda had already exchanged her costume for an old soft T-shirt featuring a small cartoon of a dog with a snorkel in its mouth. Marissa blinked back tears recalling all the nights she'd kept that shirt under her pillow. Linda stretched out on the bed, one long, lean line, and watched Marissa remove her sandals, then roll down and carefully remove her thigh-high stockings.

Marissa no longer felt awkward undressing in front of Linda. A year and then some of proof that Linda got very excited just looking at her in anticipation of the moment Marissa slipped naked into her arms had given her the confidence to take her time. She sat down on the bed so Linda could reach her zipper and bra, and without prompting, Linda undid both.

"Thank you." The gown had already slipped from her shoulders when she rose, and she held it to the front of her as she removed her watch and bracelet, then her earrings. She didn't know if the exposed curve of her back and hint that the dress would fall to the ground if she let go was anyone's definition of sexy. All that mattered was that her body made Linda's gaze follow her with hunger and desire.

"You're teasing me."

"Am I?" Marissa let the gown slide to her waist and she slowly removed her bra.

"You know you are."

"Is there something you'd rather I do?" She let her bra fall from her fingers and shinnied the dress farther down until it rested just at her hips.

"God, no."

"I don't want my dress to wrinkle." Turning her back, she lowered the dress until she could step out of it. She would bet money Linda's gaze was on the white silk panties she wore, and she smiled to herself. No one had ever made her feel as powerfully attractive. She hung the dress in the closet and finally turned around. Linda had taken off the T-shirt, and for a moment Marissa couldn't breathe.

"*Yummy-yum-yum.* Worth waiting for."

Recovering her wits, she crossed the short distance to the bed. "One last thing to take off."

"Need help with that?"

"Oh, yes." Marissa adopted her best impression of a Southern Belle. "Why, I just can't figure out how to take them off all by my little lonesome."

"Easy." Linda practically purred as she slid to the edge of the bed. "You use your teeth."

Linda's unrestrained intensity never failed to melt Marissa's confidence into an ache of desire. No longer the stalking tigress, she felt abruptly the prey. Linda first nipped at her thigh before she bit into the front of her panties and pulled them down. Marissa cupped Linda's face as heat from Linda's breath seemed to float over her entire body. With a shiver of delight, she helped lower her panties until they pooled around her ankles and she could kick them off. Linda opened her arms and Marissa settled into the shelter of their encircling strength.

Breasts, stomachs and thighs melted together as knees sorted themselves out with the ease of familiarity. The scratch of Linda's nails along the inside of one thigh drew a low moan from the back of Marissa's throat.

"Is this what you want, Marissa?"

She nodded, gaze locked with Linda's. When Linda dipped between her legs, Marissa felt herself falling into the well of Linda's eyes. Entwined on their sides, Linda seemed intent on kissing Marissa until morning while her fingertips teased lightly. It was as languid as their lovemaking had been feverish the night before. With each new kiss and whispered affection Marissa grew more and more frantic for Linda's touch inside her.

"I love the way you can move for me," Linda whispered. Her hand shifted and Marissa felt the long, welcome stroke of her fingers. "I love the way your body feels against mine."

With a sudden spasm, Marissa arched hard against Linda. The layers of sensation that radiated out from Linda's hand brought a tingle of electricity wherever her skin touched Linda's. There were stars behind her eyes, then all of that light folded inward until she glowed from the inside out.

"We could go to the lip sync contest," Marissa offered sleepily quite some time later.

"Sure."

Marissa knew that voice. Linda was asleep, but her brain's autopilot would mumble appropriate responses if Marissa kept talking.

"Will you get me a space shuttle for my birthday?"

"Sure."

Marissa laughed softly to herself, then rose to turn out the lights. She studied the sweep of Linda's hair over the pillow before faint moonlight from the porthole replaced the last lamp's glow.

She slipped back into the circle of Linda's arms and melted at the warmth of Linda behind her. "Go dancing with me tomorrow night?"

"Sure."

"Marry me?"

"Sure."

"Love me forever?"

"Abso-freaking-lutely."

"You're not asleep."

"I was."

Marissa fondly tickled the arm around her waist. "Thank you."

"For what?"

"All the tomorrows."

Linda pulled her a little closer. "Finders keepers, sweetheart. You're mine now."

Lip Sync
Karin Kallmaker

"She's doing a great job selling that song."

Dishra turned from her adoration of the woman on stage to give Brandy an agreeing smile. "It doesn't hurt that there's a strong resemblance. Add the wig, dress and the real Mariah Carey's voice, and she does put on a perfect illusion."

"You work wonders with the wigs. Peggy Lee is perfect."

Her focus back on the woman moving like a diva in the spotlight, Dishra said, "Wait until you see ABBA."

Brandy chuckled appreciatively as she moved on. Dishra hoped she got hired by LOVE—she was a delight to work with. Then she forgot all about such matters as "Mariah" exhorted the crowd to shake it off, all the while strutting in five-inch stilettos and a body-molded gown that left little to anyone's imagination.

Certainly it left nothing to Dishra's. Oozing sex appeal, lip syncing with confidence and dancing with abandon, the woman on stage moved like a real goddess. Dishra had always had a thing for Mariah. She'd always been convinced that if only Mariah met the right woman, she'd be singing an entirely different tune. Dishra had always believed, from the time she was about twelve, that she was the right woman for Mariah.

The crowd was into the number, cheering at the defiant, "Baby, I'm Gone" and applauding madly as the contestant left the stage. As she breezed past Dishra she gave her a look that was pure siren. All that exuberant lesbian energy in the room—Mariah seemed to have gotten infected. At the door to what served as a quasi-dressing room, Mariah gave her one more look over her shoulder.

Heart pounding, Dishra got Peggy Lee into position, checked that the blond page boy wig was still on straight, then followed Mariah into the chaos of the room set aside for LOVE's overflow use. The steady pulse of "Fever" followed after her even when the door had closed. Appropriate, she thought.

"Thank you for all your help," Mariah said. She put up a hand to remove the wig, but Dishra caught it and pulled the surprised woman deeper into the room. Behind the stacked high boxes of T-shirts and CDs for sale, she found a dark corner and pushed her personal diva up against the wall.

"I don't care if this gets me fired. I want to make you sing for me."

Mariah resisted until Dishra's lips were on hers, then the fever seemed to catch her too. Somebody had loved Mariah wrong, and Dishra was going to love her right.

"Yeah, kiss me," she whispered, and Dishra was happy to oblige.

The sun was lighting up the daytime from the stage speakers when she felt Mariah's hands on hers, guiding them around her hips to her ass, then up to her breasts. Dishra's head was spinning.

That soft, sweet voice asked, "How did you know what I wanted?"

It was not a moment to be shy. They didn't have much time before she had to get ABBA lined up for the stage. "I've always known what you wanted. And what you needed." She yanked up the dress and massaged the soft insides of two perfect thighs. She worked down the pantyhose just far enough, then boldly pushed her hand in.

"Oh, baby, that's right, that's what I need. God, how did you know?"

Grinning, Dishra angled her palm up to a wonderfully prominent clit while she wiggled her fingers, getting them wet and ready. From her back pocket she removed a small packet of lube. "Do you know what I'm going to do to you?"

"Whatever it is, you know I want it."

She tore the packet open with her teeth as Peggy sang about Romeo and Juliet. With a shift of her hand, the tips of two fingers sank into the increasingly slippery and sodden woman. This was her diva, her songbird goddess, and it was perfectly natural to get down on her knees to worship at the only shrine that mattered.

With a growl she locked her lips around the beautifully peaked and straining clit, and the noise Mariah made was the kind of music Dishra had wanted to hear for years. She squeezed the packet of lube and knew some of it missed her hand, but most of it went where she wanted. She was slick past her wrist, and Mariah might say she didn't know what was about to happen, but from the way she planted the stilettos and spread her legs, it was clear she had expectations.

Captain Smith and Pocahontas were burning in the fever as Dishra pushed all of her fingers into Mariah's delicious pussy. She was getting sweet wetness on her shirt, on Mariah's dress, but nothing was going to stop her from giving the moaning woman what she needed.

"Sing for me, baby," she said, low and intense, as she tucked her thumb and pushed firmly.

"Oh, oh, oh, baby!"

There was no time to pause in awe at the sight of the beautiful black-fringed cunt clasped around her hand, to wonder what an artist would make of the hues of cocoa, caramel and rich, lustrous red. This wasn't art, it was sex, and the way her hand was being squeezed and molded, obviously needed and enjoyed, had blood pounding in Dishra's ears.

She leaned in to slip her other arm around Mariah's hips and pushed gently up, once, twice, then harder. "I'm going to fuck you right off those pretty shoes."

Long fingernails dug into her scalp, then slid away as Dishra's tongue flicked over the swollen, gleaming clit.

"That's right, you fuck me. Fuck me good. That's what I need, damn it."

Every thrust of her arm was met by responsive, powerful muscles that pulled her hand in deeper, then threatened to push her out.

"No, you don't. I'm not done. I like watching my wrist go *in*, and then slide back *out*. You are so incredibly beautiful. You do give me fever, baby."

Mariah grappled for some kind of balance against nearby boxes after Dishra went in so hard and deep the stilettos slipped. "Harder," Mariah begged. "Harder!"

"Come on my hand." Dishra sucked the hard clit between her lips again as Mariah finally sang the high note she'd always imagined. Mariah's cunt shuddered around Dishra's hand until she pushed it out with a hoarse cry. She surged against Dishra's mouth, violently scrubbing her clit across Dishra's chin and lips. Her tight curls reddened Dishra's cheeks. Tomorrow, she thought, I'll look like I got too much sun, but this was a much, much more lovely way to burn.

"Jesus Christ," Mariah gasped as she started to go limp.

"I'm sorry. I'm so sorry. I have to go." The applause was rising, and Dishra knew ABBA was milling around off stage, wondering what to do.

God, I'm a mess, she realized, *wet and sticky from my nose to my fingertips.* She grabbed a T-shirt from the defects and discards pile and wiped her face and arm as she ran for the door. Peggy was just coming off stage, flushed and pleased.

"You were great. Wait right here for the results after our last act. Girls, stand right here, now do your entrance!" Dishra pushed the trio of jumpsuited platinum blondes toward the spotlight, then hurried back to the little room where she'd left that hot, beautiful woman.

When she opened the door she saw her girlfriend, Becka, perched on a stack of boxes. One stiletto dangled from her fingertips as she massaged her toes.

With a lopsided grin, she asked, "Did you make it in time?"

"Yeah, baby, just in time." Aching with affection and gratitude, Dishra pulled Becka to her feet to hug her.

"You smell like sex," she murmured into Dishra's chest.

"So do you."

"Not as much as I'd like." She leaned back to give Dishra another of those looks. "Mariah got really fucked, baby, but now I'd like something of my own."

The stage speakers pulsed out "Waterloo."

"I promise to love you evermore," Dishra said, "but this is pure Top Forty, baby, and the song is only three minutes, including the applause. I can't do everything I want in what's left."

"You can kiss me then."

No hardship, that. Dishra brushed her lips to Becka's, then went in for a long, wet kiss that promised more later. "Thank you, darling, for dressing up for me."

"It was all my pleasure."

The singers were finally facing their Waterloo, and Dishra knew she had to let go of Becka. "Why don't you join the others backstage when you've caught your breath?"

"Okay."

At the door, Dishra looked back to watch Becka slip her delicate foot into the killer stiletto.

Becka looked up and grinned. "Honey? We can keep the outfit until tomorrow, can't we?"

There was only one thing to say to her passionate, playful girlfriend in reply to such a perfect idea.

"I adore you."

Easy Loving
Radclyffe

"How many propositions did you get while I was in line for the restroom?" Honor Blake sat down on the end of the lounger while a few hundred women danced and partied on the pool deck.

"Not a single one." Quinn Maguire pulled Honor higher between her legs and leisurely traced her tongue along the edge of Honor's lip. "I was just sitting here missing you."

"Really?" Honor skimmed her mouth over Quinn's ear. "Blonde, twenty, big breasts, thong bikini."

"Oh," Quinn murmured. "Her."

"Uh huh." Honor leaned back, surveying her lover. Even wearing loose khaki shorts and her favorite T-shirt bearing the name of the girls' soccer team she coached, Quinn looked deadly sexy stretched out under the stars. Honor had observed more than a few women taking note of Quinn's Black Irish good looks and athletic body. "Did she drool anywhere?"

Laughing, Quinn lifted aside the red-gold strands of Honor's shoulder length hair with one hand and nuzzled her neck. "She asked me to dance, and I told her I reserved that pleasure for my wife."

Honor tilted her head back so Quinn could kiss the spot below her ear that always made her instantly wet. Not that she needed any special encouragement this week. The excitement of finally being on vacation, just the two of them, left her constantly horny. Being able to have Quinn whenever she wanted only made her hungrier for her. "You'd better have told her you save *all* the pleasures for me."

"I think the word *wife* did the trick."

"I guess your wedding band isn't big enough." Honor nipped at Quinn's chin. "Come on. Want to dance again? It's almost eight back home, and we'll need to head inside soon to call Arly."

"So let's just make out for a few minutes instead." Quinn shifted her focus to the area exposed by the open buttons of Honor's sleeveless blouse and kissed the soft triangle of skin between her breasts.

"Oh, no." Laughing, Honor braced both hands against Quinn's shoulders and pushed her away. "We didn't travel four thousand miles to do what we could just as easily do in our back-yard."

"With half the neighborhood, one mother-in-law and a nine-year-old daughter likely to traipse through at any moment, there's no way we can do in the yard what I have in mind right now." Quinn grabbed Honor's hand and pushed it under her T-shirt, trapping it against her stomach. Reflexively, Honor stroked Quinn's abdomen, coaxing the muscles to contract. Quinn leaned her head back with a satisfied smile. "That's a start."

"You know how much it turns me on," Honor murmured, leaning down to suck on Quinn's lower lip as Quinn's belly danced under her fingertips, "when you get all hard and quivery like this."

Quinn blinked lazily and spread her legs farther, pressing her crotch against Honor's hip. "Yeah. I know." She circled her cheek over Honor's breast. "Jesus, it feels so good when you do that. I think you could get me off if you just kept rubbing me like that."

"Honey," Honor scraped her nails lightly up and down the center of Quinn's tense abdomen, knowing just exactly how hot and how wet that would make her lover. "There are about a hundred lesbians in our immediate vicinity, and I have no intention of letting a single one of them get a glimpse of what belongs to me." She nipped at Quinn's neck. "You're beautiful when you're excited, and you're mine."

"No one's watching us," Quinn said. "But just the same, I'll pretend nothing's happening. Keep going."

Honor laughed and skimmed her fingers through Quinn's short, thick dark hair. "You might have perfect control in the operating room, Dr. Maguire, but there are some things even a big tough trauma surgeon like you can't manage." She slid her other hand between Quinn's legs and squeezed her through her shorts. "And being quiet when I make you come is one thing you haven't mastered."

"The music's loud enough so no one will notice," Quinn gasped, covering Honor's hand with hers and guiding her fingers over a spot just to the left of the seam in her shorts. "This week is the first time I've had you completely to myself, and I can't get enough of your hands on me."

Honor grew still. "I know it's tough, walking into a relationship with a ready-made family. Then with both of us heading up departments—"

"Honor," Quinn said, lifting Honor's hand from between her legs and cradling it against her cheek. "That's not what I meant. I love Arly almost as much as I love you. I love our family. I just like having all your attention."

"Oh, you've got my attention all right." Honor drew Quinn's

hand to her breast where her nipple tightened into a hard prominence against Quinn's palm. "You're not the only one who can't get enough. I'm so swollen right now I'm not sure I can walk."

"Let's go make that call, and then let's go to bed," Quinn said, her voice husky. "What did she have after school tonight? Karate practice, right?"

Honor nodded, keeping Quinn's hand in hers as they rose. "Yes. She's working on her fourth form, remember?"

"How could I forget?" Quinn circled Honor's waist with her arm as they wended their way through the crowd of laughing, dancing women. "We've been working on that backhand knife block for weeks."

"Yes, we'll be home in time for the tournament." Quinn sprawled on the couch, the phone cradled between her shoulder and ear, and grinned at Honor, who stood beside the bed unbuttoning her blouse. "You still have the schedule, right? We'll be back in Venice the day after tomorrow. I promise we won't miss the plane home."

Honor dropped her blouse on the floor, her eyes holding Quinn's. Quinn gave her a look as if she were in pain and mouthed *Have mercy*. Honor smiled.

"What, kiddo?" Quinn frowned. "Master Cho made you do twenty extra sit-ups? Oh. Well, if you leave your mark before the count, it might seem like you weren't listening."

Honor trailed her fingers over her breasts and down the center of her abdomen as she walked over and stood in front of Quinn.

"I know you just wanted to explain and weren't really arguing." Quinn hooked a finger over Honor's waistband and pulled her closer. Then she leaned forward and kissed Honor's stomach at the edge of her navel. "But Master Cho has to keep the class running on schedule, and part of learning to be a good martial artist is to follow the rules. You can do that, right?"

"Phone," Honor whispered before sinking her hands into Quinn's hair and rubbing her belly over Quinn's face.

"Your mom wants to say hi," Quinn said, stroking Honor's thigh. "I'll see you soon and then we'll talk about what happens when a rule doesn't seem fair. Here's Mom."

"Hi, sweetie," Honor said, caressing Quinn's neck. "How's everything?"

Quinn unzipped Honor's shorts, pulled them down, and let them pool on the floor around their bare feet. Then she skimmed a fingertip beneath the edge of Honor's pale yellow bikinis and kissed lower on her belly. Honor's thighs trembled, and Quinn followed the path her finger had taken with her tongue.

"Isn't it about time for you to get ready for bed?" Honor said, catching Quinn's chin in her fingers to stop her movements. "We miss you too. Bunches. We'll talk to you tomorrow, okay? Love you too. Bye, sweetie."

Honor tossed the phone onto the sofa and grabbed a fistful of Quinn's hair, pulling her head back until their eyes met. "You cannot do that to me while I'm talking to our daughter."

"I wasn't going any lower."

Honor bumped her hips forward. "Wanna bet?"

"At least not until you got off the phone." Quinn grabbed her around the waist and rested her chin on Honor's stomach. "Is she okay?"

"She's fine. Just misses us."

"I miss her too," Quinn said with a sigh.

"I remember when we first met you said you weren't very good with kids."

Quinn looked up. "It's different when they're yours."

"I know. You're great with her." Honor stroked Quinn's face. "She really wants a brother or a sister."

"Well, we're trying," Quinn said gently, knowing how hard it was for Honor not to have gotten pregnant the first two times they tried. She had been careful not to let her own disappointment show, because she never wanted Honor to think she wasn't completely happy with their life. "Sometimes it just takes a while."

"Mmm," Honor said, "it sure seemed that way."

Quinn slipped her fingertips beneath the bikinis and skimmed them down and off, needing Honor naked, needing the connection that centered her world. "Don't worry, it will hap—" She stopped abruptly and jerked her head up. Honor was smiling. "*Seemed* that way? Seemed as in past tense?"

Honor nodded.

"You're . . . ?"

"Uh huh," Honor said, suddenly sounding shy.

"How . . . how long . . . when?" Quinn rose slowly to her feet, holding Honor gently. "How long have you known?"

"Just today."

"You're sure? I mean . . . you checked?"

"I didn't say anything earlier because I wanted to test it twice. The second time was just now when I was in the bathroom." She smiled hugely. "I'm pregnant. I can tell."

Quinn briefly closed her eyes. "God. God, Honor sweetheart, that is so . . ." she framed Honor's face and kissed her deeply, carefully. Then she whispered, "I'm so happy."

"So am I." Honor grasped the bottom of Quinn's T-shirt and dragged it up her torso. "Get this off. I'm happy and really, really horny. God, I need you to finish what you started a minute ago."

Quinn glanced at the bed, then back at Honor, suddenly looking uncertain. "Maybe we should wait?"

Honor's eyebrows rose. "For what?"

"Just to be sure everything is okay."

"Baby, I'm pregnant, not sick." Honor popped the button on Quinn's shorts and unzipped her fly. She pushed the khakis down over Quinn's hips, catching her underwear along with them.

"Out of these."

Quinn stepped free. "I know you're not sick, but, you know, maybe we should take it easy."

"Okay. We can take it easy." Honor grabbed Quinn's hand and dragged her toward the bed. "We'll lie very, very still while you make me come until I scream."

Quinn groaned. "Easy will be hard. I'm already half ready to go, and you know when I get turned on I . . . forget myself."

"Stop talking. I want the other half of you going, too." Honor wrapped her arms around Quinn and fell backward onto the bed, yanking Quinn down with her.

"Jesus!" Quinn caught herself with both arms extended, her rigid body stretched over Honor's. Their breasts and bellies touched. "You said easy!"

"Lie down, baby, please." Honor let her fingers travel through the warm, damp curls at the base of Quinn's belly, and when she found her already hard and throbbing, she groaned. "Oh, look at you. You're a lot more than *half* ready." She grasped Quinn's clit delicately with two fingers, squeezing just hard enough to make Quinn groan. "Quinn?"

"Unnh," Quinn croaked, collapsing onto her side facing Honor. Her eyes didn't focus, and she blinked rapidly to clear her vision. "What?"

"You may be able to wait," she whispered, trapping Quinn's leg between her own and pressing herself hard against the taut muscle of Quinn's thigh. "But I can't."

Honor licked Quinn's neck and slowly slid her fingertips up and down the length of her clitoris. She was immediately rewarded with a quickening in Quinn's already rapid breathing and her own breath caught in her throat. "Touch me too. I love you so much, and I'm so excited right now."

Quinn managed to slide her fingers between Honor's legs without dislodging Honor's exquisite hold on her. Mirroring Honor's motion, she returned pleasure for pleasure. "God, you make me feel so good."

Honor closed her eyes and kissed her, tilting her hips to signal she wanted Quinn inside. When Quinn hesitated, she opened her eyes. "It's all right. I need you, baby. I really need you."

"Oh Jesus," Quinn groaned, easing into the welcoming depths. "You feel amazing. So hot . . . so tight."

Honor clenched inside and her breath fled on a soft sob. "I never thought . . . never thought I'd have a love like this."

"I'm here." Quinn pressed gently, spreading her fingers to fill her. "I'll always be right here."

Honor's pupils flickered and she trembled, working her hand faster between Quinn's legs. "We're going to have a baby."

"Yes." Quinn moaned. "And you're going to make me come."

"Me, too. Any second."

"Okay," Quinn gasped. She held her hips still and swept her thumb over Honor's clitoris. "You first."

Honor's vision clouded as a deep surge of exquisitely pleasurable pressure filled her belly, then she shook her head. "Uh-uh. You."

Honor rested her forehead on Quinn's, their lips barely touching. Quinn dipped her tongue slowly into Honor's mouth. Honor sucked the tip of it in and out, her fingers ceaselessly stroking. She teased and pushed and pulled and Quinn echoed each move.

"I'm about to come."

"Baby? Now?"

"With you. Want to . . . with you."

Circling firmer, faster. Stroking deeper.

"Ready?"

"Soon. Oh God, soon."

Legs twitching, hips pumping, bellies knotting. Sweat mingling on slick skin, flushed with love.

"Oh, I need to come," Quinn groaned. "I'm almost . . . so

close."

"Let me help you." Honor found Quinn's nipple and tugged. "Baby? Good, baby?"

"So good. Almost—" Quinn's voice broke on a moan.

"Feel me?" Honor clutched Quinn's shoulder. "Oh God, feel me coming? I can't wait . . ."

"Do it," Quinn gasped.

"Coming! Baby, I'm coming." Honor thrust against Quinn, climaxing around her fingers, arching to touch Quinn everywhere. Still coming, she cupped her palm over the fragile flesh that pulsed and beat beneath her fingers and stroked the slick ridge in tight, hard circles. "Oh baby, you're so beautiful. Come in my hand, baby, come in—"

Quinn's back bowed. "Coming. Coming so hard."

"Oh yes, baby, oh yes." Honor held her lover inside the protective circle of her arms, inside her body, inside her heart. "I love you."

Quinn caught her breath and kissed her. "I love you. Feel okay?"

"Better than okay. I'd forgotten how sexy I felt when I was pregnant with Arly."

"Yeah?" Quinn caressed her breast. "Good for me."

"Mmm, me too." Honor pressed her sensitive nipple against Quinn's hand. "Want to go back to the party?"

"What's my other choice?"

"Stay here and make love to me again."

"That's an easy one." Quinn pulled Honor on top of her. "So easy loving you."

Filled to Overflowing
Karin Kallmaker

"I think I've got a blister, but that hike was worth every step." Cat leaned into Jessica and closed her eyes.

"We actually stood on Lesbos. I'm blown away." Truthfully, Jessica's feet were throbbing too, but a soak in the ship's hot tub before the promised pastry extravaganza at dinner would make it all better. Some sips of nice ruby port Herine had given them as a bon voyage gift would also be dandy.

"I wonder how Kitty is—"

"Nuh uh." Jessica pointed a warning finger at Cat. "We are not grandmothers. Therefore do not mention the grandchildren. We agreed."

"I know. It's hard not to wonder, though." Cat straightened up, her gaze fixed on the ship as they rapidly approached it in the passenger sea shuttle.

"Every day for the last three years, nearly, we've been part of their lives. It's only right that Rob's parents get this week. I'm sure everyone is doing well." Jessica resolutely did not voice any of the many petty thoughts she'd found herself considering at the idea that Kitty and Hank might call someone else Meemaw.

Cat squeezed her hand sympathetically. "We were on Lesbos."

"Yeah. This was a great idea."

"And how sweet of the kids to give us this in anticipation of our thirtieth anniversary."

"I was just thinking about that bottle of port Herine gave us."

Cat made a little purring noise. "Now that sounds heavenly."

A half-hour later they shared sips from a paper cup after they'd eased their sore bodies into the hot tub. Jessica closed her eyes and let the bubbles at her feet soothe her.

"We were on Lesbos," Cat said again.

In her mind's eye Jessica could picture the time-worn temple and other landmarks of the island's history. Though there was nothing overtly welcoming to lesbian pilgrims, she had no trouble envisioning acolytes in gossamer gowns carrying laurel-scented water to wash the feet of the poetess.

Her reverie was interrupted by the noisy arrival of two young women she recalled from the tour. They plopped in the water and sighed with relief.

"I'm whacked," one said.

"Totally. I'm still disappointed, though. All that dust and ruin and that's what we're all called? Because somebody wrote some poems?"

The other woman fiddled with the spa jets. "Poetry is dead."

Jessica gave Cat a sidelong glance and then looked away with a deep breath.

"Actually . . ." Cat paused to casually sip again from the paper cup. "Poetry's immortality is what allowed our foremothers to adapt the island's name to describe a society of women for women. Had not Sappho's verse survived, there's no telling what we'd be calling ourselves, and we might still be searching for a collective identity that allows us to bond and struggle for the advancement of our rights. Without the word *lesbian* we'd not be on this cruise, or it would be called something else."

The two women were looking at Cat as if she were speaking Greek, which might not be far from the truth. Jessica wiggled her toes in the bubbles and watched her beloved through her lashes.

"If you think about it, the words we use to describe our gender describe not what we are, but what we are not. Fe*male*. Wo*man*. Not male, not man. In contrast, *lesbian* is an assertive word that states what we are in relation to ourselves and no other construct. Sappho's work, and that of her contemporaries that survives, indicates that her academy was likely only for women. Certainly, in our modern age, we want to romanticize this as an act of feminist rebellion when she was a member of a family that was overall persecuted into exile. She chose to eschew the power of men thereafter, probably because it was one of them that brought the wrath of the rulers down on her. Societies run by women *had* nearly disappeared by Sappho's time. We look back at her academy and see it as a continuation of the line of matriarchy. A bright moment in the long, dark fall of women from their place of respect as givers of life."

The poor young things were deer caught in Cat's headlights. That they were ignorant wasn't their fault—they obviously hadn't had Cat for a mother.

"I expected something more," one of them muttered. "That's all I meant. Everybody goes on and on about her poetry."

"So little has survived, it's true. But it has inspired our lives. 'For while I gazed, in transport tossed, my breath was gone, my voice was lost, my bosom glowed—'"

"Sounds like she'd had a very good time at some point," Jessica said drolly.

Cat splashed her with water. "Hush, you."

The other young thing cocked her head to one side. "That

sounds familiar. The voice lost and bosom glowed part."

"Those lines were used in one of the songs Marcy Chastain did Sunday night. She obviously found them inspirational."

"Marcy's so hot," the other said with a sigh.

They slipped into conversation between them after that, and Jessica stole a glance at Cat, who was basking in the hot water while a satisfied smile played around her lips. Leaning over, she said, "I'm going to tell Herine you used her honor's thesis to scold two baby dykes in the hot tub."

Cat snorted. "Think they want to hear about how much of dead poetry is in the song lyrics they enjoy every day?"

Given that the two girls were now making out, Jessica shook her head. "They have a few good ideas, though."

Cat gave her an amused glance. "I'm all relaxed now, what about you?"

Jessica drained the cup of the last of the port. "I'm dandy."

Cat was stripping off her swimsuit as Jessica sidled up behind her to nuzzle her neck.

"Wanna be a little late to dinner?"

"Is that what you have in mind?" Cat wrapped Jessica's arms around her waist. They still fit together exceedingly well.

"Port . . . warmth . . . thoughts of licentious acolytes and glowing bosoms."

"And you an old lady."

"Dirty old lady."

Cat turned in her arms and lifted her mouth. "Thank goodness, because I'm one too."

The days of romping across the bed in abandon had been over from the moment Jessica had first slipped a disk, and other delights were curtailed because Cat's knees protested forty-five degree or sharper angles. They'd always been *au naturel* when it came to lovemaking, but sensible crones, as Cat called them, made use of modern science.

They slid between the cool, dry sheets as Jessica retrieved the slender bottle of personal lubricant from the bedside table. "I love this stuff."

Cat grinned. "So do I. When I'm in the mood I do like to be wet."

"And when you're wet . . ." Jessica gently spread the lube over Cat with sure fingers. "You're in the mood."

"I should insure your hands."

Jessica kissed the lips curved in a fond smile, then pressed more firmly with her fingertips. Cat's response was quite gratifying. A few whispered words and they were moving together, sweet and easy, not forcing the tide, but letting it rise to wash over them. The motion of the ship lulled them into a soft pace, and kisses were long and languid until they were panting more than they were kissing.

"Touching you like this is my very favorite thing," Jessica whispered.

Cat's shivers were so familiar to Jessica. "I'm glad, because if it wasn't, you should have said so before this."

She pulled Jessica down for a wet, deep kiss, and delightful muscles gripped at Jessica's fingers until Cat gasped for breath and made that wonderful sound. Jessica went in a little deeper, drawing out every bit of response she could.

Cat relaxed and laughed. "God, that's fun."

"Well, if it wasn't you should have said so before this."

"Foo."

"Is that the best you can do? Got no brains at the moment?"

"Foo."

"There's supposed to be chocolate at dinner."

Cat abruptly wiggled and pushed until Jessica found herself on her back. "We'll get there, but there's something else I'd rather eat first."

Jessica grinned. "Do you have a reservation?"

Cat quickly slipped her hips between Jessica's thighs, then deftly tickled the sensitive patch along her underarm. While Jessica struggled and laughed, Cat continued her downward journey until the laughter faded and there was only the intimate exploration of Cat's tongue where Jessica never tired of feeling it. Today would be one of those times when she didn't climax, but the soothing, relaxing pleasure of Cat's attention left her feeling a glow that would last for hours. It was a different kind of sex for her and as meaningful to her at this age as other kinds had been when she was younger.

There was a moment she reached when it felt as if Cat had filled her to overflowing and she could take no more. It didn't matter that certain muscles no longer spasmed as easily, not when she reveled in the heat of Cat's mouth, feeling the wonder of it in all the places only Cat had ever reached. She laughed, low, and stopped Cat with a soft gesture. They smiled over the length of Jessica's body. "Better than a hot tub."

Two beautifully arched eyebrows disappeared under Cat's bangs. "I should hope so."

"Come here, you." Jessica opened her arms and they snuggled together under the covers.

"We smell a bit funky now."

"I like it."

Cat's breathing quickly steadied and Jessica decided another ten minutes wouldn't matter to whatever was served for dinner. Cat was warm and safe in her arms. Someone else might think that they'd sleep together later, so why give up a unique experience in favor of one she could have almost any time she wanted.

Then again, some people didn't get it.

Count Me In
Radclyffe

The hands were back. Sinewy tendons tented the tanned skin as tapered fingers deposited a stack of crisp $100 bills on the felt. Aidan scooped them up, counted the stack twice, and then folded them into the slot on the table that connected to the safe underneath. With practiced efficiency she slid $5,000 in chips back across the table. Only then did she look up and nod at the familiar face of the stranger. Eyes the color of winter stared back from beneath jet black brows. The surprisingly wide, full lips curled briefly into a smile. Then the flash of welcome faded, and all expression left her sharply sculpted face.

Aidan scanned the table as five different hands pushed chips into the betting circles. Some dropped them carelessly. Others aligned them precisely in the center. The new arrival let them fall from the funnel of her fingers one at a time with a *snick snick snick* that reminded Aidan of the sound of sex. She had watched those hands every night of the cruise—fingers flicking the edge of a card, caressing the faintly corrugated rim of a chip, tapping the felt delicately with a firm, round fingertip.

Aidan dealt the cards and her clit grew hard. Beautiful hands, strong and deliberate. She imagined them skimming her body with casual possessiveness, a fingernail grazing her nipple. She tilted her hips forward until her mons rested against the curved edge of the table. Her cunt throbbed.

Each of the five players took a card. Tonight, the stranger wore a fine-weave linen shirt with the cuffs rolled back to the middle of her toned forearms. Her wrists were small, her fingers long and fine-boned. Aidan imagined them folding inside of her, knuckles massaging the tender spot that forced her clit to grow and ache and finally burst apart.

Aidan dealt the cards.

Two players went over twenty-one. Losers. Two stood at sixteen and seventeen. Still in the game. The stranger took a card, her middle finger tapping twice with slow deliberation. Aidan felt the smooth, hard edge of a fingernail skim beneath the swollen flesh hooding her clit, and her thighs tightened. Aidan dealt the card.

The stranger slowly brushed her hand over the cards, standing firm at eighteen.

Aidan turned her cards over. A nine and a three. She dealt a card. Five. House rules—the dealer stands at seventeen.

"Dealer pays eighteen." Aidan raised her eyes to those of the winner. She could read nothing in the hawk-like gray eyes, but she caught the glimmer of another smile. She swept the chips of the losers from the table and paid the stranger.

Aidan dealt the cards, round after round, and the stranger won more than she lost. Chips clinked, bills whispered across the surface of felt, and stiff, crisp cards snapped between sure fingers. Hours passed and she watched those hands, feeling the press of smooth flesh in her hot, hungry places. By the time her shift ended, she was wet and swollen and mindless of anything other than the need to reach the locker room and fondle the hard length of her clitoris to a sharp, swift orgasm. She needed to come now, wouldn't be able to wait, just as she hadn't been able to wait the night before. And the night before that.

When she stepped back from the table, struggling to control her erratic breathing while the pit boss removed the safe deposit box from its rack beneath the table, she saw the gambler collect her chips to cash out.

By the time Aidan signed the receipt for the pit boss, the dark-haired stranger was gone. Intent on reaching the locker room, imagining the way her clit would pulse and dance between her fingers, Aidan twisted her way through the crowded aisles. Her skin was on fire, but even after she loosened her tie and unbuttoned her vest, she still couldn't catch her breath. Just as she yanked open the door marked *Staff Only*, a hand shot out to slam it closed. Aidan nearly moaned. She knew that hand, those fingers, those blunt, strong nails. Her clit jumped. *God, I can't last another minute!*

"I'd like to buy you a drink," the gambler said.

Aidan studied the shadowed hollows beneath the angled cheekbones, the strong jaw, the straight nose. Those winter eyes appraised her coolly in return. Aidan dealt the cards.

"I don't drink where I work."

"Where do you drink?"

"On the veranda outside my cabin."

"Alone?"

"Sometimes." Without the barrier of the table between them, Aidan saw that the gambler was younger than she had thought, although her eyes seemed those of someone much older. Aidan watched those eyes, waiting for a clue. Seconds passed. A minute. Then, for the length of a heartbeat, the stranger dropped her gaze. Aidan smiled and waited some more.

"What about tonight? Are you drinking alone?"

"Deck seven. Number seven twelve." Aidan turned the knob again, and this time the hand fell away, allowing the door to open. "Thirty minutes. And I'm drinking Stoli."

Inside the locker room, Aidan leaned against the door and contemplated the next thirty minutes. It would take all of a frantic minute to take the edge off the mind-scorching arousal that pounded away inside her, and then she'd be able to head back to her cabin for a shower without her clit screaming for relief. Or she could ignore the stiff little tyrant and wait to come later, when she'd need it so bad she'd be almost sick with excitement. Those were the times when she climaxed so hard she couldn't walk afterward. She thought about those hands squeezing her breasts, those fingers working inside of her, and she cupped her crotch. She bunched the material of her pants in her fist and ground the heel of her hand into her clit, moaning softly.

"Oh fuck," she gasped, easing her grip before she really let go. She walked on rubbery legs through the casino. Tonight, she'd shoot for blackjack.

The shower cleared her head a little but did nothing to ease the pounding in her permanently erect clit. Skipping underwear, she pulled on loose black cotton shorts and a white T-shirt. Her nipples stood out. So did her clit. She was wet again by the time the knock sounded on the door. When she opened it, the gambler stood in the hall with an unopened bottle of vodka in the crook of her arm. She'd changed into a sleeveless black shirt that buttoned up the front, khaki pants and deck shoes. An intricate black and green tattoo twined over the peak of her exposed shoulder and down her arm. It looked tribal or Celtic and definitely sexy. Traces of the design crawled up her neck.

"What's your name?" Aidan asked, still holding the door ajar.
"Fel."
"Short for anything?"
Fel shook her head. "Would you like a drink, Aidan?"
Aidan raised an eyebrow.

"Nametag."

"The bar's in the corner. Rocks with a twist of lime. I'll be on the veranda."

The sky was moonless and nearly black. The ship's lights glinted off the water and reflected on the undersurface of the clouds. Tomorrow they'd dock, Aidan would lay over for a few days, and then she'd fly back to their headquarters while awaiting the next cruise. She might meet a girl in Venice, or she might end up sleeping alone. But tonight, tonight she'd play the hand.

"Here you are," Fel said.

They drank in silence for a few minutes, then Aidan said, "You play cards for a living."

"I've had some luck at it." Fel set her glass beside her and pivoted so her back was against the railing. "I wasn't working this week, though. I'm on vacation."

"I know." Aidan drained her drink and put her glass next to Fel's. Then she stepped into the vee between Fel's thighs and settled her crotch against Fel's. "You weren't counting. I was watching."

"I know. I imagine the cameras were, too."

Aidan smiled and kissed the side of Fel's neck, feeling her shiver as she slid her tongue over and between her lips. Stroking leisurely inside Fel's mouth, Aidan pumped her crotch into Fel's. "I had to mention it to the pit boss. She said they'd check."

"I'm glad I passed inspection," Fel murmured, letting her head drop back, exposing her throat. "I would have been disappointed if I couldn't see you every night."

"Why did you wait all week to talk to me?" Aidan's kisses turned to slow, firm bites as she sucked the thick muscle in Fel's neck.

"Because watching you deal the cards made my cunt ache." Fel groaned as Aidan sucked harder. "And I like the way that feels."

"Is it aching now?"

"Oh, yes." Fel cupped Aidan's ass and thrust her hips as Aidan rocked faster in her crotch. "I'll come right here if you keep doing that."

Aidan stopped moving. "You'd better not." She opened the top button on Fel's shirt and reached in for her breast. She squeezed, rolling the nipple hard between her fingers. "Remember who's dealing."

"I know," Fel said breathlessly. "I won't come if you don't want me to."

"Get inside," Aidan said sharply, grabbing Fel's hand and dragging her back into the stateroom. "I need you naked. Now. Get your clothes off."

They stumbled in the half dark to the side of the bed, each of them flinging clothes in their wake. Aidan pushed Fel down on the bed and straddled her stomach. Heat flooded her cunt, inside and out. Fel's skin was flame. She grabbed Fel's hands and crushed them to her breasts, groaning at the first rush of pleasure.

"Finally. Jesus, I love your hands."

Fel arched beneath her, rubbing her stomach against Aidan's wet cunt while twisting her nipples and squeezing her breasts. Aidan whimpered and felt an orgasm gathering.

"Oh, not good. Not good."

"No?" Fel gasped. "It feels pretty fucking good to me. Come on me."

"Uh huh," Aidan panted. Grasping Fel's wrists, she jerked her hands away. "These are dangerous. Just watching you handle the cards all week got me so hot I had to jerk off every damn night."

Fel groaned. "Let me touch you. Let me make you come now."

"I don't think so." Aidan leaned across Fel's chest, yanked open the top drawer of the bedside table, and pulled out a wide silk tie. "Put your hands over your head."

Wordlessly, Fel complied. Aidan looped the silk around her

wrists and secured the length to a reading light that jutted from the wall. "Don't pull on this. Just lie still."

Fel's breasts, hard-tipped and gleaming in the lamplight, rose and fell rapidly. "Can I suck you off? Please?"

"Quiet." Aidan pushed down on the bed until she was lying between Fel's legs. She rested her cheek against Fel's quivering thigh and fingered the slick folds around her clit. When Fel jerked and moaned, she worked her fingers slowly inside her and then out again before lightly rimming her ass with a fingertip.

"Oh God oh God oh God," Fel muttered over and over.

"Your clit looks really hard, and I haven't even touched it yet," Aidan observed matter-of-factly as she rubbed her flushed cunt against the bed. The friction made her clit tingle and beat.

"You're driving me crazy," Fel panted. "My clit hurts. Please touch it."

"You probably need to come."

"So bad." Catching her lip between her teeth, Fel rocked her head back and forth.

"Don't pull on those restraints or I won't let you come."

"I won't I won't. Please. Do something to take the edge off. Do something. Please."

"Would you like to come now?" Her mouth was so close to Fel's clit, she could taste her tangy excitement. "Should I lick it?"

"Oh, yes, *yes*." Fel twisted the silk around her hands and pushed her hips forward, forcing her clit against Aidan's lips. "If you just suck me a little I'll come for you."

"You're right. You will. I can tell how bad you need it." Aidan leaned back on her heels and spread the puffy folds around Fel's clit with her thumb and finger. She was fully erect, her bruised looking clit wet and shiny. As she watched, it pulsed. She swept her forefinger rhythmically back and forth at the juncture of the thickened shaft and Fel's neatly trimmed mound, applying just enough pressure to pull the hood back, forcing her clit to stand up. "How's that feel?"

"Good, really good, don't stop." Fel bucked and groaned. "I'm ready. I'm ready." Her thighs trembled wildly. "Do me harder. Can you do me harder?" When Aidan milked her clit with a couple of strong strokes, her back bowed. "Oh yeah. Oh yeah, you're gonna make me come."

Aidan abandoned her clit, leaving it straining and twitching in the air.

"No!" Fel cried. "Jesus, I'm so close!"

"House rules," Aidan whispered, crawling up the bed and straddling Fel's shoulders. She grasped Fel's hair and pulled her head up into her crotch. Her breath came in short bursts and her stomach tensed so hard she nearly bent double. "All ties go to the dealer. Suck me. I want to come in your mouth."

Fel latched onto her clit like it was a lifeline, sucking it in hard, then shaking her head from side to side. It was like being jerked off by a suction pump. Aidan moaned and thrust her hips.

"Oh, you do that so nice. Feels so good." The tension in the pit of Aidan's stomach made it impossible to breathe and she gasped, struggling for air. "You like my clit? You like the way my hard clit feels in your mouth?"

"Mmm, mmm." Fel shook her head and sucked even harder.

Aidan leaned down and worked the knot loose, freeing Fel's hands. "Touch my breasts."

She rocked against Fel's mouth and stared wide-eyed at the hands fondling her breasts. Long fingers squeezing, blunt nails scraping her tense nipples. She held her cunt open with one hand so Fel could suck her deeper into her hot mouth. With the other, she caressed the hands caressing her. She started to unravel inside and her vision dimmed. "You're going to make me come. Is that what you want? Do you want me to come all over your face?"

"Yes," Fel shouted and then lunged for Aidan's clit again.

"You're doing it," Aidan cried as Fel's teeth scraped the hood back and her tongue whipped in hard circles. Clutching Fel's head, she jerked spastically. "Doing it! Damn you, you're making me . . . making me . . . unh . . . *fuck*, I'm coming."

Aidan fell forward, hands against the wall, and frantically rubbed her cunt over Fel's mouth. She could feel herself ejaculating, soaking Fel's face and neck. The pleasure was so intense she screamed.

Fel licked and sucked her gently until her clit softened and she rolled away.

"Oh, God," Aidan sighed. "I can't believe how hard you made me come."

"I've wanted to do that all week." Fel's voice was raspy and uneven.

Aidan rested her head in the palm of her hand and traced Fel's nipple with her fingertip. She flicked it rhythmically until Fel groaned. "I bet you want to come now, don't you?"

"Yes," Fel whispered, staring at Aidan imploringly. "Please don't stop."

Aidan sat up cross-legged and drew Fel's leg across her lap. Stroking the inside of Fel's thigh, the backs of her fingers lightly brushing Fel's swollen cunt, she said, "I want to watch you masturbate."

Instantly, Fel grasped her clitoris between her thumb and fingers. Her breath hissed out as she rolled it rhythmically.

"Go slow," Aidan instructed, tracing each of Fel's fingers with her own fingertip until she reached Fel's clit. Then she lightly caressed the part that appeared each time Fel stroked. "Show me how you tease yourself. That's it. Tease it."

"I'm close," Fel whispered plaintively, her fingers jerking unsteadily. "Can you help me? I need to come."

"I know," Aidan said gently. "I know you do. Would you like me to fuck you? Would that make you feel good?"

"Oh, yes," Fel sobbed, circling her clit faster.

Aidan stroked between her swollen lips, massaging the underside of her clitoris as Fel masturbated. "You're so hard. Can you slow down? If you don't slow down you're going to come."

"I can't I can't." Fel grabbed Aidan's wrist with her other hand and pushed her fingers inside her. She arched her back, her hand a frantic blur. "Oh God," she shouted. "Oh God, I'm coming."

Aidan bent down and licked Fel's fingers as come flooded between them. When Fel's cries subsided and her trembling fingers slowed, Aidan pushed them aside and sucked on Fel's still tense clit. Within seconds it hardened again and Fel grasped her head, thrusting against her mouth.

"I'm going to come again," Fel exclaimed urgently. "You're going to make me come again. Oh, oh here I come. Here I come!"

Fel writhed and moaned until Aidan finally released her. Then she cupped her cunt protectively and squeezed gently. Shivering, she held out her hand to Aidan, her fingers dripping.

"Look what you made me do. You made me come everywhere."

Smiling, Aidan slowly and carefully licked each finger clean. "You have beautiful hands. I'm going to come for a long time thinking about your hands."

"I'm not ready to stand firm just yet." Fel slid a finger into Aidan's mouth. "We've got all night, and I'm feeling lucky."

Cupping Fel's hand, Aidan drew it down her body and pressed it between her legs. Then Aidan dealt the cards.

Midnight Buffet
Karin Kallmaker

"That was certainly interesting." I wondered if I looked as feverish as I felt.

Ashley and Odette stood on either side of me, both exuding so much heat that I felt like a Tart they wanted to go Pop.

"It certainly was." Ashley had a purr to her voice. "I've never seen a woman gush like that before."

Odette, with a pitying tone said, "You haven't? Maybe someday it won't have to be in a video."

Point to Odette.

Turning toward the Lido Apollo restaurant I said, "I didn't know some of the things I saw." *Pink Pleasures* had featured several scenes that I was still reeling over. I wasn't sure how I felt about power play. I liked it rough sometimes, but I also liked it soft. Sometimes I liked to be told what to do, and sometimes I liked to tell. The idea of being only one way, all the time, just wasn't what I was all about.

I could feel the arch looks the other two were giving each other behind my back. At one point during the video I'd considered that a three-way could be a lot of fun. Certainly it had looked pleasing for the woman in the middle. I'd had my share of fun but never tried that, and sometimes it really appealed to me.

The notion had begun this morning during our tour of Lesbos. The three of us had outdistanced the rest of our group; we were two decades younger than most of the others. We'd explored the museum and temple at our own pace, making ribald remarks and flirting like mad. It had taken me a while to realize they were both flirting with me and not so much with each other. Okay, I have an ego, and it felt very nice to have two attractive, but very different, women interested in me.

At one point, after Ashley said she'd heard rumors of a real sex show during one of the late night videos, I'd suggested that we all watch the porn video tonight. With that kind of stimulation, I had imagined myself with a passport to the Land of Three-way by midnight. However, as the day had gone by, Odette and Ashley had become increasing hostile to each other.

Machismo in a woman was disappointing. My last two girlfriends had both made me feel clueless and in need of their guidance. Even when I was showing them how to wire their home theaters or set up a wireless LAN—things I got paid to do—they had to tell me how to do it better, according to them. The next time I got involved with a woman it would be because she liked and cared about the things that interested me as well. Someone who didn't make me feel silly for watching musicals and chick flicks. Someone who could cry over a book or coo over a cute puppy.

So normally the competitive attitudes Odette and Ashley were putting on would have had me running the other way from both of them. A holiday fling wasn't about puppies and tomorrow, I reminded myself. After that video it would be a damned shame if I went to bed by myself tonight. It seemed increasingly clear that I couldn't have both of them, though, but I had no idea how to pick.

"What's going on in here?" Odette opened the restaurant door for me nanoseconds before Ashley could do so.

"Dessert Extravaganza."

"Getting your strength up for anything in particular?" Ashley gave me a sidelong glance as she handed me a plate and a wrapped roll of cutlery.

"I'm just here for the calories. Oh look, aren't they cute!" I peered closely at the tiny penguins and igloos in handcrafted marzipan. The lavish spread of desserts—cream cakes, éclairs, brownies, pralines, pirouettes, baklava, on and on—included tableaus of dolphins, whales, fairies and monsters.

Ashley, in front of me in line, said, "Don't have any of the brownies, Hallie. I'm not sure how something can look so much like chocolate and be flavorless."

I shrugged. "I've yet to have a chocolate dessert I really liked on this trip, but the fruit tarts are fantastic."

Odette put her hand on my arm to get my attention. "Look, behind the centerpiece. It's a pastry pride parade!"

"Oh, how *cute*," we said in unison.

Ashley said, "I really don't like marzipan."

We carried our laden plates out to the pool deck where dancing under the moonlight was underway to bouncy party music blaring from the huge speakers. Odette found us a table after we successfully avoided joining the conga line.

I puckered in response to the first bite of lemon bar. "Oh, that's sour. And good."

"The kiwi strawberry soufflé is great, too." Odette savored a spoonful of her dessert.

"Try some of the sorbet, Hallie." Ashley offered a spoonful and I accepted. Point to Ashley.

"Very nice. Coconut and rum."

Odette offered to get us all some water and I watched her

walk away. Where Ashley was firm and sculpted, Odette was a little bit more round, softer. She had a beautifully shaped head, highlighted by tightly locked dreads, and her smile was the easiest thing about her. Ashley's long blond hair had been pulled out the back of her hat on the tour, with a jaunty flare I liked. Now it was loose around her shoulders. They were both in tailored shorts and simple tank tops tonight, as were about half the women on board. I had chosen a skirt for the evening, mostly because I was running out of clean shorts, and paired it with a spaghetti-strapped camisole. Okay, and a pair of shoes that really weren't meant for much walking.

Maybe it was the sugar and the video, or the rum and Cokes we decided we all needed, but it didn't seem like all that much later that I was dancing to "We are Family" sandwiched between the two of them. I'm not sure which one of them decided to drizzle some of the melted sorbet on my shoulders, but it was mind-altering when they both licked it off of me.

Our hips were moving in a continuous rolling rhythm, reminding me of the toy-packing scenes in the video we'd watched. I reached a point of not caring how they felt about each other. I was on holiday, a long way from my job and limited dating pool. I wanted to invite them both to any private place we could find—my roommate had been assigned by the tour company and was apparently a nun—and let them do just about anything they wanted to me.

I leaned into Odette behind me and her hands slipped around my waist. Ashley's response was to grind just a little harder into me from the front and to continue licking my shoulder and neck even though the sorbet was long gone.

Finally, I just said it. "You aren't going to make me choose between you, are you?"

Odette whispered in one ear, "I'd really like to have you all to myself."

Ashley whispered in the other, "I have plenty of things

planned for you—you won't need anyone else."

I wanted to say that it wasn't about need, it was about want. They both wanted me, so why couldn't I be selfish and have them both? My inner slut was really pouting about having to give up either. I was all worked up into a three-way fantasy, and they were very ungallantly not playing along.

Leaving the dancing behind, I sauntered back into the restaurant with the two of them trailing along behind me. I treated myself to one of the tiny ice cream cones and treated them to watching me lick it. They both promptly got cones and demonstrated their prowess. It was very silly. More slut pouting.

We were lingering near the doorway, ostensibly watching the dancing while eyeing each other, when a raised voice at the nearest table drew our attention. A young woman had paused to address a much older woman who could only be, based on many similar features, her mother. Her words confirmed it.

"Hi, Mom." She was speaking just loudly enough that it was impossible not to eavesdrop. "You'll never guess what I saw in the Lost and Found when I was looking for my sweater."

The older redhead gave her daughter a suspicious look. "Whatever it is, you're very pleased with yourself."

The younger woman unfurled a black garment—a little black dress. "This turned up on the pool deck."

The mother blushed bright red, and so fast it was almost frightening. The silver-haired woman sitting across the table from her burst into laughter.

The younger woman, with a knowing smirk, draped the dress around her mother's shoulders. She gave the other woman a broad grin. "Candace?"

The silver-haired woman, still chuckling, said, "Yeah?"

"Way to go!"

The mother dropped her head into her hands as Candace and her daughter high-fived. I was grinning from ear-to-ear.

The daughter strutted off and Candace reached across the

table to pat the redhead's hand comfortingly. "It's okay, honey. She's only going to tease you about it for the next ten years."

In a low voice, Ashley said, "Well, that puts a person off their food, doesn't it?"

Puzzled, I asked, "What?"

"Well." She gave a meaningful glance at the twosome, still holding hands. "They're a little past it. It's not really a pretty picture to contemplate."

I glanced at the couple again, and all I saw was stars in their eyes and affectionate curves in their smiles.

Before I could say anything, however, Odette said, "Quite the contrary. I am really hoping to grow up and be as lucky as they are. Finding any kind of romance at any age is hard enough. I want to be one of them in another twenty years."

"Yeah," I agreed. "What Odette said."

And then I thought, "So much for the three-way."

Odette lived almost five hundred miles away from me, and the drive from Eugene to Sacramento could be perilous in winter and miserably hot in summer. This wasn't about tomorrow, I thought as we kissed our way to her cabin. But at least she believed that romance wasn't dead. There were possibilities with Odette, while a dead end had been all that Ashley had offered. I wanted some good sex, but I also wanted possibilities if I could have them; so sue me.

"My roommate is a heavy metal groupie, and I've had the cabin to myself all week," Odette explained as she unlocked the door.

"I need to use the restroom," I admitted. Odette's cabin was an exact replica of mine, and I knew how to get inside the little bathroom and close the door without tripping over the raised sill or bonking myself in the head with the door as I freed it from its safety latch.

"I'll be right out here," she said as I closed the door and locked it.

After taking care of my urgent needs, I studied Odette's toiletries. She used the same moisturizer I did, and I was relieved to spy some toothpaste, cap firmly on. I made sure it was cinched down just as much after I squeezed some onto my finger and swished it around my mouth.

There was rustling going on out in the cabin. Given the various comments made during the video, and the uninhibited body language while they were dancing, I was pretty sure what Odette was arranging. I shinnied out of my skirt, panties and bra, leaving on only my camisole, which was decidedly not long enough to preserve any modesty. I looked ready for sin, and I hoped Odette found that sexy.

Trying to look anything but shy, I left the bathroom. Odette was closing the small closet door.

She looked at me over her shoulder. "Well, don't you look edible."

Leaving the bathroom light on behind me, I walked toward the bed that had been turned down in my absence. "I hope you think so."

I was about to turn around when Odette stepped up behind me. Strong arms wrapped firmly around my waist and warm lips nuzzled at my neck.

"I noticed, during the video, that you were breathing hard a couple of times."

"So were you," I said.

Odette's fingers found my nipples through the cami and she squeezed them firmly, making me shiver further into her embrace. "Did you like the scene where that cute girly-girl was pounced on by her lover?"

"Mmm, yes I did."

Odette pushed me forward onto my hands so I was bent over the bed. The sound of her zipper sent a hard chill up my spine.

"You're ready, aren't you?"

For an answer I reached between my legs and encountered her hand wrapped around a good-sized cock. "I'm very ready for this."

"Then why don't you put my cock inside you, hmm?"

She had lubed it heavily, and it was slick in my hand. I angled my hips, slid my feet a little farther apart and felt the head slip just inside me. And it felt *really* good.

"Am I the girly-girl and you're the big, bad girl who's gonna fuck my brains out?"

Odette pushed into me very, very slowly. "That's right, baby. I have been thinking about doing this to you all day. And that movie . . ." She groaned as I pushed back to take her more quickly.

"That movie made you want to bend me over, didn't it?"

"Got that right." She pulled out and this time shoved in so quickly I gasped. "I'm not usually so freaking hot for it, but once I started thinking about looking at the gorgeous ass of yours, feeling these—" She reached under me to squeeze my breasts, hard. "I wanted to see how naughty you could get."

"God, that feels good." I braced myself for her increasing pace while moments from the video flitted through my mind. "I feel like a very naughty girl tonight."

"Yes, you do." She punctuated each word with a sharp thrust of her cock. "You wanted to do it with both of us, didn't you?"

"Yes," I admitted through gritted teeth. "I've never done that and—damn! Don't stop. I just wanted to get fucked tonight."

She leaned hard into me, pushing my shoulders down into the bed. We'd found a rhythm and the position brought sensitive, responsive parts of me into constant contact with the bulk of her cock. "As long as we're clear about that. You're going to get fucked."

"Ye-es, yes," I moaned. The backs of my thighs were starting to shiver and my clit ached for attention in that way that made the inside of my cunt all the more wet and open.

There were several minutes where I'm not sure I said anything coherent, and her earthy, sweaty words boiled past my ears, making me hotter and hotter. She was suggesting that I play a starring role in every scene in the video we watched when I pushed up onto my hands, helplessly gripping her cock with muscles I wasn't sure I'd ever used before. Of course I had, I thought a bit later, after I had collapsed on the bed with her on top of me. It had just been a while.

For the rest of the night we used the video as fodder for our fantasies. On top of me, on top of her, me on the floor, her tied to the chair, fucking with our hands and mouths—I was on fire and so was she. The lack of a porthole helped us lose track of time, but I wouldn't have been surprised to learn it was approaching dawn as she sprawled back across the damp, sticky bed while I licked and played between her legs.

"I love how red you are, and how tight your lips are." I parted her cunt again with my tongue. "And I love that you like getting your brains fucked out, too."

She laughed softly and cupped my head. "I don't think I can come again, but your tongue feels incredible."

"Is that a challenge?"

She moaned as I pushed my tongue inside her. "We can do this again tomorrow night. Even tomorrow afternoon, you know."

I savored the delicious taste and texture of her cunt. I wanted to go on doing that for a long while. After kissing her clit, I raised my head to say, "Pity we didn't run into each other earlier in the week."

"There's quite a buffet of women on board—we might not have noticed each other then."

"I'd have been a fool to have overlooked you."

"I quite agree." Her mouth curved in that easy smile of hers.

"I still wish we had more time."

The hand on the side of my head pulled me back down to what I'd been doing. "It's only about five hundred miles from Eugene to Sacra—fuck, yes, like that."

She was thick and wet against my lips, and remained that way for the next few minutes. When we finally fell into exhausted sleep my last thought was about the possibilities.

Points of Departure
Karin Kallmaker

"Smile, ladies!"

From my comfortable seat on one of the sofas lining the Piazza Casanova, I enjoyed the sight of yet another couple having their formal photograph taken. The dark-haired woman, six feet if she was an inch, was truly beautiful, and when she smiled it was hard not to believe she wasn't in films. Her arms were nestled around a curvy gal with an infectious smile. A hand casually cupped around a hip illuminated their intimacy.

They finished their time with the camera. The beauty said to the next couple waiting their turn, "That's the first time we've taken a formal portrait."

"It's been ages since we had one done." A much older dyke with curly silver hair had, like me, been waiting for a while for her partner to appear. Her partner, cute and bubbly, had arrived in a bustle and rush, complaining of zipper woes. I had smiled to myself as a kiss along the neckline had been stolen while the troublesome zipper was adjusted. The bubbly woman's reaction to the kiss had been delightful to watch.

She was engrossed now, looking at something on the curvy gal's finger. There was a hint of tears, ripples of laughter, then the photographer cleared his throat and the couples separated. The younger pair headed for the champagne reception and the older twosome took their place in front of the camera.

I wondered if my dear girl was having trouble with her zipper or something, because she was running later than her estimate. She'd said she had something special planned for our formal portrait and she didn't want me to see it beforehand.

As I watched the ebb and flow of women, I let a short film play out in my mind's eye. I was helping my girl dress, but not being very successful. The zipper just wouldn't go up as my mouth nuzzled the nape of her neck. Bad zipper, horrible zipper. My tongue traced its way down her spine until I buried my lips in the heat at the small of her back. The low zipper allowed the dress to curve around the alluring heart-shape of her ass. Rising, I snuggled my front to her back, pushing the dress forward so I could wrap her close. Years of lovemaking told me that the sudden baring of her breasts would harden her nipples. I didn't need to touch them to know that for certain. Not touching them would make her even crazier. I could bend her forward slightly and let the dress fall all the way to the ground. She was naked against me and starting to pant.

The wonderful rise of her moan at my touch was broken by someone close calling out, "Hey, Hana!" I reluctantly opened my eyes and was glad I had. The voluptuous Asian woman in a long, glittering gown was well worth the effort.

A leather-clad butch swung around to face her, looking annoyed.

"I have your T-shirt," the Asian woman said. She handed the butch a folded white bundle. "I even had it laundered."

"Why thanks," the butch said with what I thought was

feigned nonchalance.

"See ya," was the only response she got, and in a glittery glow, the Asian woman headed in the direction of the Medusa. Slinky was far too mild a word to describe her walk.

I looked back at the butch just in time to catch her smelling the shirt. Cast aside like a dried-up piece of fruit, I wagered. Crossing between us was a picture of happiness, though, and I followed their progress across the Piazza as the redhead said firmly, "I'm not getting off this ship until we go to the Internet library and book something that will let us be together again sometime next month."

"Have I told you that one of your attractive features is that you know what you want?" Her lover looked at her with such fondness that I was reminded of my girl when she saw that I'd made her breakfast in bed.

Breakfast in bed . . . the last time was a wonderful memory. I'd brought in a tray with her favorite tea, buttered crumpets and a special surprise she felt the moment I slid back into bed next to her. I loved her body sleep-soft and melted. She was pliable and easily aroused when she'd had enough sleep. Her mouth opened to me, her body opened to me, and we rose and fell together until, in her abandon, she'd rolled atop me, fully awake and ready to ride me into sunset.

Eventually we had the breakfast.

An elegant couple arrived in my line of sight, walking arm in arm toward the dining room. It would take most observers a little while to figure out why they moved so sinuously together, as if they were merged at their hips and arms. The smaller woman was a subtle guide, navigating the scattered crowd with ease that kept her partner's blindness from being apparent. Their animated conversation was interrupted when the blind woman pulled her partner to her for a kiss that ought to have set off the sprinkler system.

"Let's do it, Gab." A blushing woman in a pretty cocktail

dress pointed out the photographer. Leaning into her girlfriend's side, she added, "We won't be able to find a photographer at home who'd do a picture like that for two women." Gab, it seemed was amenable, and they joined the short queue on the other side of the piazza.

The photographer continued to exhort smiles from the couples and I drifted again, wondering where my darling girl was. All around me were loving, happy women, holding hands, all of them looking at the future with shared visions. I wanted my beloved at my side, too. We were going to dance all night and then I was going to exhaust her by morning.

We loved dancing together. We'd met at a local dyke dance, both surprised to find a jive partner who could keep up. The later it got, the more the lights dimmed and the more she melted into my arms.

I was enthralled by her shoulders. We danced slower and slower until her hands were down the back of my trousers and my lips and tongue were exploring the slope and breadth of her shoulders. I had never recovered from that night. Before her, I knew what sex was all about. One night with her and I knew what love was all about.

There seemed to be nothing but couples deeply in love everywhere I looked. If love could float a boat, we'd all be dancing in the stars tonight. Just across the way one woman touched another's belly—the gesture was unmistakable. Their future was taking on a new life.

I thought about the redhead wanting to plan her next date with a new love. I wanted to plan my next date with the love I had. I wanted to know when I'd see her smile and when I'd breathe in her perfume. I wanted to plan to spend the holidays in New Zealand, spring in France, next summer in Victoria, and after that I wanted to know the shape of every day, the time of our next kiss, how many times I could count on seeing her smile.

I was desperately, completely in love, and the future was all I wanted.

"Smile, ladies!"

The photographer shook me again out of my reverie. My gaze focused on the luscious curves of a lissome brunette leaning against the bar. Since she was facing away from me, I admired the playful dark curls that cascaded down her bare back and acknowledged that the slinky blue silk dress was extremely flattering to her fair skin.

The sheer stockings and skimpy high heels awakened even more lustful feelings, and I imagined her on her back, under me, those long legs wrapped around my hips. I left my perch to see if her perfume was as delicious as that dream of a dress.

Moving in behind her, I whispered, "Can I buy you a drink?" just before I put my hand on her waist.

"I've been waiting forever for my lover to notice I'm here, so yes." She turned and those bright blue eyes gave me that look, the one that had been instantly fatal to my heart. "Yes, you may buy me a drink."

The future was all that I wanted. Tonight, tomorrow, next week . . . next year. After a hard swallow, I said, "You look fantastic. That dress is a crime."

"I thought you'd like it." She smoothed the midsection with one hand. "I'm afraid I've put on a few pounds this week, what with the good food and lazy days."

"Don't worry about it, darling." I loved our past, but all that mattered was the future. "They'll come off after you start the chemo on Monday."

I folded her to me, holding my future in my arms.

Dream Date
Radclyffe

Kay wasn't certain she was really the diamond drop-earring kind of girl. She wouldn't even have *had* diamond earrings if her great-grandmother hadn't left them to her, and in the five years that she'd had them tucked away in her jewelry box, she'd never worn them. They weren't overly large or blatantly ostentatious, but they *were* bright and bold and, . . . okay, a teeny bit showy. In short, they just weren't her. She wore small gold posts. Unassuming and reserved. Like her.

Well, she thought, *today was a day of firsts, so I guess for tonight at least, the diamonds are me.*

Brushing her thick, curly blond hair back from her shoulders, she shook her head and watched the diamonds sparkle in the mirror over the dresser. She had spent the afternoon in the salon, having a massage and a facial and getting her hair done. That wasn't something she ordinarily did, not just because it strained her teacher's salary, but because she didn't pamper herself.

Tonight, for a few hours, that was going to change. Tonight, the last night of the cruise, she was going to finish up an unusual day with a night like none she'd ever known. Taking in her strapless red dress with the plunging neckline and cutaway hem that left most of one thigh bare, she laughed, knowing that none of her friends back home would recognize her. And that was part of the fun—she had come on the cruise alone so that she could do what she wanted and not have to hear anyone say, "Oh Kay, that's so unlike you!"

She was going to the formal dance, and she was going to look the way and dress the way and act the way she had always dreamed. The only other thing she needed to make the evening complete should be arriving any moment.

At precisely seven thirty p.m., a knock sounded on her cabin door. For one second, Kay had a moment of sheer panic. What had she done? This was so absolutely not her!

"And that's the point," she whispered as she pulled open the door and smiled brightly. "Hi. I'm Kay."

Her dream date smiled back.

"Hi, Kay. I'm Ryan."

I don't care who you are, you're perfect. And of course, she was, because Kay had chosen her based upon her photograph and date profile on the escort Web page. "5 feet 8 inches and 140 pounds of blue-eyed, black-haired sex on the prowl. A butch for all seasons—tops with ease, bottoms with expertise." Tonight, she looked even more edgy and exciting than her picture or the glimpse Kay had caught of her, quite by accident, earlier in the week. Lean-hipped and lithe, her plain-fronted tuxedo shirt revealed the barest curve of small breasts beneath the starched fabric. Unable to resist, Kay glanced down and thought, but she couldn't be sure, that she saw a slight swelling to the left of the fly in Ryan's silk tuxedo pants. Just thinking about what might be tucked away in there made her pussy clench.

"I'm sorry," Kay said somewhat breathlessly, "I'm staring,

aren't I?"

"That's all right," Ryan said, grinning. "So am I. You look fantastic."

Kay stepped back. "Come in for a minute. Is that all right?"

Ryan stepped inside. "Anything you want is all right. Tonight, the only thing I want is to please you."

Kay wasn't sure how Ryan managed it, but she sounded sincere. Practice, she guessed. It didn't matter. She was getting wetter by the second.

"Would you like a glass of champagne? The dance doesn't start for at least an hour and I'm a little nervous. Maybe if we—"

Ryan gently lifted aside Kay's hair and kissed her softly on the neck, just below the angle of her jaw. Her lips were warm and very soft.

"You have nothing to be nervous about." Ryan framed her face and kissed her lips, slowly and carefully. "Anything you want. Anything at all."

Weak-kneed, Kay steadied herself with both hands on Ryan's shoulders. Her breasts felt heavy and she knew her nipples were hard and pushing out against her dress. She didn't usually get so excited so quickly. Maybe knowing that whatever she did or said was all right, no matter how *unlike* her, had unleashed something in her she hadn't even known she wanted. "Can I ask you questions?"

"Of course." Ryan slid her arm around Kay's waist and directed her toward the sofa in the sitting area. A champagne bottle sat in a wine cooler on a small low table. "Sit down while I pour."

Kay studied Ryan again as she popped the champagne and filled two flutes. She was clear-eyed and confident, moving with easy grace. Her hands were long-fingered and slender. And as she watched Ryan bend to pour the champagne, she saw that her first impression had been correct. A sizable cock nestled against the inside of her left thigh.

"Isn't it uncomfortable like that . . . for hours?"

Ryan followed Kay's gaze. "Not with the right fit. It can get a little intense when I'm excited, but that's natural."

Kay took the glass Ryan held out, feeling her face flame. "I have absolutely no idea where that came from. I'm so sorry."

"There's no need to be." Ryan sat down next to her, leaving her champagne glass on the table. "If it's not what you want—"

"It is," Kay said quickly, not caring if she sounded a little desperate. She felt a little desperate. Desperate and breathless and terribly terribly terribly horny. She took a generous swallow of the champagne. "Sometime tonight I want to touch it."

Ryan drew a sharp breath, and when she spoke, her voice was deeper. "I'd like that." She leaned closer and kissed Kay's neck again, then cupped Kay's face and kissed her mouth.

She was a wonderful kisser, softly teasing and stroking with her tongue as she caressed Kay's neck and shoulders with both hands. She let the diamonds at Kay's ears play across her fingertips as she kissed along her jaw, but she didn't touch Kay's breasts. And after a few minutes of Ryan's mouth on her skin, Kay ached to have her nipples massaged. She was getting too excited too fast and she finally pulled away. Ryan was breathing quickly, too. Realizing that Ryan enjoyed what they were doing made Kay even more excited.

"You're really not pretending, are you?" Kay whispered.

"You're very beautiful. Very sweet." Ryan traced a fingertip over Kay's chin, then down the center of her throat. "Feeling your excitement excites me. Thinking about you touching my cock makes me hard and wet."

"Are you? Now?"

"Yes."

"I don't think I'd better kiss you anymore right now," Kay said, moving away but keeping her hand on Ryan's arm. "All I can think about is going to bed, and I spent all day getting ready for tonight."

"There are a lot of pleasurable things we can do outside of bed." Ryan retrieved her champagne glass and emptied it in several long swallows. Then she stood and held out her hand. "You look too beautiful not to show off. Let's go dancing."

For one second, Kay contemplated blowing off the dance. She wanted to kiss Ryan again. She wanted Ryan to play with her breasts. She wanted to caress the hardness in Ryan's pants and make Ryan's breathing get harsh again. "I don't know how long I can wait. I don't think I've ever been so unspeakably aroused in my life, and we've only kissed."

"Whatever you need," Ryan whispered, kissing her, "whatever you want."

"Oh God. We'd better leave now."

Kay took Ryan's hand as they left the cabin and walked down the hall. They rode the elevators to the main deck and followed the sound of music and laughter. The night was dark but the ship was blazing with light, and Kay imagined it must look like a roaring inferno from a distance. She certainly felt like one.

"Did you want to ask me something else?" Ryan said, releasing Kay's hand and putting her arm around Kay's shoulders.

Kay circled Ryan's waist and leaned against her. "It might be personal."

"Whatever you want, remember?"

"I saw you Sunday night in the theater. You were with a woman, a really beautiful blonde in a short leather skirt."

"Yes."

"Was she a date?"

Ryan guided Kay to a shadowed area along the railing. "You're my only date this week."

"I watched her come with your cock inside her."

Ryan's arm tightened around Kay. Her voice sounded tighter too. "Yes."

"It was very sexy. When I got back to my room I thought about it and masturbated. I came three times."

"Kay," Ryan groaned.

"Can I touch your cock now?"

"Yes."

When Ryan reached for her fly, Kay stopped her. "I want to take it out while you kiss me again."

Ryan leaned against the railing and pulled Kay close, kissing her more intently than before. Kay felt the hardness between Ryan's legs pressing against her belly and she rubbed herself against the prominence, clutching Ryan's hips. With her mouth against Ryan's, sucking her tongue and her lips, she slid Ryan's zipper down and worked her hand inside the opening. When her fingers closed 'round something full and firm, she gasped.

"Oh my God. It's warm. It feels . . . so soft."

"It's cyberskin," Ryan murmured, her fingers sifting through Kay's hair. She nipped at Kay's earlobe and ran her tongue along the rim of Kay's ear. "Do you like it?"

"Yes," Kay said, tightening her fist and massaging the bulge. Ryan lurched against her and groaned. "You can feel that?"

"Oh yeah," Ryan said shakily. "You're jerking off my clit when you do that."

"I want to see it."

"Take it out."

Kay angled her body against Ryan's so they faced the ocean and no one could see what she was doing. She worked the cock out through the opening in Ryan's pants. It looked long and pale in the moonlight, and when she closed her fingers around it, just the head was exposed. She tried sliding her hand up and down its length, and when she did, Ryan's hips lifted and fell. "Does that feel nice?"

"Very nice."

"Will you come?"

"Is that what you want?" Ryan's chest heaved and she grabbed the rail. "Kay? You have to tell me what you want."

"Kiss me."

Ryan's mouth was insistent, her kisses urgent and harsh. The harder Kay pulled on Ryan's cock, the deeper Ryan plunged her tongue into Kay's mouth. She loved the grunting sound Ryan made deep in her chest each time she stroked her. She'd never felt so powerful.

"Tell me how to make you come," Kay demanded, watching Ryan's face.

"Faster." Ryan's eyes were beseeching. "Faster."

When Kay wrapped both hands around the cock and worked it rapidly up and down in Ryan's crotch, Ryan's knees buckled and she sagged.

"I'm going to come," Ryan said through gritted teeth. She grabbed Kay's waist for balance. "Do you want me to? Can I? Tell me what you want."

"I want to know how it feels," Kay whispered, "when I do this to your cock."

Ryan groaned and closed her eyes briefly. "Like there's a fireball in my belly . . . getting ready to . . . explode." Ryan stiffened and stared down at Kay hammering her cock. "Oh fuck . . . I'm going to come. Right. Now."

"You're so sexy." Kay kept up the motion as Ryan thrust into Kay's hands, pumping her hips in short, hard jerks. Even when Ryan's fingers dug painfully into her waist, she didn't stop. Not until Ryan groaned and went limp against the railing. "So sexy when you come."

"Oh baby," Ryan sighed. "You're good at that."

Kay smiled. "Really? I've never done it before." She leaned against the front of Ryan's body, bending Ryan's cock so it nestled against her stomach. "I wish I could put it inside me right now. I'm so wet from feeling you come I know I'd come in a second."

"We can go back to your room." Ryan cupped Kay's breast and thumbed her hard nipple. "I'd love to fuck you."

"Was that your girlfriend? The one who came in your lap in

the theater?" Kay found Ryan's other hand and put it on her breast, catching her lip between her teeth as Ryan squeezed both nipples simultaneously.

"My mistress."

"Oh." Kay reached down between them and tucked Ryan's cock back into her pants. Then she carefully settled it against Ryan's thigh again. "Is that good there?"

"Perfect."

Kay zipped the fly and patted Ryan's cock gently, thinking about how the blonde had touched her own clit when Ryan was inside her. "She doesn't mind when women make you come? She doesn't get jealous when you fuck other women?"

"No."

"Will you tell her that I made you come standing out here where anyone could have seen us?" Kay swayed, rubbing her pussy back and forth against the prominence in Ryan's pants. Her clit jumped in time to the pull of Ryan's fingers on her nipples.

"Do you want me to tell her what you did?" Ryan rolled Kay's nipples harder. "That you played with my cock until my clit was so hard I came in your hands?"

"Uh huh." Kate nodded and covered Ryan's hands with hers. "Feels so good."

"If I tell her what you did, she'll get wet and she'll want to come."

"What will she do?" Kay felt almost drunk on sensation. Her pussy swelled and tightened.

"She'll make me kneel on the floor between her legs while she plays with her clit. When I tell her you jerked me off on deck, she'll order me to kiss her clit."

Kay shivered. "Will her clit be very hard?"

"Very big and very very hard." Ryan bit down gently on the side of Kay's neck. "When I tell her that I asked you for permission to come, she'll let me lick her cunt. Then she'll come in my mouth."

"She's beautiful when she comes." Kay's eyes slid closed as the sharp pleasure in her breasts spread to her belly and focused in her clit. "After I watched her with you that night, I kept seeing her face and coming and coming."

"Would you like to watch again?" Ryan breathed the words into Kay's ear.

"Oh yes." Kay dropped her head on Ryan's shoulder. "I want to come so hard right now."

"Anything you want."

"I want you to put your cock in me."

Ryan nuzzled Kay's neck. "Do you want to go back to your cabin?"

"I want to dance with you and feel your cock rubbing against me and know that I'm going to come on it later." She shuddered and pulled Ryan's hands off her breasts. "I'm going to need it so bad by then."

Ryan linked fingers with her. "Dance with me."

Kay followed her into the huge ballroom where a sea of women in tuxedos and gowns and leather and lace danced and caressed and celebrated. Ryan danced like she kissed, sensuously and totally in tune with Kay's body. Kay rested her cheek against Ryan's shoulder and floated, feeling her body ripen as the hours passed and Ryan continually caressed her shoulders, her back, her bare thigh. Her breasts ached against Ryan's chest. Ryan's hard cock brushed rhythmically against her mons, ever so lightly tapping her clitoris, taking her just to the edge of release and leaving her aching inside.

"I've never felt so wonderful in my life," Kay murmured as the last song finished. "Thank you."

"You don't need to thank me. I'm having a great time. You feel fantastic in my arms."

Kate tilted her head back, knowing her eyes must look heavy with sex. "I want you to have a good time, too. I know it's work—"

Ryan touched her finger to Kay's lips. "This is not work."

"Will you . . . will you make love to me now? I'm past needing you to make me come. I think I might die if you don't."

"I would love to." Ryan circled Kay's waist, held her close and kissed her temple. "I want tonight to be even better than you dreamed."

Kay smoothed her hand down the center of Ryan's chest and over her abdomen. Fleetingly she touched the cock between her legs. "I want this."

Ryan tightened her hold but didn't hurry her pace as she led Kay through the crowd toward a staircase. "As many times as you want."

"Where are we going?" Kay asked as she realized they were headed to an unfamiliar part of the ship. She stifled a gasp of surprise as Ryan spun her against the wall and pinned her there with the force of her body.

"You know where."

Then Ryan was kissing her, and Kay forgot her next question. She clung to Ryan as Ryan's kisses went from gentle to fierce in a heartbeat. She dug her fingers into Ryan's shoulders and parted her legs, her dress riding up her thighs as Ryan's hips ground against her. The floating feeling was gone and in its place, she burned. Her clitoris pounded and her pussy contracted powerfully each time Ryan plunged her tongue into her mouth. She fumbled at Ryan's fly.

"I need you to fuck me."

Ryan caught her wrist and pressed Kay's hand to her cock. She skimmed her teeth up Kay's neck. "I need to fuck you. I've needed it for hours." She pulled Kay along the hall by the hand. "Hurry."

Kay followed. Tonight was her night to be bold.

Ryan slowed before a cabin door and pulled the key card from her pocket. She kissed Kay softly, as softly as she had ravished her mouth just moments before. "Anything you want. And nothing that you don't. All right?"

"Open the door, Ryan." Kay tightened her grip on Ryan's hand and stepped inside.

A small blonde sat reading in a large upholstered chair on the far side of the room. She wore nothing except black bikini panties and a see-through black silk tank top. The outlines of her breasts and nipples were clear. She put her book carefully aside, her gaze shifting from Ryan to Kay. She smiled softly. "Hello."

"Allie," Ryan murmured softly in the dimly lit cabin, releasing Kay's hand. "I'd like you to meet Kay." She gently cupped the back of Kay's neck, stroking her lightly. "Kay, this is my mistress."

"Hello," Kay said, the crystal-clear image of Allie climaxing as she rode Ryan's cock flashing through her mind. Her stomach rolled with a wave of arousal, and she knew from the way Allie's smile flickered on the edge of laughter that she saw it.

"Has Ryan been good to you?" Allie asked, fanning her fingertips, one after the other, over her right nipple.

"Yes, very," Kay said, her gaze fixed on Allie's breasts. "She's a magnificent dancer."

"She dances like she fucks." Allie shifted in the chair and parted her thighs to expose the thin strip of black silk covering her sex. "Has she made you come yet?"

"Not yet," Kay said, aware of Ryan breathing rapidly beside her. Ryan's hand trembled against her neck. "I'm afraid I was a little eager and I made her come first."

Allie jerked infinitesimally and her fingers tightened on her nipple. "Did you?"

"Yes."

"What did you do?" Allie's voice was slow and deep. She cupped both breasts, thumbs brushing her nipples rhythmically.

Kay took a deep breath. "I'll tell you while Ryan licks you."

Allie's lips parted soundlessly and her eyelids fluttered before her gaze fixed on Ryan. "Come here."

To Kay's surprise, Ryan drew her along until she was close enough to see the wet sheen of excitement seeping beneath the silk onto Allie's legs. Then Ryan knelt and carefully skimmed Allie's panties down and off.

"I thought about her fucking me every day since I arranged for her to be my escort tonight," Kay said, watching Allie's face. "I wanted to masturbate tonight before she picked me up, but I made myself wait. When I saw her at my door, I was already wet."

"Ryan," Allie said softly without taking her eyes from Kay's face. She sighed when Ryan leaned forward and put her mouth against her cunt.

Kay slid a little closer and rested her fingertips against the back of Ryan's head. Her clit ached and she wanted to touch herself. "We kissed and I was so excited. I felt her cock against my leg." Allie moaned. "My pussy throbbed and I wanted her inside me so much."

Allie arched forward, her stomach contracting, and slid her hand behind Ryan's head, her fingers just touching Kay's. "Lick me harder, Ryan."

"I waited all this time so I would need it so much I'd come over and over and over when she was finally inside me." Kay twined her fingers through Allie's. Allie was gasping, her eyes shining brightly. Her thighs trembled against the outside of Ryan's shoulders.

"You're going to make me come in her mouth," Allie said breathlessly, staring at Kay. Her hips rose and fell against Ryan's face.

"I know," Kay said. "I made *her* come in my hands while I jerked her cock—"

"Oh God." Allie made a choking sound as her shoulders lifted into the air and she curled forward.

Kay knelt quickly and circled Allie's shoulders, her fingers still joined with Allie's behind Ryan's head. She held Allie as she shuddered and climaxed in wrenching jolts. Kay was so excited she could barely breathe. She'd been on the edge of orgasm for so long she couldn't wait any longer. She pulled her dress up and pushed her panties aside.

"Wait," Allie said sharply and Kay stopped.

"Ryan, lie down and get your cock out." Allie opened a drawer in the small table next to the chair and pulled out a condom. She quickly knelt beside Ryan and rolled it down the cock that stood up from Ryan's open trousers. Then she grasped Kay's hand and pulled her forward. "Ride her."

Kay was already straddling Ryan's hips, her dress pulled up to her hips, one hand gripping Ryan's cock and the other holding herself open. She lowered herself until the cock pierced her lips. The first jolt of pleasure was so sweet she cried out. There was no way she could stop until she had it all, and she took it all in one long sweep, driving the cock head deep inside her. Her back arched and she screamed.

"Don't come yet," Allie ordered, taking Kay's face in her hands. She licked Kay's lips and slid her tongue inside her mouth.

Kay rocked on Ryan's cock, sliding up and down, working it in and out while Allie fucked her mouth. Distantly she heard Ryan groaning, felt Ryan's hips thrusting to match her strokes. Her pussy clenched on the cock and her clit swelled against it.

"I'm coming on this cock," Kay exclaimed.

Allie swiveled sharply and straddled Ryan's shoulders, facing Kay. She lowered her cunt to Ryan's mouth and caressed Kay's face. "Wait for me, baby."

"Oh God, it's good," Kay whimpered. "She's so good." She grabbed Allie's shoulders, unable to support herself as her thighs went soft and her belly rolled. "You're beautiful. Oh God, I really need to come."

"So do I," Allie said through clenched jaws. "Just one more minute . . . give me one . . . oh yes . . . she's got me . . ."

"Oh," Kay wailed, exploding on Ryan's cock. "I'm coming."

Allie cried out and Kay crushed her mouth to Allie's, swallowing her pleasure. Kay came so hard she thought her pussy would never stop pumping. Allie finally slid off Ryan's chest and curled beside her, rubbing her palm in slow circles on Ryan's stomach. Kay leaned forward and braced her arms on either side of Ryan's shoulders with Ryan's cock still curled inside her. Ryan looked dazed, her face covered in sweat.

"Are you okay?" Kay kissed Ryan lightly.

"Perfect."

"You need to come?"

"Already did." Ryan grinned lazily. "With you."

Kay nibbled on Ryan's lip. "Good." She glanced at Allie, who rested with her cheek on Ryan's outstretched arm. "I can't think of anything better than watching you come while Ryan's cock is inside me."

Allie smiled. "I'm glad Ryan brought you by."

"Me too." Kay carefully rose, sighing as Ryan slipped out of her. "I guess I should go."

"Ryan," Allie said sharply, sitting up. "Get yourself together."

"Yes, Allie." Ryan tucked her cock back in her pants and disappeared into the bathroom. A minute later she returned and took Kay's hand. "I'm going with you."

At the door, Kay turned to Allie. "Thank you . . ." She glanced at Ryan. "This has been a wonderful cruise, but tonight was the very best part."

"The night's not over." Allie smiled and opened the door. "And neither is your date."

Kay wrapped her arm around Ryan's waist as the door closed silently behind them. She could hardly wait for the next cruise, and the next dream date.

Acknowledgment

To the reader—

Before you finish this volume you may have realized that several of the characters in my stories are familiar to you. Brandy of "Cruising Solo" first appeared in *All the Wrong Places*. Linda and Marissa of "Gladiators" are from my most recent novel, *Finders Keepers*. From my earliest novel, *In Every Port*, Jessica and Cat appear, celebrating their approaching thirtieth anniversary.

Revisiting old friends is as much fun as dreaming up new ones. But even more fun is the morning e-mails I would discover from Radclyffe containing everything from shocking announcements like "I'm just here for the sex" and equally shocking meek sentiments such as "Yes, dear." (Be still my little femme heart.)

Of course, all was eclipsed by the arrival of her storyboard in a tidy Excel spreadsheet categorizing each story by accessories (or lack thereof), power play and number of bodies. Talk about putting a girl in the mood for her day's work! Most people just get coffee in the morning.

This collaboration has reminded me just how much I love my work. From the first conversation with Radclyffe it was clear we shared a common passion for romance, erotica and especially for writing romance and erotica, all of the lesbian variety. I am eternally grateful to the friend who introduced us in New Orleans. Our poor partners were consigned to talking about their careers while Rad and I communed on our joy of lesbian books.

From the moment we started planning this project, on the suggestion I believe of Linda Hill, she was an oh-so-delightful dance partner who could lead or be led whatever the music. She let me take her on a sea cruise, so it's only fair I let her take me to Vegas in our next volume. Our love of our work is a huge common ground, while our different styles and approaches provide a consistent source of creative energy and positive friction. Friction, after all, is one of the key elements of both romance and erotica, leading to very happy endings.

— Karin, April 2007

Acknowledgment

Every artist has an ego (often a fragile one), or so I've been told, having no experience with such things personally. Writing has been called a solitary pursuit, something one does alone in a room. However, even though we may write in private, we share the product of our imagination, our hopes, our dreams and our fears with strangers throughout the world, often never knowing if what we write will be understood or enjoyed or ridiculed. That process alone can be intimidating, and trying to do it with another author presents even more challenges. I have never written anything of this scope with another author before. I had no idea how Karin and I would manage to meld our individual styles and vision of the work to create something we and the readers would be happy with. Even more importantly, how in the world would we work out who would top and who would bottom?

Without sharing all our secrets, let me say it was amazingly easy. With no fanfare, no strife, and no safe words, we navigated the murky waters of artistic temperament and not inconsiderable egos with no difficulty. As I look back at the process which began two years ago over breakfast in Provincetown, I realize that the reason this project went so well is because Karin and I share something very fundamental—we both love the work. I recognized that shared passion the first time Karin and I sat down to dinner in New Orleans during Saints & Sinners three years ago and talked about writing. We immediately discovered not rivalry, but common ground. We love to write about women passionately loving other women. We love writing romances. We love writing erotica. So when it came time to write together, it was all about sharing what we love. That is the perfect power dynamic no matter what your favorite flavor.

So, my thanks go first and foremost to Karin Kallmaker for being an outstanding professional and a true pleasure to create with. Happily the next trip is right around the corner. In 2008, Bold Strokes Books will publish the second volume in this collection, *In Deep Waters 2: Cruising the Strip* by Karin Kallmaker and Radclyffe, set in Las Vegas. I can't wait to see how Karin follows up on the Wandering Lube Lady.

It's exciting both as a publisher and an author to break new ground. I have Linda Hill to thank for so many things, but in this instance for being willing to consider something outside the norm—the collaboration of two publishers producing a two-volume collection, one from each publishing house. It's a bold and beautiful adventure.

Also, much appreciation to Cindy Cresap for not believing everything she'd heard about Karin and me, and for doing such a fabulous job with the edits.

See you all next trip, and thank you for reading.

—*Radclyffe, 2007*

About the Authors

Karin Kallmaker

The author of more than twenty romances and fantasy-science fiction novels, Karin expanded her repertoire to include explicit erotica saying, "Nice Girls Do." Her works include the award-winning *Just Like That, Maybe Next Time* and *Sugar*. Short stories have appeared in anthologies from publishers like Alyson, Bold Strokes, Circlet and Haworth, as well as novellas and short stories with Bella Books. She began her writing career with the venerable Naiad Press and continues with Bella.

She and her partner are the mothers of two and live in the San Francisco Bay Area. She is descended from Lady Godiva, a fact which she'll share with anyone who will listen. She likes her Internet fast, her iPod loud and her chocolate real.

All of Karin's work can now be found at Bella Books. Details and background about her novels, and her other pen name, Laura Adams, can be found at www.kallmaker.com.

Radclyffe

Radclyffe is a retired surgeon and full-time author-publisher with over twenty-five lesbian novels and anthologies in print. She is the recipient of the 2003 and 2004 Alice B. Readers' award for her body of work and has been short-listed for the Lambda Literary Awards and Golden Crown Literary Society Awards multiple times, winning the 2005 Lambda Literary Awards with *Erotic Interludes 2: Stolen Moments* ed. with Stacia Seaman and *Distant Shores, Silent Thunder* and the 2006 Golden Crown Awards with *Justice Served*. She has selections in numerous anthologies including *Call of the Dark*, *The Perfect Valentine*, *Wild Nights*, *Best Lesbian Erotica 2006 and 2007*, *After Midnight*, *Caught Looking: Erotic Tales of Voyeurs and Exhibitionists*, *First-Timers*, *Ultimate Undies: Erotic Stories About Lingerie and Underwear*, *A is for Amour*, and *Naughty Spanking Stories 2*.

She is also the president of Bold Strokes Books, a publishing company featuring lesbian-themed general and genre fiction.

Her forthcoming works include *In Deep Waters, Volume 2: Cruising the Strip*, an erotica collection written with Karin Kallmaker (2008).

Story Attributions

"Uncharted Course" features characters from "Executive Agenda," an erotic short story by Radclyffe in Erotic Interludes 4: *Extreme Passions* (2006, Bold Strokes Books)

"Music on the Wind" features characters introduced in the novel *Love's Melody Lost* by Radclyffe (2002, Bold Strokes Books)

"Easy Loving" features characters introduced in the novel *Fated Love* by Radclyffe (2004, Bold Strokes Books)

"Dream Date" features characters introduced in the erotic short stories "Top of the Class" and "Bonus Night" by Radclyffe in Erotic Interludes 3: *Lessons in Love* (2006, Bold Strokes Books).

Also by Karin Kallmaker

Writing as Karin Kallmaker:

Finders Keepers
Just Like That
Sugar
One Degree of Separation
Maybe Next Time
Substitute for Love
Frosting on the Cake
Unforgettable
Watermark
Making Up for Lost Time
Embrace in Motion
Wild Things
Painted Moon
Car Pool
Paperback Romance
Touchwood
In Every Port

Writing for Bella After Dark:

18th & Castro
All the Wrong Places
Stake through the Heart: New Exploits of Twilight Lesbians
Bell, Book and Dyke: New Exploits of Magical Lesbians
Once Upon a Dyke: New Exploits of Fairy Tale Lesbians

Writing as Laura Adams:

Sleight of Hand
Seeds of Fire

Feel free to visit www.kallmaker.com

Also by Radclyffe

The Provincetown Tales:
Safe Harbor
Beyond the Breakwater
Distant Shores, Silent Thunder
Storms of Change
Winds of Fortune

The Justice Series:
A Matter of Trust (prequel)
Shield of Justice
In Pursuit of Justice
Justice in the Shadows
Justice Served

The Honor Series:
Above All, Honor
Honor Bound
Love & Honor
Honor Guards
Honor Reclaimed
Honor under Siege

Romances:
Fated Love
Innocent Hearts
Promising Hearts
Love's Tender Warriors
Love's Melody Lost
Love's Masquerade
Passion's Bright Fury
Shadowland
Tomorrow's Promise
Turn Back Time
When Dreams Tremble

The Erotic Interludes Series:
Erotic Interludes: *Change of Pace*
Erotic Interludes 2: *Stolen Moments* (edited with Stacia Seaman)
Erotic Interludes 3: *Lessons in Love* (edited with Stacia Seaman)
Erotic Interludes 4: *Extreme Passions* (edited with Stacia Seaman)
Erotic Interludes 5: *Road Games* (edited with Stacia Seaman)

Visit Radclyffe at www.radfic.com